The Sloth's Eye

The Sloth's Eye

Linda Lombardi

FIVE STAR
A part of Gale, Cengage Learning

Detroit • New York • San Francisco • New Haven, Conn • Waterville, Maine • London

Five Star Publishing, a part of Gale, Cengage Learning.

Set in 11 pt. Plantin.

LIBRARY OF CONGRESS CATALOGING-IN-PUBLICATION DATA

Lombardi, Linda, 1961–
The sloth's eye / Linda Lombardi. — 1st ed.
p. cm.
ISBN-13: 978-1-59414-962-7 (hardcover)
ISBN-10: 1-59414-962-3 (hardcover)
1. Zoo keepers—Fiction. 2. Zoos—Employees—Fiction. I. Title.
PS3612.O44S58 2011
813′.6—dc22 2010051991

First Edition. First Printing: April 2011.
Published in 2011 in conjunction with Tekno Books and Ed Gorman.

Printed in the United States of America
1 2 3 4 5 6 7 15 14 13 12 11

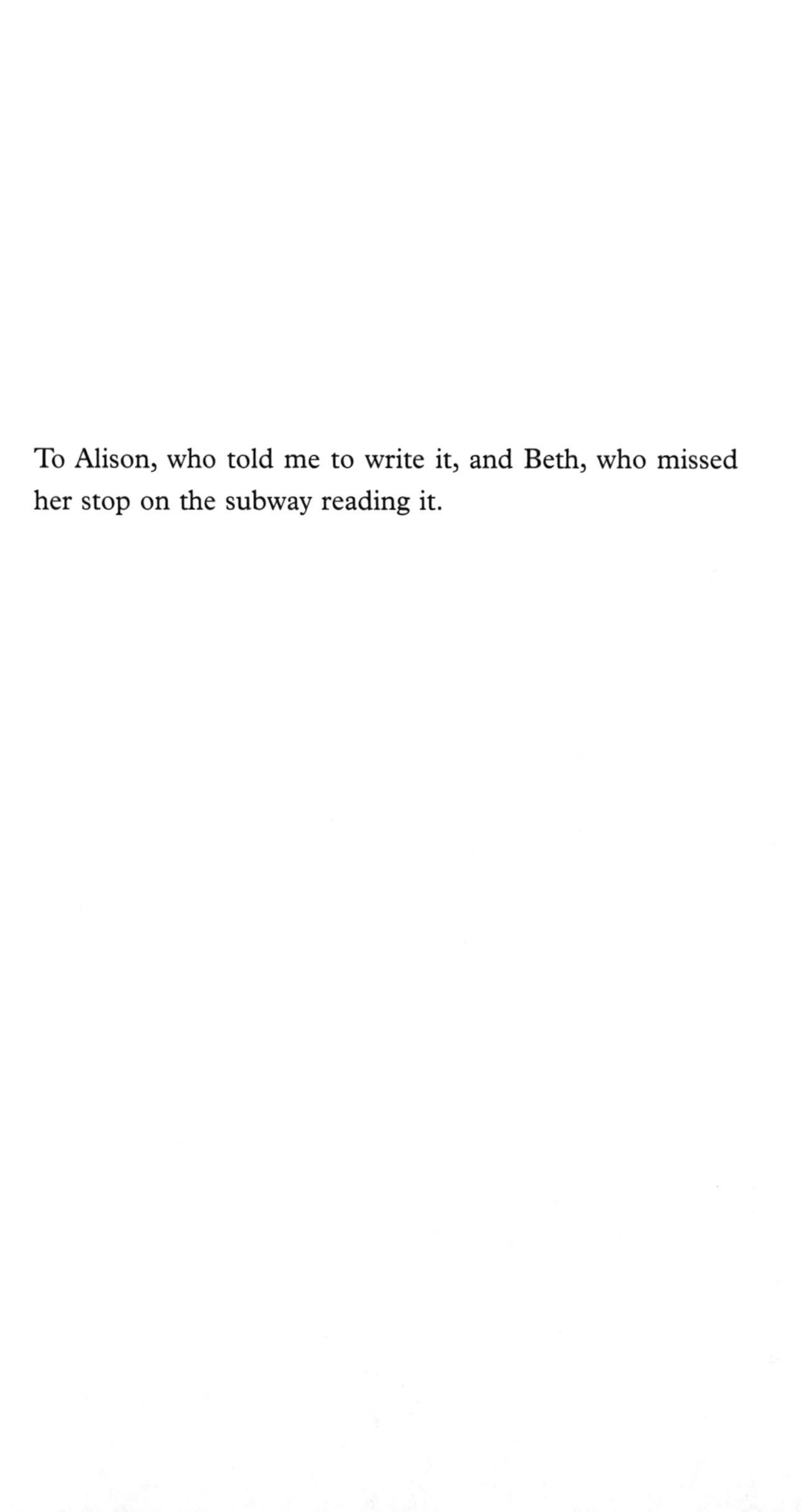

To Alison, who told me to write it, and Beth, who missed her stop on the subway reading it.

Chapter 1

"Do the capybaras get any of these?" I asked, scraping the seeds out of the fourth pumpkin and passing it to Jeff so he could do the carving. I liked the messy jobs best.

"No, their keepers aren't as much fun as we are," Chris said, setting another jack o'lantern on the dumbwaiter.

"Can I have these pieces?" Jeff asked Chris, pointing to the chunks of pumpkin eyes and mouths on his cutting board.

He nodded. Jeff took them and said, "This one's for the chinchilla. I'm going to give it chinchilla ears and a tail."

Jeff was too cute. If he wasn't way too young for me, I would totally have a crush on him. And if I wasn't already preoccupied with a certain other coworker of mine.

Speaking of whom, Chris looked at the clock and said, "I've got to go. I'll be back around noon." Chris is senior keeper at the Small Mammal House, so it's his job to go to the boring meetings. "I have total confidence that you two can handle this."

I watched him go up the stairs and then turned to Jeff and made a silly face. "Poor us."

"Yeah, how come we don't get to go with him instead of carving pumpkins," Jeff said.

Our work as animal keepers was more fun than sitting in meetings, even though we didn't usually spend the day carving pumpkins. But tonight was the special Halloween event with trick or treating at the zoo. The office staff and volunteers decorated the hallways of the building, but only we could do the insides of the exhibits. Pumpkins were safe to put in with the animals, who either ate them or ignored them. Or if they were little enough, they ran in and out of them, which was cool.

I watched Jeff biting his lip in concentration, carving a notch in the pumpkin to fit a chinchilla ear-shaped piece into. He had been working here for about three months now, and he was still so impossibly young and enthusiastic. I felt kind of protective of him, despite how silly it was to feel like that toward someone a foot taller than me. Although since everyone was taller than me, what difference did that make?

He put the ears on the chinchilla o'lantern and held it up.

"Oh, that's cute," I said. "Maybe I should make one with Radar ears." Radar is a fennec fox. Fennecs have very big ears.

"Oh yeah." He started to rummage around in the pumpkin pieces strewn all over the table. "But none of these pieces are big enough."

This was getting a little too fancy to possibly count as work. We both probably should have been upstairs cleaning up poop. But Chris had told us to carve pumpkins, and he outranked us. So there was nothing we could do about it, right?

"I could start a new one and cut really big eyes and use those pieces," I said. "Or maybe I could use something else?"

I dug into the bins of food that we'd be using if we were doing our real job of preparing the diets for the animals. "Look, we have turnips. I read that they used to carve turnips at Halloween in Europe before they got pumpkins from the New World."

Jeff looked skeptical. "That wouldn't be nearly as good."

I nodded. I took out some big sweet potatoes and contemplated whether they had fennec ears inside them. Nobody on earth had a better job than me.

★ ★ ★ ★ ★

The dumbwaiter was full of jack o' lanterns, and it was time for lunch. It had been a very productive morning in a certain way, but the pumpkin art had put me way behind on my routine work. Poop needed to be cleaned up and animals needed to be fed every day, no matter what else happened. You couldn't put it off to tomorrow. It was too nice out, though, not to take a little bit of a lunch break, when soon it would be too cold to sit outside. So I'd have to stay late, but what else was new?

My favorite spot to sit was behind our building, where the lemurs had access outside. I could sit on the low brick wall opposite their exhibit and watch them, or I could lie down behind the wall on a nice private patch of grass, where no one could see if you fell asleep for a few minutes. It looked like I would never really get used to getting to work at seven A.M., but I had found ways to deal with it.

I ate my lunch on the grass and then decided to watch the lemurs for a few minutes before going back inside. I stood up and looked at the wall. There was a big flat rock on my favorite spot. Even though the wall was in a public place, I kind of felt like it belonged to me. Some kid had probably put the rock there, I thought irritably as I moved it. I don't know why I assumed it was a kid instead of, say, one of the landscapers who had needed to move it out of the way to work in the flowerbed. I'm sure it had nothing to do with the fact that there were often way too many kids at the zoo and a lot of them were way too annoying.

Underneath the rock were a bunch of those little roly-poly bugs. I remembered how those bugs had always reminded me of trilobites when I was a kid. I don't think trilobites could roll up, and I can't explain why trilobites in particular had caught my fancy, but I liked the bugs for that reason. Now I found myself sitting and staring at them like I was seven years old again. I forgot all about the lemurs and was transported to the pill bug world for I don't know how long.

The sun came out from behind a cloud, and a shadow fell over the bugs. I looked up. Chris was watching me. He was standing there in a relaxed way like he'd been there for a while.

I stared back at him. I could interact with him normally for hours on end, but then I'd suddenly notice again how blue his eyes were. Or how his hair, sandy blond and always a little too long, would blow in his face with the wind. Or worst of all, he'd smile at me in the way he did now, the way that made me feel like my insides had turned to armadillo gruel. Don't worry, by the way, that's gruel that we feed to armadillos, not gruel made from armadillos.

I realized I had bent over so far that my nose was only a few inches from the bugs, and I felt silly and blushed for a number of reasons at once.

"Hey," he said cheerfully, "looks like you need a microscope."

I thought he was just teasing, but then he brushed some of the bugs into his hand and said, "Let's go," like he didn't know what I was waiting for.

I got up and walked along with him, and when we got to the door of the Invertebrate House I realized where we were going. There was an exhibit in there where kids could put things under a microscope. But you were supposed to use it to look at the stuff they already had in the building.

I stopped at the door. "Are we allowed to do this? We wouldn't like someone bringing some small mammals into our building."

It was surprising that no one had ever tried that, I realized. People had dumped pet birds and reptiles that they didn't want anymore at those houses. It was only a matter of time before some idiot left their chinchilla or ferret at ours.

Chris put his bug-filled hand in his pocket. "Don't know

what you're talking about," he said and pushed open the door.

It was dark and cool and calm in there, as it always was. We stopped and looked at the cuttlefish. The cuttlefish looked back calmly today, without flashing colors at us. We continued past the tanks of the nautilus and octopus. I loved this building, but I was glad I didn't work here. They had even more freaking glass to clean than we did, all easy for people to reach and get their sticky fingerprints all over it. I hated cleaning the glass of my exhibits so much that I would sometimes briefly consider asking for a transfer to work with some nice, outdoor, unenclosed-by-glass large mammals. So far, though, I'd always stopped when I was reminded—usually by walking outside for a minute—that our wonderful mid-Atlantic climate is unbearable for about nine months of the year, and that one of the reasons I was lucky to work at Small Mammals was that it was indoors.

Chris sat down at one of the microscopes in the corner and put the bugs on the counter. He picked one up and put it on the slide and adjusted the eyepiece. As the other bugs unrolled, I poked them a little so they'd roll up again and not run away. After a minute he got up and said, "Go ahead," and took over the bug-poking duty.

I looked in the microscope. "This is hopeless. All I can ever see in one of these is my own eye."

He leaned over and put his hand on my shoulder. "Move your head a minute." He looked into it, crouching down to my height, fiddling with the dials. "Okay, try again." He moved aside.

Now I could see. "Oh, that's cool." I sat there enjoying watching the bug roll and unroll and the feeling of Chris's hand that he had left on my shoulder while he herded the rest of the bugs with the other hand. Some people really know how to have a good time, I thought.

Just as I was thinking how I would be content to sit there

forever, I heard footsteps behind us and Chris stepped away from me. I figured we were about to get in trouble about the bugs, but then I heard a large and cheerful voice that didn't belong to an Invertebrate House keeper.

"Chris, Hannah. How nice to see you." I turned to look.

"Allison," said Chris flatly.

Allison was the director of the zoo. She was larger than life, the kind of person who always seemed to have a spotlight focused on her. Which made it all the more striking when she turned her attention your way. For that moment, it felt like the universe revolved around you. Chris was one of the few people who seemed to be resistant to the effect.

"Hannah, how are the pugs?" she said.

Like a politician, she always remembered everyone's name and some detail about them, even if she had only met them once for half a second. I found this amazing, since I swear I only remember my own name because I have it written down in a lot of places. She knew I had pugs because the first time we met, at a big event for new zoo employees, she had remarked on my pug earrings. It was kind of a trick, I knew, to be able to do these things, but somehow it still made you feel special.

"The pugs are great." Normally I could talk about my pugs for hours, but I reminded myself that she was just being polite. She was the director of the zoo and I was no one important, after all.

"It's so nice to see the two of you getting out and enjoying the zoo. So many people get into a rut and lose their passion, don't you think? I'm so glad to see that's not happening to you. Well, see you around."

She sailed away, with heads turning as they always did after her long mane of golden hair and her air of owning the world.

But I looked at Chris instead. He didn't like Allison. I didn't know why. I knew they'd known each other a long time, that she had been curator of our unit when Chris started as a keeper. She didn't act like she disliked him, but I suspected she could act any way she wanted no matter how she really felt, so that didn't mean much. What I did know was that she had spoiled the mood for him.

"Well, better get back to work," I said, trying to sound cheerful, and started to scoop up the roly-poly bugs.

He looked worried and distracted for a moment. But then he looked back at me and smiled. "Yeah." He seemed to forget about her again, and we walked back to Small Mammals together in a quiet little bubble of Invertebrate House serenity.

At the end of the day I ran home to shower and take care of the pugs so I could come back to work the Halloween event. I got back to the Small Mammals building and was passing through the vestibule to the public area when a dark figure in a black cape jumped at me from behind and covered my eyes with its hands.

"Ray," I said.

"Oh." He made a big show of sounding disappointed. "Am I so obvious?"

"No one else would do it so well," I said soothingly.

He took his hands off my eyes and turned me around. Then he grabbed me by the waist and bent me over backward and started to bite my neck.

"Ray, I'm sure there's a federal regulation against sucking my blood while I'm on duty."

He stopped. He looked at me, a pleased expression on his face. "You never let me have any fun," he said, letting me go. He did make a good Dracula, there was no doubt. He had slicked back his black hair and trimmed his beard in a way that made him look even more sinister than usual. And yet simultaneously attractive, to an extent that it was better to try not to think about.

"Are you working tonight or just being a nuisance?" I said, feigning annoyance. I knew he'd be disappointed if I didn't.

"You must come over to Reptiles and see my coffin," he said, ignoring my question. "It's the highlight of the evening."

Was he serious? That would be going to new heights even for Ray. "You have a coffin? Yeah, right."

"Well, only rented," he admitted. "If you owned a coffin, then you'd feel obligated to dress as Dracula every year. You know I hate to be tied down."

This was something I'd have to see to believe. "I have to work, but I'll come over at the end of the night. Get out of here now, okay?"

"Yes, your highness," he said, making a dramatic exit.

My job was turning out to be easy, because nearly everyone was too busy running around getting candy to stop and look at the animal I was supposed to be talking about. I think the kids mostly went by so fast that they didn't even notice I had a tenrec in my hand. They had their priorities clear.

On the other hand, I had to admit I wasn't exactly shouting at them to stop or anything. I was happy to sit there holding Clark and watching everyone rush past in their costumes. No one wore cheap plastic masks anymore like when I was a kid. They had full-length plush dinosaur suits and other amazing getups.

"Hannah, how's it going?" I heard someone say as I stared in wonder at a stroller full of triplet babies dressed up as pumpkins.

It was Victor, who was in charge of public relations for the zoo. He was wearing his usual business suit, but as a concession to Halloween he had little tiny horns on his head, peeking out of his fox-colored hair.

"Hey, nice horns," I said.

"What's that?" he said. "Some kind of hedgehog?"

"No, it's a tenrec. It's called a hedgehog tenrec because it's the kind of tenrec that looks like a hedgehog, but it's not closely related. They live in Madagascar, and they're the only insectivore family there, and you know, since it's an island, the tenrecs have evolved to look like hedgehogs and shrews, because they use the same ecological niches."

Victor nodded. He could have done PR anywhere, but he worked at the zoo because he loved it. If he were a regular visitor I would either have to go into a lot more detail or just forget about it, but Victor didn't need a long explanation about convergent evolution. He knew more than he needed to know just to do his job.

I watched him peering at the tenrec. It was a lovely scene. Victor wasn't my type—he was a little too perfect. But Allison really knew how to pick them, Victor being not only the PR guy but also the zoo director's current more-or-less significant other. You kind of hoped she had a better reason for her relationship than the fact that he would look great in photos with her, but he sure did.

"What do they eat?" he said.

"The usual insectivore stuff. We feed them mostly cat food and mealworms. They forage on the ground and in trees too. It doesn't look it, but they are pretty good climbers. I know this because of where they ended up the time I accidentally let them out of their exhibit."

He smiled. I wouldn't have joked about something like that to most people on the office staff, but Victor was one of us. He didn't stay cooped up in the admin building any more than he absolutely had to. He was a lot like Allison that way. He was always looking for any excuse he could find to get out into the park and hang out with animals. He could say he knew more and could do his job better that way. It was a good rationalization.

"Can I touch him?" he asked.

I wasn't supposed to let the public touch the animals, but surely that didn't include him.

"Okay, as long as no one's watching."

He stroked Clark's spines gently with one finger. "Not very painful."

"He's relaxed. He's used to this. But they don't hurt as much as some spines. They're nothing like an African hedgehog," I said. "I hope all the predators on Madagascar have really sensitive mouths and gum disease and all, or these probably don't do much good."

He looked at Clark closely for a while. I left them alone. It was clear I wasn't there for them for the moment.

After a bit, Victor looked up and smiled. "Thanks. So how's it going? Everyone enjoying themselves?"

"Oh, it's great, but hey, what's with all the dried fruit and nuts we're giving out for treats? I really had to scrounge around for actual candy," I said, trying not to whine, since after all I was here to work, not trick or treat.

"It's part of Allison's rainforest conservation campaign. They're sustainably harvested."

"Yeah, but didn't you always hate the kinds of people who gave out stuff like raisins for trick or treat?" Really, that was one step up from giving out toothbrushes. It gave me a nostalgic urge to throw some eggs, except I knew that I'd be the one who'd end up having to clean them up.

He smiled. "I'm not part of the decision process. I just represent the company line." He looked around conspiratorially. "I'm about to head out and stop in at all the other buildings. Can I look for anything to bring back?"

"Chocolate. Why isn't there any chocolate? Chocolate grows

in the rainforest too, and you can buy all kinds of politically correct brands now. Organic and everything, all those small companies that work with local farmers instead of big plantations," I said. "We should support that kind of thing, right?"

"Well, yes. But no one's making fair-trade fun-size bars yet, unfortunately."

"I guess," I said, deflated. I'd been so swept away by my argument that for a moment I'd almost been convinced that my motives were purely environmental. Now I was suddenly desperately in need of a hit of caffeine and sugar.

"You know, though," he said, "I think we might have bent the rule. I'll be back if I find anything."

"Hey, thanks." Now I was smiling again. "See you around."

I got suckered into helping clean up, so the park was almost empty by the time I managed to get away. I passed a last few straggling tyrannosauruses and Harry Potters looking overtired and a little queasy, their parents encouraging them, promising that they had almost made it to the parking lot if they could just go a few more steps. The door to Reptiles was locked, but I peered in through the glass and could see a caped figure leaning against something a little way down the hall. I knocked.

Ray strode down the hall with the cape flying behind him. He unlocked the door and leered at me. "Welcome to the crypt of Renos Tsakanikas," he said with a flourish.

"Ray, that doesn't work. Horror movies are never set in Greece," I complained.

He shrugged. "I have to work with what I've got. We can't all be Transylvanian." Then he smiled evilly again and held out his hand. "But please. Come right this way."

I ignored the hand. "Okay, let's see this coffin you promised me."

I followed him down the hall, and there it was. It was black and shiny and lined in red silk with a red silk pillow. And naturally, it was also surrounded by reptile exhibits. This added to the creepiness in my mammal-person mind, which was full of all the usual reptile stereotypes.

"I'm impressed," I admitted. I liked a person who knew how to do Halloween right.

He looked at me significantly. "Don't you want to try it?"

"Try it?" I said, confused.

"We'll all get to have one someday, but we won't know what it feels like, will we? Here's your chance."

I laughed uncomfortably. "Um, thanks but no thanks, really."

He came and stood behind me and put his arms around me so I was enclosed in the cape with him and rested his chin on my shoulder. His beard tickled my neck. "Don't worry," he said in his best worry-inducing tone, "you'll be safe with me."

Well, I had come over here instead of heading straight home, and I was impressed by such a serious attitude toward Halloween decorations, and what was the point if I didn't go sit in his coffin for a minute. Right? Anyway, I was getting a little too much enjoyment out of the way he was holding me, and I needed a reason to put a stop to it.

"Okay," I said, "So let go and let me try it."

"Mmm," he said, lightly biting my neck as he released me. He stepped over to the coffin and opened it all the way with a dramatic gesture.

Now I was a little sorry. The whole thing was a bit too eerie. But I couldn't look scared of a silly wooden box full of pillows, could I? I was a tough little zoo-keeping woman. I had been bitten by ravenous chinchillas. I could leap tall piles of animal poop with a single bound. I shoveled shit and carried bales of hay and handled live crickets with my bare hands. Well, okay, mostly at Small Mammals we hosed the shit, or swept it up with a dustpan, rather than actual shoveling, but that was beside the point. Nothing scared me, right?

I sat down uncomfortably on the edge of the coffin.

"Oh, that won't do," he said. He climbed in in his nimble catlike way and lay on his side smiling mischievously. "I made sure to get the biggest one."

He tugged on my ponytail just a little bit, and the next thing I knew I was sitting inside the coffin leaning awkwardly against him. My efforts to rectify the situation, not entirely unaided, ended up with us both lying stretched out in the coffin on our sides facing each other.

"Isn't that better?" he said softly.

I couldn't decide if this was funny or scary, like I often couldn't decide if Ray was scary or just putting on a show. I also couldn't figure out how I'd ended up with his arms around me. Again. But lying down this time.

"This isn't a very realistic preview, is it? I said, flustered, trying to keep my mind on the topic of the coffin.

"Ah. The grave's a fine and private place, but none I think do there embrace. But," he said with a cheerful look, "this is a coffin, not a grave, isn't it?"

"Um," I said, eloquently.

He considered. "Dracula's coffin wasn't in a grave. It would have made it dreadfully inconvenient to get in and out of it every day, don't you think?" He raised his eyebrows. "I think he just kept it in his bedroom, don't you?"

He pulled me closer, and I stared into his eyes. Even this close they were so dark, you couldn't really see where the pupils ended and the irises began. It was probably why it was so hard to read his expression sometimes, aside from the fact that he made it hard on purpose.

He looked back at me with a wicked little half smile and then kissed me lightly on the lips.

I closed my eyes and wondered what I should do if he did it

again. I felt my heart racing. Everyone knew there was something irresistibly sexy about a guy in a Dracula outfit, I rationalized. It didn't mean anything. There was no need to worry about whether he'd locked the front door behind us.

I sat up abruptly.

"Right," I said.

It would really be better if Ray and I were to keep on being just good friends, I told myself. But if that was ever going to change, it was certainly not going to happen in a coffin in the hallway of the Reptiles building.

I climbed out. He stretched out and put his hands behind his head and crossed his legs, totally relaxed, like he lounged in a coffin every day. He looked content, which I noted because I couldn't decide whether I was sorry that I'd gotten out or not.

"Ray, thanks for a memorable Halloween, but I really have to get going now," I said a little too loudly.

He just nodded and closed his eyes and smiled. He's going to sleep here in that coffin, isn't he, I thought. Or he wants me to think he is. Well, I won't spoil his fun. I walked quickly down the hall and out of the building.

Ray was the sort of person who had no trouble sleeping with people who were just friends, I thought as I trotted down the path. I'd gathered this from various remarks he'd made, although it had taken me a while to realize that the topic probably didn't come up by accident. I wasn't sure I was that kind of person. Anyway, I wasn't the kind of person who'd do it in a coffin at work, for Pete's sake. Which he surely knew. So it was all just kidding.

Who was I saving myself for, though—No, shut up, not Chris, I said with irritation to the part of my brain that always insisted on bringing him up in this context. No, it would be stupid to get involved with someone I worked with every day. I loved my job. He loved his job, too. What if it didn't work out between us? Imagine how awful it would be if one of us had to leave. Imagine how awful it would be if we both stayed and tried to act like it didn't matter. It was a perfectly terrible idea.

I should probably turn around and climb right back in that coffin, I thought. But I didn't. I waved to the zoo police who were standing guard at the back gate and headed out toward home.

Chapter 2

I had a restless night. Don't blame me for your dirty mind if you think it was because I was dreaming about sex in coffins. I'm sure it was just all that dark chocolate that Victor found for me. So I was, amazingly, at work early, trying to get my counts done. We all have to count our animals every day, because they are little and not easy to find. If a bear was missing you'd notice it right away, but if you have five squirrels that look almost exactly alike in a big fake forest with lots of hiding places, you have to work to keep track of them.

The Halloween decorations were gone from the hallways but the pumpkins were still in the exhibits, most of them now looking gnawed-on to various degrees. Which just made them even better as far as I was concerned. I was admiring my jack o'lantern with the fennec fox ears when I heard footsteps, brisk confident steps that covered the ground like the whole planet was her private domain.

"I love your Halloween pumpkins," Allison said. What was she doing here at this hour? Who knew? She could be anywhere at any time. "I adore the Halloween event. What could be better than combining trick or treating and a trip to the zoo?"

"Yeah." I nodded. I had to agree. Candy and animals: did it get any better than that?

"I thought when I came through last night that you are all doing such a nice job, but this building needs some attention. You haven't had anything new in a long time, and the collection is a lot less diverse than when I was the curator here. Maybe you could give me some advice about what we could do."

Somehow, under the magic touch of her attention, I didn't think of how strange it was for the zoo director to be asking advice from someone as lowly as me.

"A wombat," I said dreamily, almost to myself. I knew we'd never get a wombat. I'd had this conversation with Larry, our curator, dozens of times. A wombat was a lousy exhibit. It would sleep all day and take up a lot of space with nothing interesting for visitors to see. A big snoozing mound of fur that might as well be a stuffed animal. "Waste Of Money Brains And Time," Margo had sneered.

But I loved wombats. I longed for a wombat the way other women longed for babies, as far as I could tell about how other women felt. I had clearly somehow imprinted on the wrong species as a newborn. I had no idea what it felt like to want a baby. But, oh, how I imagined a sweet little round wombat pup in my arms.

"A wombat!" Allison exclaimed, jolting me out of my marsupial reverie. "What a splendid idea. We don't have anything quite like that."

I looked at her dumbly for a minute, waiting for her to laugh at her joke, but she didn't. I surreptitiously pinched myself. Surely this was some kind of crazed zookeeper fantasy dream, where the director swoops down and gives you the animal you've always longed to work with. I was sure that in a minute I'd wake up and go into work and tell people about it, and I'd find out that everyone had had this dream, like we'd all had the dreams of our animals getting out, or those moments where we woke up in the middle of the night, positive we'd left some shift door in the wrong position.

"Um," I said, "but . . . won't it sleep all day?"

"I'm sure we can figure out a way to deal with that. We can

make sure its den is visible to the public. That way you'll always see something even if it's asleep. After all, that's better than an animal that's hiding all day when it's awake, isn't it?"

"Where will we put it? Where can we get one?"

"Details, details," Allison said. I seemed to be awfully good at dreaming that particular cadence she had, the tone that assured you everything would always go her way. "Don't worry, that's why I have a staff. If we want a wombat, we'll have a wombat. Do you know which species you want?"

I'd never thought about it. The idea had never gotten anywhere near close enough to reality for it to matter. "I don't know. Can I go and do some research?"

"Of course. Just email me when you decide. I'll come by again soon, and we can talk about what renovations we need to do to house it."

I gazed off toward the pygmy marmoset exhibit in a daze. The plant wall needed watering, and tons of mossy stuff had fallen down and needed to be replaced. I decided I wasn't dreaming after all, because in my dream Small Mammal House, the plant wall in that exhibit waters and re-mosses itself, instead of me having to crawl in there and hit my head and get soaking wet and covered with moss.

"But you know," I said reluctantly, "wombats aren't from the rainforest. It doesn't really fit with the master plan, does it?"

"That's no problem." Obviously my attempt to think of problems was going to be thwarted at every turn. "You're always going to have animals from all different habitats in this building. We can do other things with the publicity for this. Don't concern yourself. The animals are your job. I have a staff for all those other boring things," she concluded with a brilliant smile.

She said goodbye, and I watched her stride down the hall toward the exit. I felt like I'd just jumped on a speeding train. Didn't we need to ask Larry? He was supposed to make acquisition decisions. I didn't mean to be going over everyone's heads like this. She'd asked me a question, and I'd just been daydreaming in answer. Suddenly I'd set this whole thing in crazy motion. Wasn't everyone going to be mad?

But then I found myself wondering if I should have asked for more while I had the chance. Maybe I should have asked for an anteater too. If I ran the zoo, we'd definitely have anteaters, even if they would only eat custard with a sauce made of mustard and required full-body massages twice a day. We'd have a giant anteater and a tamandua at minimum. And then . . .

I dreamed of wombats through the morning meeting. I had finally learned how to usually get to work more or less on time, but the morning meeting was still a challenge. Sitting still and listening to people talk was not one of my talents. Nor was being fully awake at that hour. The fact that Chris ran the meetings didn't help. When I did manage to focus my foggy morning brain on him, I usually found myself thinking how perfectly beautiful he was looking, and how it was too bad that I really couldn't do anything about it.

But today I was completely off in the wombat dimension. Even Chris's blue eyes couldn't compete. So I was startled when Margo helpfully elbowed me at the end of the meeting to wake me up. Margo's that unbearable type of person who gets up at five A.M. even on her days off and generally beats me to work in the morning despite having to drive all the way from Baltimore. She's perpetually entertained by my tardiness. I guess to her, watching me try to get to work on time is like watching the dog try to get a box of biscuits open without the advantage of opposable thumbs. I used to think that was funny to watch, too, until I thought of the comparison.

"And where were you this morning, hon?" she said as I followed her into the kitchen and started to get my food pans out of the fridge. "Not in the usual place, it looked like." She smirked. "So it must be something special."

I ignored her second remark. Margo lost no opportunity to tease me when I was gazing dreamily at Chris, or apparently, even when I wasn't.

"Wombatland," I answered, sighing contentedly.

"What does that mean?" she said, scowling a little.

"Allison just sailed through the building this morning and promised to get me a wombat." I tried not to grin. Margo would also tease anyone who got too excited about a particular animal.

"What?" she said. "You mean here in Small Mammals?"

"Well, yeah, not to take home with me," I said, trying to sound jaded and cynical, while my heart was jumping up and down going WOMBAT WOMBAT WOMBAT!

Margo shook her head hard, tossing her wild red curls into even more of a mess than usual. "Well, that's typical of her idea of collection planning. Any inspiration or brainstorm she might have becomes the next big thing that everyone has to drop everything to work on. She was serious?"

"She acted like it. Why would she pretend?" Really, the only reason I could believe the whole thing had happened was that it would be too strange a joke for the director to play on a lowly keeper.

"That woman," Margo said with exasperation. "She thinks she can do whatever she wants."

"Well, she is the director," I said uncertainly. I wasn't sure I wanted to defend Allison, since she seemed to annoy so many other people. But she was getting me a wombat. She was getting me a *wombat.* I felt there was some possibility that it would be appropriate for me to kiss her feet.

"She's the director. Not the queen. She makes the rules, but then she doesn't have to follow them. Oh, don't get me started," Margo said, heading up the stairs with her food pans. "We'd be here all day, and I have work to do."

I got my food pans and dropped them off behind my line and went back to trying to count my animals. I couldn't find the agoutis. I was too busy thinking about what parts of the building we could redesign to hold a wombat. Inevitably, I guess, I couldn't think of any of my own animals that I wanted to replace, so I found myself contemplating what space I could usurp from boring animals on other people's lines. Like those shrews of Robin's that never came out of hiding. And even if you explained that they were almost the only large tree shrews left in captivity, the public still thought they just looked like uninteresting little brown jobs. What was the point? Couldn't I have that exhibit for my wombat?

I was pretty full of myself. I thought life couldn't get any better. Then I heard Chris's footsteps coming down the hall. Of course, that's what could be better. How could I forget?

"Hey," he said.

"Hey, yourself," I said, peering into the exhibit.

"Do you need . . . ?"

"Your agouti-spotting superpowers? Maybe."

He sat down on the floor, leaning against the bench I was sitting on. Just like you had to go into a phone booth to turn into Superman, he said you had to sit on the floor to turn on your agouti-spotting powers. Because where he got them in the first place was sitting on the floor of a forest for a whole summer looking for agoutis in the wild. I thought this was pretty amazing every time I thought about it. I was better at keeping still while looking at animals than keeping still any other time, but I couldn't imagine having that kind of superhuman patience.

I glanced at him as he sat serenely beside me and thought he was really more like a Zen monk than a superhero. I was so restless, I'd never even get to be an apprentice to that Zen state.

I could only envy Chris sitting perfectly still and centered in the middle of the forest, or the middle of the Small Mammal House, at one with the agouti universe until it provided enlightenment. But I was lucky that at least I got to be here with him and share it sometimes.

Something brown flashed by. "There's the male," he said. This was why I needed him. I couldn't have told which one it was without a better look.

"I saw the baby earlier, so now we just have to see the female."

Yeah, I would have found them myself eventually. And if I wanted help, it would have made more sense for us to sit at opposite ends of the exhibit so we'd cover the whole thing effectively. Really it was just that it was soothing to sit with him, like it was soothing to feed oranges to the sloths. It was one of the things I liked about my job. Did it all have to be about the animals?

Just then there was a flurry of activity high up in the exhibit.

"Hey, cut that out," I said, pointlessly, at the golden lion tamarins chasing each other around. Primates. Why do they have so much trouble getting along?

Chris got up to look more closely, then, satisfied that the GLTs were just being their usual noisy and quarrelsome selves, sat down on the bench beside me.

We had the building to ourselves, so there was no reason not to lie down, stretched out on the bench. I put my head on my hands. The top of my head was almost touching the side of his leg. I could feel the little hairs on the top of my head touching him, even though I knew my hair didn't have nerve endings. I repressed an urge to rub my head against him like a cat.

"Hey," I said after a few minutes.

"Mmm?"

"How did you grow up to be a zookeeper? Like, what did you do with animals as a kid and all?"

He looked at me. "You might not want to know," he said with an odd little smile.

"What does that mean? Your family ran a slaughterhouse or something?" I couldn't imagine what there could be that had to do with animals that I wouldn't want to know.

"Not that bad, but it did involve dead animals."

He was dragging this out on purpose to tease me. Not that I really minded.

I wrinkled my forehead. "Of course now I have to know," I said crossly.

"Okay, but don't say I didn't warn you."

I just waited. The lemurs started to call on the other side of the building. With the building not open yet, it was quiet in the public area, the only noises coming from the animals. Mostly the primates, as usual. We were the noisiest order at Small Mammals, no question about it.

"My grandfather was a taxidermist for the Smithsonian," Chris finally said. "He worked on the old Hall of Mammals."

I looked up at him and was about to say "eeuw," but managed to stop myself just as he looked at me with raised eyebrows and said, "You were about to say 'yuck,' weren't you?"

"No!" I blurted. Which was, strictly speaking, true. "Well, okay," I admitted. "Kind of. I mean, wouldn't that just give you an interest in dead animals?"

He shook his head. "A good taxidermist has to know a lot about animal behavior. You can't make a mount look realistic without knowing how the animal acts when it's alive—how it moves, what its expressions are, its typical behaviors. He went to zoos to observe and take photographs and sketches, and I got to go with him. Since he worked for the Smithsonian, we could talk to the keepers here and get up close to the animals."

Wow. I was overcome with envy, even though it was years ago.

He continued, "Also, sometimes when it was a small animal, we'd get to keep a live one for a while for him to observe, and it was my job to take care of them. Some of them we kept as pets. We had a chinchilla for a long time, and a couple of kinds of armadillo, and a kinkajou."

Now I was so jealous I wasn't sure I could be his friend anymore. "Wow, you were really lucky. It was a big deal I had a guinea pig."

"Really?" He looked surprised.

"Yeah. I was born in New York and went to the Bronx Zoo all the time when I was really little. But then we moved to Boston, which hardly has a zoo to speak of. And my parents were kind of uncomfortable with animals. I had lots of stuffed animals and plastic animals. I didn't have any dolls, just animals. I can still remember some of them, like a little plastic lion cub. And a black horse that I took outside with me to shovel snow, and I lost it in the snow and never found it. I was so heartbroken. Oh, and I was so mad after I went away to college and my mother found my old box of plastic animals and threw them away! I never forgave her for that, really."

I glanced up and saw that he looked as fascinated by my exotic story as I'd been by his.

"Anyway, I hardly got to spend any time with real animals until I left home, and I had those summer jobs at the pig sanctuary and the wildlife place—well, you know, that stuff. It's all there on my résumé." I finished, "So I guess I'm making up for lost time, now I get to be around real animals all day."

He turned away and focused on the exhibit again. "Experience teaches you a lot," he said, half to himself. "But some of it, you have to be born with."

I felt a little shiver all down my back. What he meant was that I had it. The thing you had to be born with to be good with animals. He thought that about me. I felt so happy, I was afraid

I was going to float off the bench into the air. I put my hand out and held on to the side just in case. It was a good thing he changed the subject.

"They're taking down most of my grandfather's work now, with the renovation of the Hall of Mammals."

"Oh, that's kind of sad."

He shrugged. "They don't last forever, any more than live ones do. There's only so much you can do."

I lay there quietly for a while, still glowing from the idea that he thought I was pretty good with animals for someone who had had mostly plastic ones as a child.

"I guess it sounds boring that I've never worked anywhere else. Not for a real job, anyway," he said. "You've lived in all those different places."

"No," I said, and I meant it. Why would you want to ever leave here? "You're really lucky. That's all much more exciting than anything I ever did."

"Really? You lived in New York. That must have been exciting."

"I guess," I said, flailing around unsuccessfully for something that was as good as keeping armadillos at home and watching agoutis in the rainforest. "We had, um, really good bagels," I concluded lamely.

We sat quietly for a while again, thinking about each others' exotic childhoods, I guess. I gazed down the hall to where the chinchillas were popping around on the rocks in their exhibit. Chris was looking for the agoutis, so it was okay if I contemplated some other nice rodents for a moment instead.

After a while I said, "Wasn't it odd to live with all those dead animals around?"

He shrugged. "It was normal for us. Although my grandmother did complain about him taking up space in the freezer."

I saw him looking at me expectantly. "Oh," I said, neutrally, in a tone as far away from "eeuw" as I could manage.

It was a little creepy, but interesting too. Growing up surrounded by dead things and the black art of making them come back to life. And you had to know all about life to know how to do it. Maybe that's where Chris had inherited the magic from.

I thought of something else. "Did your grandfather ever work on animals people hunted?"

"He did before he got the Smithsonian job. It's how most taxidermists make a living."

"Did that bother you?"

"I don't know. I was so young then. I think it was just unpleasant but normal. Animals kill other animals, and so do we."

A flash of brown dashed out of the underbrush and jumped over the stream.

"There she is," Chris said. Oh, too fast, I sighed, a little disappointed, until he continued, "Now we can go see the pumpkin stomping."

"Oh yeah! I almost forgot."

The pumpkin stomping was a Halloween tradition. Every year the elephants got a huge pile of pumpkins that were donated to the zoo. They played with them and ate them and, best of all, stomped on them. I must have been very distracted by wombat thoughts to have forgotten about the pumpkin stomp.

"Did someone tell Jeff?" Since he was new, I wasn't sure he knew about the pumpkin stomping. We couldn't let him miss it.

"He already went ahead with Margo."

We left the building and started up the hill. Margo wouldn't normally go to the pumpkin stomp, I knew. She probably wanted to get Jeff alone to pump him about whether he had a girlfriend or a boyfriend. We actually weren't sure yet which it would be, which frustrated Margo to pieces. How was she going to try to match him up with someone if she didn't know?

But this was no time to worry about Margo's matchmaking problems. It was a beautiful fall day. I was full of leftover candy from yesterday that I'd had for breakfast. I was going to see the pumpkin stomping with Chris. I was going to get a wombat. It didn't get any better than this.

Wait. I realized Chris didn't know about the wombat. I couldn't believe I hadn't told him. No, I could believe it. Because I knew he wouldn't like how it had happened. But come on. Even if he didn't like Allison, surely he could only be thrilled about a wombat?

"Hey," I said, "a weird thing happened this morning."

He looked at me expectantly.

"Allison came by—wait, it's a good story anyway—when I was in early doing my count. I don't know why. But she said she thought we needed something new in the building and asked me what I thought. And the next thing I knew she said to email me about what kind of wombat I wanted, and she'd arrange everything."

I watched him, worried about his reaction. It would spoil the whole thing if he didn't think it was terrific.

"I know that's kind of crazy," I continued, "but a wombat would be so cool. And we really haven't had anything new in a long time, right?"

He looked blank for a moment, like he was trying to decide which way to go. Then he smiled, reluctantly at first, and then for real. "You really love wombats," he said.

"Oh, yeah. It would be so great. I know she just charged in and decided without consulting you guys, but—"

"Don't worry about it," he interrupted, "that's how she does things. It's nothing new."

"I didn't, like, try to talk her into it or anything . . ."

"It's okay. It's great. It'll be fun." He smiled like he meant it.

I tried not to jump up and down. And then we were talking about where we would put it, and how we could make interesting keeper talks about it even when it was sleeping, and he was telling me neat wombat facts that even I didn't know. I was the happiest woman on earth.

"Do you see Margo and Jeff?" Chris said, looking over the crowd that had already gathered around the elephant yard.

"No." Probably because I wasn't trying. I didn't care where they were. I was happy to be able to talk to Chris without Margo hanging on my every word and glance for something to torment me about in the ladies' room later. I was going to enjoy the pumpkin stomp, and if part of that was enjoying having Chris to myself, it was none of anyone's business.

We grabbed a place by the railing and waved to the staff hanging around in the elephant yard. It was warm for early November, with a blue sky full of unrealistically fluffy clouds, and there was a big crowd for a weekday. Elephants were so popular, people must take time off from work to see this, I thought. No one took a day off from work to see something happen at the Small Mammal House. And no one would send all these TV station cameras. Sometimes we felt a little second-class.

Still, a crowd of people who'd made a special trip to see animals do a cool thing were my kind of people. For today I would forgive them for liking the elephants better than small mammals.

The pumpkin stomp was always preceded by a lot of waiting. We leaned against the railing and watched the staff doing more or less nothing in the yard. There were a few pumpkins placed here and there, but we were waiting for a truck to come with more. There was no reason the pumpkins couldn't all be there ahead of time—it was a ritual left over from the days when a dump truck would come and dump a whole pile of them. But the vets had declared that unsanitary, so now a cute little farm truck came, just to make an event of it, and more pumpkins were unloaded by hand.

I only had a vague idea of who most of the people were. I knew Bruce, who was standing around the yard talking on his cell phone, because he was the curator in charge of the capybaras as well as the elephants. I mulled this fact over resentfully for the millionth time. Sure they were large for rodents, but surely capybaras weren't really large mammals? Really we ought to be in charge of them, and I ought to be their keeper. Probably Bruce should have been talking to the press, and I wondered if he was just avoiding them instead of making some vital last-minute pumpkin-related communication. Instead the reporters were all clustered around another guy. He was tall and blond, and he looked like he spent way too much time on his hair.

"Hey," I said, "I should know these people's names. Who's this guy who thinks he's a movie star over here?"

Chris, trying not to smirk, said, "That's Matthew."

"Matthew, king of the elephants," I said, making a face. "He's enjoying the attention."

He only got it for another moment, though, because then Allison came sailing in like she was the woman we'd all been waiting for. Matthew stepped aside more graciously than I expected. He knew who ran the show.

As if her appearance really had started everything moving, just then the pumpkin truck arrived and started to back up into the elephant yard. The reporters couldn't figure out whether to film the pumpkin truck or interview Allison, and it was funny to watch all of them in a bunch try to get around to the side where they could get both of them into the shot. It was a little feeding frenzy, like when you threw crickets into the meerkat exhibit and the animals couldn't decide which cricket to go after first.

The truck backed up to the far side of the elephant yard, and the driver got out. He looked like everyone's dream of a wholesome young farm dad. Probably like us zookeepers, he was usually all dirty and sweaty in real life and had cleaned up special for this. The truck was like an adorable toy farm truck, with a red cab and a perfectly clean wooden railing around the cargo part in back. Definitely no dump truck. Like so many things at zoos, this event had been cleaned up a lot, for better or worse. But it was still pretty cool.

A little girl got out of the passenger side and started to help the crew unload pumpkins. The way she was acting, you'd think she did this every day, and I wondered if she knew how lucky she was. Little girl, I wanted to yell, you are in the elephant yard! I would have given anything when I was a little girl to be in her position, right inside an exhibit at the zoo. I'd had to wait until I was all grown up!

The giraffe in the adjacent yard came up to the wall and looked over it, checking out the odd interruption. I wondered if she could remember the same thing happening in previous years. I wished I had a camera. I loved the Elephant House, one of the zoo's old-fashioned stone buildings. What a perfect picture it would be of the truck and the giraffe and everyone unloading the pumpkins in anticipation, with the blue sky and fall leaves and the Elephant House in the background. The elephants weren't even out yet, and it was wonderful anyway.

It was a good thing I was having such a lovely time without any elephants, since there was still more waiting. The truck drove away, and Allison continued to talk to the press. The elephant staff milled around, and the curator was on his cell phone again. The zoo photographer fiddled with fiddly bits of her cameras. I momentarily thought about putting one of my arms around one of Chris's, but then came to my senses and just stared at the sky. The crowd waited patiently. They'd only spend ten seconds trying to find a small mammal that was hard to see in its exhibit. But they'd wait many long minutes to see elephants.

There was a disturbance in the little knot of staff standing around the yard, and everyone looked in that direction. Surely it was time for the elephants to come now? But no. Allison had to say a few words to the crowd.

"Thank you all for coming," she began. Chris gazed off in another direction, trying to look indifferent. I sighed and watched the clouds.

Finally the door opened, and the crowd oohed. Out came the mother elephant and the two-year-old baby, who was really the one everyone had come to see. Grownup elephant pumpkin stomping was one thing, but baby elephant pumpkin stomping was almost too much to stand. You could feel everyone tense up with anticipation of nearly intolerable cuteness as he trotted across the yard.

He ran to a pile of about half a dozen pumpkins and plowed right through them. I don't care if it's anthropomorphic, he looked totally pleased with himself. He kicked a few in different directions and then, the moment we had all been waiting for. *Stomp.*

Pieces of pumpkin flew all over. People laughed and cameras clicked. The zoo photographer moved around looking for a better angle. The curator kept talking on his cell phone. Everyone watched as the baby eyed another pumpkin with mischief in his heart. *Smush.* More laughter.

Hanging around in the back of the elephant yard was a tall blond Valkyrie sort of woman who looked a little like she would be able to wrestle an elephant to the ground. But her expression and posture were uneasy, and she seemed to avoid the other staff. Sometimes you could tell who the submissive animal in a group was, even when there wasn't much going on. She was big, but that wasn't enough to put her on top.

"Who's that blond woman in back?" I asked, leaning over to watch the baby elephant as he trotted off to an inconveniently distant corner of the yard. Why didn't they put all of the pumpkins right in front of me?

"That's Stephanie."

"Why don't they carve the pumpkins into jack o'lanterns first?" I suddenly wondered.

"That's a lot of pumpkins," Chris said.

I looked at the big pile, thinking of how it had taken us all morning to carve our jack o'lanterns while our other work wasn't getting done.

"Or it might be too gross," I said. "Too much like smushing someone's head."

Yeah, maybe stomping on pumpkins with faces on them would just be a much less wholesome family activity. Probably it was better to stick with the idea that they are squashing squash, even at Halloween.

The mom elephant was stomping on one pumpkin at a time, and then actually eating it. That was the grownup way. Baby was still running all over trying to find as many as he could, getting dibs on all of them. He kicked one in a way that made him look just like he was playing soccer, and the crowd laughed again.

The curator was still on the phone. I guess he'd been to a lot of pumpkin stomps already in his time. "Do you think Bruce is ever going to hang up and pay attention?"

"Did you come here to watch the elephants or the staff?" Chris said.

"They're both just as interesting. Can I pretend he's

unimpressed because he likes the capybaras better than the elephants?"

"I don't know. Can you?"

Bruce finally put his cell phone away and watched as baby stood both of his front feet on one pumpkin. *Splat.* I'm not sure why this whole thing was so fascinating and adorable, but it was, even though I didn't care about elephants that much. I guess it's partly just that there's nothing like a baby mammal, no matter what kind of mammal it is.

Then the baby finally seemed to notice the group of people standing around the yard watching him and got distracted from the pumpkins. He walked up to them and put his trunk out to the photographer. He was about the same height as the grownup people looking at him. The photographer put her hand on his trunk, and it looked like they were shaking hands. How nice of him to stop being a bad little boy and greet his admirers so politely.

"Oh my God, that's so cute," I moaned.

I didn't want to be an elephant keeper, because I wasn't that thrilled with the idea of working with an animal that might kill me. Elephants kill more keepers than any other animals. But it was hard to remember that right at this moment when I was so insanely jealous of people who got to shake hands with the baby elephant's trunk. I needed to make friends with some elephant keepers, I thought. Maybe then they'd let me do it sometime.

I saw that in the other yard, the sad woman was now bringing another elephant out.

"Why is that one separate?" I said.

"She wouldn't get any of the pumpkins if she was with the others," Chris said.

With animals like the elephants, often the whole zoo staff knew about their personalities and family history. I wouldn't expect Bruce to know which of my pygmy marmosets was the submissive one, but if I asked Chris about elephants, he could tell me all sorts of stories about each of them and what happened to them long before I worked here.

The sad elephant walked up to the pumpkins and gave one a tentative kick. I saw the keeper talking to her, encouraging her. Zoo people were like other animal people—there was the type who always wanted to rescue the blind dog with three legs, who liked trying to draw the timid animals out of their shells. But that kind of thing just made me impatient. There's a pumpkin, dammit. What are you waiting for? Seize the day!

The sad elephant put a foot on a pumpkin, and left it there for a moment. Then she put her weight down and it was crushed. It didn't give the same satisfying *splat* that the others had. But there was a little scattered applause, from the three-legged-blind-dog crowd, the people who were happy to see the sad elephant make an attempt at what came naturally to all the others.

I turned back to where the baby elephant was making a mess of crushed-up pumpkin bits. I didn't feel guilty about liking the animals that were more fun, I thought. Which reminded me of something.

"Do we have time to go visit the capybaras?"

"Not really," Chris said, "but let's go anyway."

Wombat and pumpkin stomping and capybaras. I wanted to skip down the path holding his hand, but I managed to keep the feeling hidden inside.

I looked at the clock as I sat down at the computer. So I was going to be leaving late again. When I got home, the pugs would gaze at me with those tragic pug expressions, shaped by generations of selective breeding by people who apparently enjoyed feeling guilty every time their dogs looked at them. But I had to email Allison about what species of wombat we were going to get. I was afraid if I waited, I would seem unappreciative, or she might discover some reason to change her mind.

I knew that common wombats were the cutest kind. They were the roundest. But there was no point in picking an animal I couldn't get. It was nearly impossible to get animals out of Australia, even ones that weren't endangered. So I had to find out what was a realistic possibility.

Chris had already checked the surplus list for me, where zoos listed the animals that they were trying to get rid of. There were no wombats on it. But the list wasn't always up to date, and I knew Allison had her special powers of persuasion. So I needed to find out what zoos had any wombats to begin with.

There's a website where you can find out where animals are in zoos all over the world. It's called Isis, for International Species Information System. Zoo staff can get more detailed information, but anyone can go and find out the basic species holdings. Before I worked at a zoo, I used to use it all the time to find out where they had some good animal that I wanted to go on vacation to see.

Sometimes the answer is discouraging. If you want to see an aye-aye, you'd better be able to get to North Carolina. Otherwise you are out of luck. But if you want to see capybaras, you can probably find some pretty nearby. Either way, it's fun to be able to find this out before you get there.

I logged on to the computer and checked the wombat holdings in North America. There was only one place that claimed to have one common wombat. That was worse than I'd remembered. There was a biggish handful of zoos that had the hairy-nosed wombat, so we'd have to take our chances with that. Still, there sure weren't a lot of them. There were more hairy-nosed wombats than aye-ayes, but not by much.

So, anyway, I just had to email Allison, and then I could go home. But somehow I found myself reading my other email first. I shouldn't be wasting time like this with the pugs waiting for me to come home, but first let's just clean out all these pointless memos about computer viruses and blood drives and lectures that I'd never have time to attend and—oh, not more email about the pandas. Don't get me started on the pandas. Why was everyone supposed to be so fascinated by every move the pandas made? I could probably teach marmosets to tap dance and still not get as much attention as—

I hit delete. I needed to go home. I started a new message.

Dear Allison, I typed.

Wait, is that okay? I can't just write to her using her first name, can I? I wondered. But it sounds funny to use her title. Email was pretty informal, and everyone called her by her first name. No, they *referred* to her by her name—did they really address her that way? I certainly never did. But then what? "Dear Ms. Craine"? No one called her that. "Dear Director"? That was totally bizarre.

Okay, there was nothing I could do but skip that part for now . . . I left a blank line and typed some more.

> *I checked on Isis and nearly all the wombats in North America are the hairy-nosed, so I guess we'll have to try to get one of those, even though the common ones are cuter.*

I read it over. No, better take out the "cute" remark. It made it sound more informal, which might make it okay to address her by her name, but still . . . I backspaced. I was beginning to understand why I'd avoided starting this. Going back and rereading all the spam and memos was starting to seem like an attractive option.

I checked on Isis, and nearly all the wombats in North America are the hairy-nosed, so I guess we'll have to try to get one of those.

Um, but is that it, then? Now I just say "Love, Hannah," and that's the whole message? That's no good. Wait, maybe I need to be making this less like it's just between the two of us. I typed some more.

All of us at Small Mammals are very excited . . .

No, is that not businesslike enough? This was giving me a stomach ache. I backspaced and tried again.

All of us at Small Mammals are eagerly awaiting . . . are looking forward to . . .

I moaned and highlighted the whole sentence and hit the delete key.

"What a face. What are you doing?"

I looked around. It was Margo, on her way out.

"Writing to Allison about the wombat," I said, trying not to wail.

"Be careful what you wish for," she said, airily, and walked out.

I desperately typed some more and read it over.

Hi

I checked on Isis and the only wombats in North America are the hairy-nosed, so I guess we'll have to try to get one of those. We're all really looking forward to it.

Thanks,
Hannah

Oh God. I probably sounded like a moron, but what would she expect from a lowly poop-shoveler? I wasn't expected to be able to write fancy memos, just push a broom and lock the cage doors behind me. Right?

I stared at the screen for another minute. I went back and put a comma after "Hi" and stared at it some more. I wondered if I should just forget about getting a wombat if it meant I had to sound like a moron in front of the director of the whole zoo. She always seemed so friendly and interested in me when she was there in the same room. But when she wasn't, you heard all the stories about how she threw her weight around, and you got the definite impression that she didn't suffer fools gladly. Was this an email that a fool would write?

I might have stared at the screen all afternoon, but just then Chris came in the door from outside that was right next to the desk. He stopped to look in his mailbox before walking around me. The idea of him reading the message over my shoulder was suddenly my most immediate and overwhelmingly terrifying problem. It would be bad enough to sound stupid in front of Allison, but for Chris to see how stupid I sounded in front of Allison would be unbearable.

I quickly hit *Send.* Of course, now that I was in a rush to get rid of the message, the computer hemmed and hawed for a moment before sending it and making it disappear from the screen.

Just as he turned around, the "message sent" notice appeared and I sighed, I guess noticeably, because he looked at me a little funny.

"Are you okay?"

"Fine," I said, forcing a bright tone.

He put his hand on the back of the chair. I closed my eyes and tried not to lean back against his arm.

"Hairy-nosed wombats are probably the only kind we can get," I said.

He nodded. "Hairy-nosed is a good name."

Oh, it was. I hadn't thought of that. "Oh, yeah," I said happily.

I opened my eyes and saw that he was smiling at me like it was adorable how I felt about wombats. I blushed and turned away, looking intently at my email.

"I'm heading out," he said.

"I'll lock up," I said, not looking at him.

"See you tomorrow."

He went back out the door. I stared at the screen for no reason for another minute, then got up to get ready to go.

Chapter 3

I looked at my watch as I walked past the capybaras. They were immobile piles of brown shagginess, their eyes closed, dreaming about chewing grasses all day. I was early again. All that leftover Halloween candy was definitely giving me extra energy. Maybe a steady diet of chocolate after every meal including breakfast was something I should consider more seriously.

As I neared the building, I realized that my early arrival wasn't the only unusual thing about this morning. I heard sirens. We could hear sirens from the streets all the time, but these sounded much closer. And now, looking up the path past the entrance to Small Mammals, I saw flashing lights up near the Elephants building.

This would have been a good day to have forgotten to put my radio away and brought it home by accident. Whatever was going on, there must be a ton of radio traffic right now, even this early. I thought about running to get one so I could eavesdrop. No, the heck with it. Why not take the direct approach?

They might need help, I rationalized as I started to trot up the hill, despite knowing that an escaped animal situation never involved flashing lights. And an animal emergency wouldn't call for the ambulance that I saw as I got closer.

There were police, too. And the biggest surprise was that they were in the outdoor elephant yard.

More police were blocking the way into the building. But a group of people was gathered on the path overlooking that yard.

I didn't know most of them—Large Mammal staff who were familiar only by sight. But one of them had his back to me, and I recognized that black spiky haircut. No surprise—Ray would be in the middle of trouble whenever he could manage. He'd know what was up.

I ran up and touched him on the shoulder. "Ray."

He turned and looked at me. His face was so serious that it scared me. His goofiness on Halloween was typical, but he had a dark side too. This wasn't either, though, and I wasn't sure what to think.

"Hannah," he said, putting his hands on my shoulders, "you don't want to see this."

"Don't want to see what? How can I tell before I know what it is? What happened?"

He walked me a little bit away from the group of other keepers.

"There's a body in the elephant yard," he said quietly. "One of the keepers found it this morning."

"Oh no," I said, "One of the elephants attacked a keeper?"

"No. It doesn't look like it's one of us. And it wasn't just the elephants. Because someone had put a pumpkin around his head."

I stared at him. It was the day after elephant pumpkin-stomping. He didn't have to explain any further.

"Oh," I said. Kind of a stupid reaction. But I was stunned. Why would anyone do such a thing? It was so bizarre and sick, I wondered if I was dreaming. But I was sure I'd never felt so realistically queasy in a dream.

I looked over toward where the police were searching the elephant yard. It was weird to see people in a different uniform in there. Only elephant keepers were allowed in the elephant yard. Because elephants were dangerous. They could kill you.

Once I looked, I started walking in that direction like an irresistible force was sucking me in.

"Hannah," Ray said and reached his hand for mine.

I shook my head without knowing what I meant by it. I looked into his dark eyes. I found the words I was searching for. "I don't want you to protect me."

He looked unhappy but said nothing. He waited till I had gone a few more steps and followed slowly behind.

I got as close as I could and leaned against the railing. Ray came and stood next to me. I could feel him watching me.

The body was lying on its stomach. You could tell it was a man from the clothing. If it had been a keeper, the clothing wouldn't have told you anything, since we all dressed the same. But he was wearing a men's business suit.

Without being told what had happened, it might have been kind of hard to tell at first. Which parts were just smashed pumpkin, and which were smashed something else, wasn't all that clear. Fortunately, I guess. And there was the disbelief, too—surely it was just some trick of the light. But eventually there was no choice but to believe it. His head must have been inside the pumpkin.

I was oddly calm. My first thought was, it's a good thing Robin is on vacation. She can't even stand it when we find a mouse on a glue trap and have to kill it by hitting its head against the counter.

Maybe the reality of the situation hadn't sunk in. Or maybe I was getting used to death. The first time I found one of my animals dead, it was devastating. The second time, well, you had to accept it; none of them lived forever. The first time I saw a chunk of one of my animals cut up on the table at pathology rounds, it was horrible. The second time, I was interested to understand what it had died of.

I suddenly thought of something.

"No one would just lie still while that happened," I said. "He must have been already dead. Or at least drugged."

Ray nodded, like he'd already thought of that.

"Do you know who it is?" I said.

He shook his head. "But we could see they found a wallet, so the police must know."

I realized that I had a more immediate problem. It was not my job to figure out who was dead in the elephant yard. I had a different job entirely, and it was almost 7:30, and I wasn't at work yet. I didn't have a radio, so I wouldn't know if anyone was looking for me. Surely this was such an exceptional circumstance that I wouldn't get in trouble? But it was hard to tell. People could be such sticklers for the rules and regulations around here.

But before I decided what to do, it didn't matter, because just then the one who'd have been looking for me found me.

"Do you know who it is?" I said to Chris without any preliminaries.

He looked at me with the blank expression that meant that he knew something he thought he shouldn't tell me. I held his gaze while the part of him that was one of us wrestled with the management part.

After a moment he looked away and said, "It looks like it was Victor from the ID he was carrying."

"Oh," I said stupidly, again. Yeah, obviously they'd have to do a little work to identify the body for sure, I thought with a shudder. Poor Victor. What a horrible way to die. Just two days ago I'd been showing him the tenrec and complaining about the Small Mammals building having nothing but stupid trick-or-treat rainforest raisins. It was hard to believe.

And poor Allison. Their relationship had been quite public, so now she was going to have to deal with it in public. Even though she was used to being the center of attention, surely that was going to be hard.

"Does she—" I stopped, because following Chris's gaze I saw the answer to my question. A car had just pulled up, and Allison was getting out of it.

Whatever she already knew, you could tell that she was just as in charge of the situation as she always was. We were used to watching creatures interact without conversation, but you didn't need any professional expertise to interpret her body language, even at a distance. An officer outside the door of the building started to say something to her. She barely slowed down to snap at him, and you could just see him flinch. She disappeared into the entrance. After a moment I saw her stride out into the elephant yard.

I don't know how I expected her to react, but I guess it wasn't surprising that there were no hysterics. She knew how to conduct herself in public, whatever was going on inside her.

She looked at the body and talked to some important-looking police person, and after that, they started to take it away. Had they waited for her to identify it? Or had she stopped them from taking it away till she'd seen it? This was her territory, and nothing important happened without her being a part of it.

Police were still swarming over the elephant yard, I suppose looking for evidence. She looked at them with what was, even at this distance, clearly disgust, and said something to the police official. It was pretty obvious that his reply was not what she wanted. There were a few things in the world even she couldn't control. She wasn't happy, but the only way she could deal with the situation was by making a dramatic exit.

She passed back through the Elephant House quickly. She came out the same door she'd gone in and barked orders at various members of her staff who were waiting nervously around the car. She didn't get back in, though, and I remembered it probably wasn't her car—she lived right outside the back gate of the zoo and didn't need to drive here.

She strode up the path. No one followed her. That must have been one of her orders, or they'd all have been flocking around her. Her long golden hair streamed behind her. She had the kind of hair that would have been the center of attention even if her personality wasn't, and that was probably as much work to take care of as a pet. I remembered how Margo always said she'd been promoted to director because of her hair. It was an exaggeration, but since her job was to be the public face of the zoo, her looks didn't hurt.

I was lost in thought and didn't realize Chris was saying my name until he touched my arm lightly.

"We should go," he said.

I looked around and saw Ray was sitting on a bench behind us. "Can I catch up in a second?"

"Sure," he said, starting to walk away. He'd never get through all those knots of people without stopping anyway. It looked like half the keeper staff had found their way here. Nothing was going to happen quickly today.

I walked over to the bench and told Ray I had to go.

"This is awful," I said, reluctant to leave. "I feel so bad for her, such a terrible shock, and to have to deal with it in public."

He was unmoved. "Knowing her, she was probably about done with him anyway. It's good timing."

"Ray, don't joke. That's horrible." Although he was unnervingly correct, in fact. Allison's love life was conspicuously serial. Still, this was a dreadful thing to say out loud right now. Changing the subject, I said, "You know she says she's going to get me a wombat at Small Mammals."

"No wonder you're on her side," he said, like he could sympathize. There was probably some special reptile that he'd always wanted the zoo to get, too. "But be careful of who comes bearing gifts."

I sighed. He didn't hate Allison like Chris clearly did, but his attitude had always been hard to interpret, like a lot of things about him. This wasn't the first time he'd warned me against Allison in his usual dramatic and mysterious manner. Sometimes he seemed to admire her, but in a way that implied she had evil talents. Yet other times he hinted he'd been on Allison's long roster of conquests back in the mists of time, which to me was any time before I'd started to work here. Such a thing was believable if only because you couldn't imagine him refusing the experience. But I had no idea whether it was true, much less what feelings it would leave him with.

"I really have to go," I said, looking over to where Chris had made his way to the outermost gaggle of standing-around people. He was about to make his escape back to Small Mammals, and I should be going with him. Animals didn't stop pooping or needing to be fed because someone had died, no matter how horribly. We had work to do.

Ray nodded. I hated to leave him alone in the mood he seemed to be in, but there was nothing I could do about it. I gave him a regretful backward glance as I ran after Chris, who was finally disengaging himself from a last conversation and trying to start down the hill back to the building.

"Hey," I called, and he turned and waited for me.

We walked together in silence for a moment.

"They're going to keep the park closed at least for the morning," he said. "It's too hard to keep people away from the elephant yards."

That was good. I didn't want to have to keep explaining to people why the Elephant House was closed.

I noticed he kept glancing over at me in a funny way, but I was lost in thought. I was thinking of the last time I'd seen Victor, bringing me back chocolate from the Reptile House at the Halloween event, conspiratorially confessing that it was politically incorrect candy with no connection to rainforest preservation. It was hard to believe he wasn't going to be popping up all over the zoo anymore.

We stopped at the door. I stared into space while Chris got out his keys. After a moment I noticed nothing was happening, I guess, and I looked over and saw he was looking at me intently.

"Are you okay?" he said.

I looked back at him stupidly, I think, because the inappropriate thought that was going through my head was that his eyes looked like heavenly blue morning glories on a cloudy day.

"I'm okay," I said after a moment.

He nodded, and we went into the building.

Jeff and Caleb were working in the kitchen when we got there. "Where've you guys been?" said Jeff. Somehow both of them had missed all the commotion and didn't know what was going on.

I didn't really want to listen to a description of what I'd just seen. I went in the ladies' room and changed into my boots. I sat there for a while, feeling sad that I'd never get to show Victor the three-banded armadillo that we used for demos. He would have appreciated the story about how its closest other relative in the building was the sloth. He would have been interested in how visitors were often confused about whether it was a mammal. He would have really liked it.

When I returned to the kitchen, Jeff looked pale and was asking Chris all kinds of questions that no one could answer yet. That seemed like a normal reaction. Caleb was weird, though. He'd been an elephant keeper till recently—you'd expect him to be especially interested. But he seemed completely unmoved.

Maybe he was just being his usual lugubrious self, I thought. Caleb was big and bearded, the sort of person you would describe as bearlike even if you didn't work at a zoo. His hair was reddish, starting to go gray. Reddish brown was like a bear, but I thought that when he went grayer he would remind me of a musk ox, especially when he let his beard get shaggy. Jeff was so different standing next to him, bony and leggy, more like some kind of tall deer or antelope, maybe even a giraffe.

That got me thinking of what different animals all the men were. The rest of them were definitely not hoofstock. Ray was dark and feline. Compact muscles ready to spring, and a little undercurrent of scariness even when he was just lazing around. Victor had been foxlike, not just his hair, but how he was kind of quick and graceful. And how he popped up where you didn't expect him, but it was always a nice surprise.

Chris was a problem, because what animals had blue eyes? I couldn't imagine him any other way. There was a blue-eyed lemur, but lemurs were lovable but dumb, which was definitely wrong. Maybe he was a wonderful purebred dog of some kind. Sometimes you saw a dog that was so perfectly put together and moved so beautifully that it took your breath away. But why was he the only one I thought of as a domestic animal, I wondered. Maybe because he was the one I wanted hanging around my house—

"Hannah," someone was saying. Repeating, it sounded like.

I looked around. It was Caleb. Jeff and Chris were gone. I hoped Jeff hadn't been so upset that he'd needed to go sit down. Jeff was a delicate flower. Caleb was a big old tuber.

"Sorry," I said. "I was kind of out of it. What did you say?"

"Could you pass me that sweet potato?"

I picked up a big old tuber from the table in front of me and looked at it stupidly for a moment and then handed it to him. I thought how it was a good thing that we didn't normally feed pumpkin to any of our animals. I was especially glad that I'd already cleaned the jack o'lanterns out of my exhibits.

"I was thinking about Victor," I said, only partially lying. "It's so awful. It's so hard to believe."

Caleb just grunted. And then I remembered something. Hadn't I heard that he was one of Allison's previous boyfriends?

How could Margo be off today, I thought, frustrated. She was the only one I could ask. It was weird, suspicious even, that he had had so little reaction to the news. Maybe I was wrong. But suddenly I felt uncomfortable about being with him.

"I'm going down to the mara yard," I said. Not that it was any of Caleb's business. But I felt like I needed to cover my urge to flee. I wanted out, and the maras, my only outdoor exhibit, were as out as I could get and still be working.

Caleb nodded without looking up. I grabbed my mara pans and meds out of the fridge and trotted out the door.

This was going to be hard, I thought as I walked down the path. The animals were all used to their routine at a certain time, and the maras were hard to medicate, not like the greedy little primates who would gladly take poison if you hid it inside a grape. Maras are the second largest rodent in the world. After the capybara, of course. They are also called Patagonian cavies—cavies, like guinea pigs. They are like very large guinea pigs on long deer-like legs, with Vulcan ears. Visitors always had strange theories about what they were—huge bunnies, little kangaroos, rabbits crossed with dogs. Don't ask me why they don't just read the sign, which says very clearly that they are rodents. That would be too easy.

What was relevant about them at the moment right now, though, was not their appearance or the order they belonged to, but their personalities and behavior. They are skittish, like the little deer that they resemble. And what I had found lately is that they were incredibly fussy eaters. It's a typical herbivore thing. They had ancestors who were afraid to eat unfamiliar food, and so more likely to skip eating something poisonous, and so also more likely to stick around to leave descendants—who were also afraid to eat unfamiliar food. Great in the wild;

not so great when your keeper is trying to make you feel better with medicine.

I climbed over the wall, sat down in their yard, and held out a leafeater biscuit. “Here, babies,” I said, “come have your cookies.” Leafeater biscuits are little red crunchy things that are supposed to be apple flavored. They don’t taste like anything to me. But the maras and lots of other animals love them. So I assume I just don’t know what I’m missing.

The maras both turned and looked at me for a few moments. They were prey animals, so they couldn’t help being cautious. It was in their nature. I tried to be patient. It was a beautiful morning, and I had a nice view of the Reptile House from here. It was another of the old buildings, made of red brick with stone reptiles decorating it. Usually I was happy to sit here and look at it against the blue sky, wondering what Ray was up to, listening to the gibbons in their nearby exhibit starting to hoot and holler.

The female mara came up to me slowly and took a biscuit. “There you go, mousie-pie,” I said, happily. The first one had no medication on it. I quickly squirted a little of the liquid onto the second one. I held the medicated end, and pointed the plain end into her mouth. She took the end with her teeth while she was still chewing the first one, and I pushed it in gently, feeling her soft lips with my fingers. Success! I grabbed another one and squirted a little more medicine onto it and held it in the same way.

She took it in her teeth and then stopped chewing. And then she dropped it.

Okay, maybe she was just clumsy. I picked it up and tried again. She took it again and dropped it.

Maybe she just didn’t like the dirt that was sticking to it now. I gave her another plain one, and she ate it right up. I put a tiny bit of the meds on another and held it out. She touched it with her teeth, dropped it, and walked away.

This problem had been coming on for a while. At first, she'd actually seemed to like the medicated biscuits better than the plain ones. Then she gradually stopped eating as many of them, so now, most days she was getting somewhat less than the full dose.

But walking away from the second biscuit with a tiny drop on it. This was bad news.

"Silly tasty prey animal," I said. "Silly girl. I'm not trying to knock you out and then eat you. I promise."

She sat and blinked.

"Come on, munchkin. You need to have more of this. It's good for you and tastes good too. Yummy grape flavor," I cooed. "Please."

She got up and walked toward me. I watched a jogger run by as the mara came slowly closer. I waited anxiously while she sniffed my offering. She took the plain biscuit and chewed it up. "Good maragirlie!" I held out another with a tiny bit of meds on it. She took it and started to chew, and my heart leapt with joy, and then she dropped it and walked away.

I felt my eyes start to water. Then I sniffled. Wait a minute. This is stupid, I thought. This is frustrating, but it's nothing to cry about. But I had been so happy that I had managed to train them to hand feed and that we'd found a flavor of meds that she would eat. Now we'd have to start all over again from scratch. And now I was really bawling.

I felt like a lunatic sitting in the dirt crying over my mara not taking her medication, but I couldn't help it. I rubbed my eyes with my sticky fingers and got grape ibuprofen all over my face, and that just made me cry harder.

I leaned back against the little tree I was sitting under and stared helplessly out of the mara yard. Through my tears I saw the red brick of the Reptile House. And I remembered Victor's red hair, and Ray, this morning, and why we were outside the Elephant House.

Now it made more sense why I was crying. And for some reason, that made me stop.

I rinsed my fingers in the maras' pool, and tried to wipe the tears and sticky grapeyness off my face with my wet fingers. I got up. There was no point in spending any more time on this. We were just going to have to find another kind of medication. Rodents 1, Hannah 0. Humans had these big convoluted brains, but we so often lost these battles with the allegedly "lower" species. They were good at what they did. And what these guys did was be careful not to eat funny-tasting things that might be poisonous. It was hard to fight millennia of evolution.

I put the rest of the unmedicated biscuits in their food pan. The female came over while I was still putting the pans down on the ground. She purred as she started to eat. You know that little trilling noise that a guinea pig makes? The maras make almost the same noise, but much louder. It was such a sweet little sound, I wanted to cry again, but I got my broom and swept up some mara poop instead.

Chapter 4

Yesterday our routine had been disrupted by a murder. Today's disruption was fortunately more mundane. There was an all-employee meeting that had been announced the previous week. Allison held these meetings regularly. She said they were to make sure she kept the lines of communication open with the staff. Sounded like a great idea, sure. But no one really wanted to go, and in every unit the meetings were preceded by a few minutes of negotiation while people argued about whose turn it was to put in an appearance.

This time was different. The auditorium was full to overflowing ten minutes before the 8:30 start time. There was a buzz in the air. Obviously, it wasn't the meeting agenda that caused the excitement—no one cared about the construction budget or any of those other boring subjects. No one understood why she had meetings about those things when she could have just sent out mass emails that we could all conveniently delete. But this time we were all sure she'd talk about something else.

"Thank you all for coming," she began. She was a little more subdued than usual, as you would expect. "I'm glad to see there is such an excellent turnout. Before we turn to the business of this meeting, I want to say a few words about the unfortunate death of Victor Reynard, our public relations director."

"What?" hissed Margo in my ear. "You mean she's going to go ahead with the agenda?"

"I won't go over the details you've all heard and read about in the newspaper," Allison continued. "I can't tell you any more than that the police are still working hard to solve his murder, and we're cooperating fully. What I did want to say, although this is rather personal to talk about in front of a meeting like this . . . But I know we're really all a family here. Most of you know that Victor and I had had a relationship for some time. This wasn't any secret. So I felt you all should know that our relationship ended a few days before his death, by mutual agreement."

Margo elbowed me, and I turned to look. She made a face at me like she couldn't believe it. "Brilliant timing," she whispered skeptically. But why would Allison lie about such a thing? I wondered. Maybe because she thought this would let her have her feelings more in private? It seemed simpler to believe she was telling the truth.

"This isn't the sort of thing I'd normally announce at a meeting," Allison said, with just a little bit of an embarrassed laugh, but then she turned serious again. "But so many of you have been kind enough to express your sympathy. And while I am devastated by his death and by its horrible manner . . ."—she sounded a little choked up—"still, it is a little different than it might have been if our personal relationship had been continuing."

She was silent for a moment. Then she seemed to brighten up. "Well, there's really nothing else I can say about that subject. I hope you will all be as helpful as you can if the police ask for your assistance. And in speaking with the public, please do what you can to reassure them that this was a unique event, and that everyone is much safer here than in the rest of the city, in fact." She looked around expectantly, and a few people nodded obediently.

"So I would like to continue now with the announced agenda. Our regular business does have to proceed as normal despite this distressing event. I know that Victor would have wanted the zoo to continue its onward progress. He was more than just an employee here. He sincerely cared about the welfare of this institution and would not have wanted to upset our normal functioning. So I feel that as a tribute to him and his nearly ten years of service, we should all try to go on as normally as possible."

"Oh, honestly," Margo whispered. "She is just too much. I'm going to hurl." She rolled her eyes dramatically.

I could understand how Margo felt. I thought Allison was right, though, even if she put it in that stilted, managerial way she always had at these meetings. Victor worked here because he thought the animals were cool. He'd chosen to write press releases about animals rather than work somewhere else for more money. He'd be sorry the stories in the newspaper were about his murder instead of about some neat animal thing that was happening here.

"As I'm sure you all remember from previous meetings, the new five-year master plan is designed to tie in to the general theme of rainforest conservation."

"I can't believe she's doing this," said Margo in my ear. "She's trapped us here."

She sure had. Just like we sometimes caught up our animals by putting their favorite treats in a live trap. They ran in to get the grape, and they couldn't get out. Margo had come to the auditorium thinking she'd get her favorite treat of gossip, and now she couldn't get out.

Allison turned to her computer and started up a slide show of blueprints for new construction.

"Believe it," I said despairingly.

"Some of the plans involve programs that don't require physical changes. The travel packages we sponsor have been modified to emphasize the ecotourism aspect of the trips, and we're concentrating on making sure that we give our business to companies that hire the local people, keeping them from needing to destroy the environment to make a living. We hope to teach them that they can make a better living by preserving a pristine environment that people will want to visit. We're also encouraging all the lodges to only buy food and supplies that have been sustainably farmed locally."

I squirmed. Of course these were all important issues. But we'd heard it all a million times before with exactly the same slideshow, and the floors of my exhibits were still all covered with poop that wasn't going to miraculously disappear while I sat here looking at blueprints of buildings that hadn't even been built and exhibits that no one had excreted in yet.

"We are also cooperating with one of the reserves that's involved with our tours to sponsor an adopt-an-acre program. People who donate will receive materials explaining what lives and grows in their own little acre of rainforest. We hope people will learn that each acre of rainforest contains thousands of individual plants and animals . . ."

Which, she would carefully not mention, were mostly insects, of course. Like the insects that were crawling all over the old food pans I hadn't taken out of most of my exhibits yet this morning. But no, those were rare and exotic rainforest insects, some of which had not yet been described by science, I thought, as she predictably continued. ". . . some of which are as yet unknown to science. So every acre that's destroyed could be an irreparable loss—organisms could be going extinct before we even know what we're losing. Each individual, then, will feel that they may have personally saved a species from extinction. With the proper promotion, this should be quite an inspiring program."

I was starting to feel drowsy from sitting still too long. I would only adopt an acre that had some of that organic fair-trade chocolate growing on it, I thought, so I could make sure we had some at Small Mammals next Halloween . . .

I felt Margo's elbow in my side and opened my eyes. It looked like it must be the question period, because Allison was peering into the audience at someone who was talking. Good, that meant the meeting was almost over. No one ever asked serious questions at these meetings, so this part should go quickly.

But as I woke up a little more, I realized I was wrong. The atmosphere in the room was totally different from when I had drifted off to sleep. I could feel the tension. Something serious was going on.

Stephanie, the elephant keeper, was in the middle of an impassioned speech of some kind. She was the big blond one who had looked so sad at the pumpkin stomp with the sad elephant.

"Elephants are social animals," she said. "You know that perfectly well. And they form lifelong bonds with other individuals. Tami and Lucy have been together for fifteen years. It's cruel to separate them. She could stay here and be artificially inseminated, like we did with Amber."

She was talking about the plans to move Lucy the elephant to another zoo where she could breed. This was a perfectly normal thing that zoos did all the time. Since there was a limited number of members of any one species in captivity, it was important to maintain the genetic diversity of the population. The best genetic match wasn't always an animal at the same zoo, so moving animals around for breeding purposes was common.

Not being that interested in elephants, I hadn't paid much attention to the talk about these plans. But now I realized that Lucy must be the sad elephant who had to get her pumpkins alone so the others wouldn't steal them from her. And that she must be Stephanie's favorite.

"She just wants her own baby elephant," Margo whispered.

Elephant people were fanatics, I thought. Oh well, I guessed I was a fanatic, too. I was a wombat fanatic. And I wanted a sloth baby. That seemed normal to me. But then when you saw it in another person, with an animal that didn't push any of your buttons, you realized it was a little weird. I couldn't understand wanting to work with elephants. I didn't think I'd love wombats if they were as dangerous as elephants. Or would I?

Allison smiled and put on a patient face. "Stephanie, I appreciate your concern. But you know better than anyone how valuable Lucy is genetically. And we don't have the facilities to breed any more elephants here right now. We have to consider the good of the species. And in this case I don't see that there is great harm to Tami or Lucy. Tami has other elephants here for company that she's known almost as long, and Lucy will have the opportunity to be part of a more normal family grouping. I think it's really a win-win situation all around."

You could see the fury mounting in Stephanie's face. "You're just parroting your own press releases." Really Victor's press releases, I thought. "You just don't care about the individual animals at all. You think about conserving habitats and the good of species and raising more money for the zoo. All you care about the individual animals for is to have your picture taken with them."

People were on the edges of their seats. No one ever argued like this with Allison anywhere, anytime, much less in public. Stephanie's colleagues were pulling at her sleeve and trying to get her to calm down and sit down, but she shook them off, staring at Allison and waiting for a reply.

It was an odd picture. Allison stood, tall and stately, in front of the room in her expensive business clothes and her long golden hair that people couldn't help staring at. Stephanie was like a distorted mirror image of Allison. She was also tall and had long blond hair. But she was rougher. It wasn't just that she was wearing a keeper's uniform instead of a fancy business suit. Her hair was less golden and glossy, she had bigger bones, and she didn't have that perfect complexion. Or the stage presence. She was the pet store puppy to Allison's grand champion.

I remembered that I had thought Stephanie looked like a big blond Valkyrie. Weren't they some kind of warrior women? I sure wouldn't want to meet her in a dark alley, especially if she was as angry as she was right now. But Allison wouldn't bother to beat you up. She'd just put you in your place with a stare. She'd win the fight before it even started. The alpha female was the one that didn't need to physically fight to maintain her position.

"Let's talk about this in private," Allison said calmly. "We can meet in my office right after this meeting. Which could be right now, if there aren't any other questions?"

Stephanie scowled. She obviously preferred a public scene and had probably hoped to get support from other keepers. Caring about the individual animal, against management's view of the big picture, was something that happened to all of us. We knew what she felt. But she'd miscalculated if she thought anyone was going to go against Allison in public. And now she could hardly complain about the offer of a private meeting with the director.

If there wasn't going to be an interesting fight, everyone was anxious to get the hell out of there—something Allison had surely counted on. People started to make little preliminary getting-up wiggles.

"Fine, then, let's get back to work, shall we? Thank you all for coming."

Everyone made a break for it like a herd of stampeding wildebeest. Once we were outside, I said to Margo, "Wow. If it was

Allison who'd been killed, I'd sure think Stephanie might have done it."

"Quite a performance." Margo nodded. "Well, you know, maybe she killed Victor to get back at Allison for trying to take her elephant away from her. But she didn't know they'd broken up. Poor Stephanie, it's just the kind of thing that would happen to her."

Poor bottom-of-the-pack Stephanie. Nothing ever went quite her way.

"It had to be someone who could get close to the elephants, right?" I said. "Get them not to spook when they saw this pumpkin was, um, a little different. A stranger couldn't do it."

I wondered if they knew which elephant had done it. Was it Stephanie's favorite? It wasn't the sort of thing you'd expect the police to think about. An elephant was probably an elephant to them.

She shrugged. "Someone could have had help. Honestly, there are so many people here who dislike Allison. If we're going to entertain the idea that the murder was a way to get at her instead of being directed at Victor himself . . . well, it's easier to think of who doesn't have a motive than who does."

Surely that was an exaggeration, I thought. But still, considering just the people in our own building: Margo didn't like her, Chris had some mysterious problem with her. And Caleb—

"Hey," I said, looking around to make sure no one could overhear, "I meant to ask you. Wasn't Caleb one of Allison's—"

"Yes," she interrupted. "And he was quite a good elephant trainer, I understand."

Jealousy. That was a classic motive. Maybe I was right that his lack of reaction yesterday was suspicious.

"And then there's Matthew," she continued. "He's supposedly very unhappy that they're going to start a new no-contact policy with the baby elephant, since he's a male. He's known him since he was born and all that. And obviously—" She rolled her eyes. "He can handle anything his way, he thinks, so it's an insult."

Allison really should have announced her breakup with Victor right away, I thought, suppressing an inappropriate giggle. A mass email might have stopped all these people from killing him. And it would have been a lot more interesting than most of the junk they sent us.

"Matthew seems like a jerk," I said. I'd only seen him from a distance, but he had the stage presence of a jerk, for sure.

"Tell me about it. Yeah, let's root for it being him," Margo said flippantly as we pulled open the back door of Small Mammals and had to stop talking about it.

I ran downstairs to do some paperwork before I forgot. I was supposed to record the medication for the mara every day, whether she took it or not. As usual she hadn't, but I had to record my failures faithfully, despite how depressing it was.

I saw that the medication record sheet for the mara was almost full, which should mean that we needed to order new meds. I checked the package and saw that it was almost empty. I stuck my head into Chris's office.

"Hey," I said, "was the mara's medication on the list of stuff you ordered this week?"

"Yes, I cc'd the email to everyone. You didn't get it?" He turned to the keyboard and started to type. "Did it get bounced back? I didn't see it . . ."

"Uh, wait . . ." I began, embarrassed.

"I sent it yesterday afternoon," he said, continuing to type, looking at the screen intently.

"Yeah, but, I haven't looked at my email since . . ." I hesitated. "Since the day before yesterday," I said in a rather small voice.

He stopped typing abruptly and looked at me, confused. He

knew that for me not to check my email four or five times a day, including from my decrepit old computer at home, would only happen if I was in a coma. A few inconvenient murders and so forth wouldn't be adequate to stop me.

I felt stupid. "I, um, sent Allison an email about the wombat, um, thing, and, I—I was just nervous about what she'd say, is all. It's . . . I know, it's dumb. I'm sorry."

His expression turned dark. I tensed up. He didn't say anything for a long moment. It was stupid of me to miss work emails for such a childish reason. I waited for him to yell at me. Not that he ever actually yelled, but coming from him even a gentle chiding was hard to take.

But he wasn't mad at me. He looked down at the desk and started to poke at a pencil, staring at it. I knew this meant he was about to say something not entirely work related.

"I knew this would happen," he said.

"What?" I said, uncomprehending.

"She's playing mind games again."

"What do you mean? She's not doing anything," I insisted. "She asked me to email her, and I'm just being silly. I just felt funny emailing the director of the whole zoo, you know? But it was her idea, so I'm just being dumb. It's not her fault."

He looked pained. He was silent for a bit. Then, still not looking at me, he said, "Never mind. It's none of my business."

"But—" I stopped. I had been trying to convince him he was wrong. But it hurt for him to say it wasn't his business as much as it did to have disappointed him about how I was doing my job. My stomach started to ache.

He went back to typing and didn't say anything else.

"I'll go look at it now." I heard the pleading tone in my voice and wanted to kick myself. This was why you shouldn't have a crush on your boss, I told myself for the millionth time. He'd always say he wasn't my boss—he'd put on his management voice in a jokey way and say that strictly speaking his job description did not include responsibility for personnel supervisory duties. But that didn't change how it felt in my stomach.

I went and sat down at the computer. My head began to hurt, too, as I waited for my list of new messages to load. I'd forgotten how much junk email we got until I saw what happened when I hadn't cleaned out a whole day's worth of it. I sifted through the garbage, looking for something from Allison. Half of these messages had already become irrelevant—like one about a parking lot closing for construction for the day, and then another message announcing its reopening. And the usual mass emailings keeping us up to date on every breath taken by a stupid giant panda.

There was no message from Allison. Was I not going to get a wombat after all? And Chris, what was the matter with him? My thoughts were a worse mess than my clogged inbox. I logged out and headed upstairs to find something sweaty to do to clear my mind.

I'd almost finished changing out the mulch in the hutia exhibit and I was feeling a lot better. I had dumped all the clean stuff in, and now all I had to do was spread it around. I was pretty much covered from head to toe in the stuff. But it went so much faster if you didn't worry about staying clean.

The door of the exhibit opened, and Chris stuck his head in. He looked me over, his expression like he was trying not to seem amused. So what? Not having people laugh at me wasn't a good enough reason to avoid getting covered in mulch.

"Go ahead, laugh," I said. He wasn't upset anymore, I could see. So he could laugh all he wanted, and I wouldn't mind.

He gave up trying not to smile. "I'm not laughing. You wear it well."

"That's what I like about working here," I said, climbing out. "No one thinks you're less ladylike for being covered all over in poop and stuff."

We grinned foolishly at each other for a moment.

"So what's up?" I said.

Chris took some pieces of mulch out of my hair. It gave me a nice companionable primate feeling, and I wished we could just sit down on the ground and do it all day. "You have a phone call," he said, in a carefully neutral tone. I had a feeling I knew who it was.

I picked up the phone, watching Chris as he walked away.

"Hi, this is Hannah."

"Hannah, you'll never believe our luck," said Allison without any preliminaries. She always expected you to know who she was. "I've found a place with a wombat that is ready to ship out immediately. It was all ready to go when arrangements with another zoo fell through—it's a great piece of luck. The zoo that's got it has already gotten in the animal that was going to replace it, so they're about to be out of space, too, since that animal's almost ready to come out of quarantine. So everyone's thrilled that we can take him on such short notice."

I was speechless for a moment. Normally it took months to get an animal, especially a new species. "So we can just take him?" I finally managed to say. "What about the paperwork?"

"We'll figure out how to hurry the paperwork. Don't worry. That's what I've got a staff for. And the exhibit doesn't really need that much renovation. We'll have it done on a rush basis and do most of his quarantine on exhibit."

The animals were supposed to go through a quarantine period up at the hospital for a month. Allison was always finding a way around this for special cases. Big animals had to be quarantined on exhibit because they didn't have space for, say, a giraffe at the hospital. Once you made that exception, then you had procedures in place you could use for a smaller animal, too. It made the vets angry, but there'd never been any complications from it yet, which made it easier to justify every time. Not that Allison needed to justify anything. She did what she wanted.

So not only would I have a wombat any minute, it would be on exhibit almost immediately. This was more like having jumped on a runaway train all the time. But wow, I was going to have a wombat any day now. Not six or nine months from now as usual. It was hard to believe. I felt like I was going to float away. Good thing we didn't have cordless phones, I thought; at least the phone cord would keep me from getting too far.

"I'd like to rush it so we can have something positive in the newspaper to take people's minds off Victor's death," she said. "We'll have an opening and invite all the feature reporters. You won't mind talking to them, will you?"

Ah. I should have known this couldn't just be about me. But it was a clever plan. "Of course not." Actually I hated the idea of being in the newspaper, but how could I complain? I was getting a wombat.

"Terrific," she said. "I'll put you through to Jessica now, and you can talk about scheduling, okay? This will be so much fun."

Jessica was Allison's right-hand person. Whenever her name came up, debate raged on how she could stand to do the job, with people generally breaking into three camps: the ones who thought she was a saint, the ones who thought she'd sold her soul, and the ones who thought she'd just lost her mind a long time ago.

The conversation about when to schedule the wombat exhibit opening went on for an awfully long time considering the end result, which was that there was only one day that it was possible to do it so that Allison could be there. And as always, Allison was the most important person to be there, second only to the wombat, and maybe not even that. But Jessica felt compelled to explain to me all the reasons we couldn't move it to another day. It couldn't be later, because a couple of days after that Allison was scheduled for a trip to the Smithsonian research center in Panama—something to do with trying to get them involved in her rainforest conservation project. It couldn't be much earlier, because they had to have time to finish the exhibit construction. So it could only be Tuesday or Wednesday, and Tuesday Allison was supposed to tape a TV program where she was going to talk about sustainable products from the rainforest, and they weren't sure how long it would take and then—

I figured Jessica was so used to telling people about the wonderfulness of Allison's activities that she didn't know how to stop, so I just waited for her to finish, trying not to sigh audibly about the work that was still left undone. I was getting a wombat, after all, and any minute now. Nothing else mattered.

Chapter 5

I walked into the kitchen carrying my cardboard cup of coffee like it was a precious relic from one of the museums downtown. "When did the coffee at the snack bar triple in price?"

"It's bird-friendly," said Jeff with enthusiasm. He hadn't been here long enough yet to be jaded by all the big zoo-wide projects that eventually came to nothing.

"Yeah, I'll bet it's dolphin-safe, too, but it sure isn't keeper-salary-friendly." I peered more carefully at the cup, now seeing the little bird logo that I'd been too stunned to notice earlier.

"It's good for the rainforest, don't you know," said Margo, rolling her eyes. "Get with the program, hon."

On the one hand, I knew that certified coffee was one of those things that was for real, not just a marketing gimmick. Coffee could really be grown in a way that fit into the local ecosystem, and there were independent bodies that enforced the standards. And of course it was theoretically a good plan, to try to sell these kinds of environmentally friendly products in the zoo shops. If we didn't seem to care, how could we expect anyone else to?

But on the other hand, I thought, taking the tiniest precious sip, how was I going to be awake enough to help save the planet if I couldn't afford coffee?

"Did I sleep through a part of a meeting where they said that this conservation initiative included giving us all raises?" I whined.

Margo threw back her head and laughed. Then she started to sing "It's Not Easy Being Green." We knew that, fortunately, she didn't know most of the words, so we didn't have to be patient for long before it stopped.

"Aren't you cutting up those pieces awfully small?" I said to Jeff, looking at the pan of tree shrew food he was working on. It was going to take him all day if he was going to cut stuff up like that.

"Um," he said, uncertainly. "They're pretty small. They have small mouths."

"Robin trained you to make that food, didn't she," I said.

"Yeah. Why?"

"I wonder who cuts it up for them that small in the wild." I knew my pygmy marmosets could handle grapes that were practically the size of their heads, and it was silly to worry about chopping their food in tiny pieces, but it was hard to resist doing it anyway. Robin probably cut the food up into a different size for every single species.

"Well," he said.

Margo laughed. "Don't let her tease you. You make that food any way you want."

I walked into the keeper room and saw Chris was on the phone in his office. He wasn't having a good time. He stood stiffly at his desk and just said "yes" every once in a while. He waved me in. He handed me the phone. "She wants to talk to you."

That could only be one person. Was she going to be calling every day? Did he always have to end up picking up the phone? Wasn't there some way to keep her from bugging him so much? It was hard to stay friendly with both of them when they made me feel like I was trapped in the middle of some mysterious battle.

"Hi," I said.

"Hannah," said Allison in her brightest voice. "I have a favor to ask of you. I know how busy you all are, but Chris was nice enough to say that he could spare you for a couple of hours."

It wasn't like he had a lot of choice, I thought, glancing at him. He was watching me, looking unhappy.

She continued, "There's a reporter who wants to do a story about me. I don't really like to encourage that kind of attention to me personally that isn't about the zoo. But it's been impossible to avoid that lately, and it's been a rather bad sort of attention that hasn't been helpful to us. She seems to be doing a straightforward feature story, just a profile, and we can hope it will be a little more sympathetic. In any case, she wants to talk to other staff at the zoo about me as well as interviewing me, and I wondered if you could help out?"

Ugh. I hated this sort of thing. But she was getting me a wombat. I couldn't say no. "Um, sure. So what should I do?"

"Oh, that's wonderful. Thank you so much. Here's what I'd like you to do. Come up to my office, and I'll have you read some of our press material and background information, just so you feel like you know what you're talking about, even if it doesn't come up, okay? She's supposed to be here in about an hour, which should give you plenty of time."

"Um, sure, I'll be right up," I said, looking at Chris a little uncertainly as I hung up. I glanced at my watch.

"I'm sorry," I said to him. "I fed out, but I've hardly started on cleaning or food prep . . ."

"It's okay. I'll get Caleb to help." Caleb did my line on my days off, so he could do some of it pretty quickly. That would be good.

"It would be nice if she'd given us a little advance notice." Yeah, for one thing I would have skipped cleaning the glass, which I hated anyway.

"At least this building is getting some attention," Chris said.

"We have to pay a price. I just wish it didn't have to be you."

"It doesn't bother me, really, like it does you. She's kind of interesting to be with. It's more a problem for everyone else to have to do my regular work."

"That's not what bothers me," he said.

He wasn't looking at me; instead he was staring at the desk and poking a paperclip around with his finger. He was trying to get up the nerve to say something he wasn't sure he should say. I waited.

After a moment he said, without looking up, "She uses people. I don't want you to be the next one."

"Well, come on, if it gets us wombats, she can go ahead and use me all she wants."

Now he looked unhappier, although he didn't say anything. He really was worried. I kind of liked the feeling of him worrying about me. I didn't want him to say it was none of his business again. But I didn't like seeing him look so unhappy about it either.

Well, I didn't know what she'd done to him, but she wasn't going to do it to me. "I'll keep my wits about me, okay? Don't worry. We'll use her instead, right? I'm going to try to get us anteaters next, you know," I teased.

He looked up. He smiled a little and seemed to relax. "Okay, get out of here and do your dirty work then."

"I'm off to be the mole in the director's office," I said as I turned to go. "It's a small mammal kind of thing, right?"

I hesitated at the entrance to the director's suite. I peered through the glass door and the receptionist looked up. It was obvious from her expression that it was weird for me to be standing there like that, so I had no choice but to open the door.

I explained who I was. She acted like she already knew. I

guess when she looked at Allison's schedule, there was only one person on it I could be. She probably didn't have a lot of other appointments with people with poop on their clothes and mulch in their hair. I felt like a penguin waddling around the Grand Canyon. I didn't belong here.

"Have a seat," she said.

I looked around, feeling awkward, trying surreptitiously to check my pants for disgusting substances, and perched on the edge of a chair. God, it was clean in here. I had kind of forgotten what offices were like. It had, like, carpet. I almost laughed, thinking about what would happen if we had carpet anywhere at Small Mammals. Even in our keeper room you couldn't put your lunch down on the table for a second if you didn't want ants to find it. The ladies' room got cleaned, I don't know, once every couple of weeks if we were lucky. And we tramped through in our muddy, poopy boots without thinking twice. I wasn't civilized enough for a room like this.

Just as my stomach was really starting to hurt, Allison appeared in the door of her office and, with her usual brilliant smile, told me to come in.

"Hannah, thank you so much for coming." As if I actually could have said no when the director of the zoo asked me to do something, especially when she was going to get me a wombat. But somehow when she focused her attention on you, she made you believe she was sincere. I couldn't help feeling this little glow about the fact that she had picked me out of everyone.

"I know it must be inconvenient to take time out of your busy day to do this. But," she said, lowering her voice, "after Victor's death, I felt I should take some responsibility to divert media attention elsewhere. I'm sure you understand. So when the idea for this article was presented, it seemed like a good idea to go along with it."

I just nodded. Whatever. Her strategy for dealing with the

press wasn't part of my lowly poop-shoveling mandate. I was just following orders.

"Here, first let me show you these. They're the plans for the wombat exhibit. I want to know what you think."

I could never really understand those kinds of drawings. I didn't care what they built as long as it ended up with a wombat in it. But I leaned forward and looked anyway.

"See, here's where the otters are now, and we combine it with the adjacent space," she said, pointing. The drawing didn't make much sense to me, but I nodded. "Then we'll redo the rockwork inside, with a den here in the front so people will see him when he's asleep. And here's a sand pit for him to dig in. You can put in some branches for him to scratch himself on, and otherwise, since it's a desert habitat, you won't have to worry about a lot of plants."

"We're getting rid of that high rockwork in back?" I said, trying to figure out the symbols on the blueprints.

"Yes. He won't use it, and it's in the way of breaking down the wall. Is that okay with you?"

I nodded. "It's hard to keep clean. And I hate climbing on it."

"Afraid of heights?"

"Not really," I said, probably not very convincingly. Really, I wasn't afraid of heights as such, so much. Just of the possibility of, well, suddenly no longer being high up in a quick and uncontrolled fashion.

She continued, describing how they were going to go about the construction process, and I just nodded and grinned stupidly. Most of it didn't mean anything to me, but the more she talked about it, the more I realized I really was getting a wombat.

"What do you think?" she finally asked.

"It's great." Oh, brilliant. I hoped I wasn't supposed to come up with some subtle insight into exhibit design. All I could think about was that soon I was going to have a *wombat.* Come on, wouldn't your brain be a little addled, too, under the circumstances?

"I think it's going to be fun," she said. If she thought I was a complete dimwit, she wasn't letting on. "We should start to think about what to do next. Maybe we could get some more Australian animals."

"I can't have all the fun though. Maybe we should ask some of the other keepers." I wondered how obvious it was that I was just saying this to be polite. Like every other keeper, I thought the collection would be much more interesting if we only had my personal favorite species. I didn't really want anyone else's input.

"That's a nice thought," she said. "How are things going there, by the way? How are the staff getting along?"

"It's fine." It was great, actually. No one had murdered anyone in our building, for one thing. No one even wanted to, as far as I could tell, which I couldn't say about every place I'd ever worked. I didn't say that, of course.

"How does Caleb seem to be finding it?"

She sounded as if she could have been asking about any employee who had recently transferred.

"He seems fine," I said, trying to make my face very neutral, like that of someone who hadn't recently considered whether Caleb had killed Victor out of jealousy over his stealing Allison from him. "It must be a big change from elephants, having to climb all around making sure all our little guys are alive every day. It's a lot harder to lose track of an elephant," I joked lamely.

She smiled, politely or for real, I don't know, because she's too good at what she does.

"I'm glad to hear it. And the new boy, Jeff? Isn't he a sight for sore eyes? Aren't you lucky to get to work with him all the time?" She laughed.

"He's so sweet. Everyone thinks so. We were lucky to get him," I said.

"I know I often ask for you to do the donor tours, but I hope you don't mind if I ask for him to give tours once in a while now. It's nice to have a choice, depending on who I'm trying to work on," she laughed again.

"No problem." As long as she left Chris alone, she could do what she wanted as far as I was concerned.

"And how's Chris doing? I never seem to run into him when I'm there." Again she sounded like this was a perfectly casual question, but I thought she was looking at me more closely than before.

"He's fine," I said, trying to sound uninterested.

"He's been there such a long time," she said, as if musing to herself. "I wonder if it isn't time that he moved up. He'd be such an asset to the curatorial staff."

"Oh, no," I said, before I could stop myself, "he really likes his job."

Idiot, I snapped at myself, you shouldn't have said that. Well, at least I didn't say, "No, he hates you and doesn't want to have to talk to you all the time like he would in that job," or, "Please don't take him away from me." I felt flustered. I tried to think of cold places that would make my hands and feet and face turn blue to keep myself from blushing. I stared back at her, trying to look blank, and furiously visualized arctic foxes.

"I know he does," she said. "But I do like to pay attention to staff development. Some people need a nudge before they realize that they can handle bigger things."

It took all my concentration to suppress the impulse to bite my lip and look heartbroken.

"He should at least lead some of our tours to Central America," she continued. "I wonder why he hasn't asked to go—most of the staff think it's such a privilege. He's got the perfect expertise for that area. It's a waste not to use it."

I wished she would stop sitting there coming up with plans to send Chris away, and then I realized that it really should be no concern of mine where Chris went, either on a trip or permanently, and then I just sat there stupidly, not knowing what to think. I almost thought she was saying all this on purpose to see how I reacted. But that was crazy. How would the zoo director know about my personal private extremely secret crush? And why would she care? Obviously I was so obsessed with Chris that it made me think ridiculous things.

"Well, that's neither here nor there," she said. "We should get down to business, I'm afraid." I tried not to moan with relief at the change of subject.

She went over to a shelf. Watching her, I suddenly realized how huge the office was. It seemed like she had to walk a long way. I started to feel very small and very dirty again. Her office was almost as big as my whole apartment. The furniture was perfect, with no scratches on the tables or desks, and no clutter anywhere. The lighting was some kind of tasteful recessed fixture, not your usual office fluorescent lights. There were actual decorations, like statues on shelves. The pictures on the walls had frames, instead of being taped-up posters with curling edges. Oh my God, she didn't just have carpet—it was some kind of fancy Oriental rug. I started to feel painfully out of place again and wondered what I might have stuck to my shoes.

As I was trying to peek at the bottom of my boots without being noticed, Allison came back from the very-far-away-seeming other side of the room with a big stack of papers. I tried to keep my face from falling.

"Here's what I want you to look at. It's a file with my biographical material and some previous news coverage that we particularly liked. Anything we can do to get her to spin the article our way, you know, helps with the fundraising. And helps us get things like wombats, right?"

I sat carefully in the very nice chair and started to look through the file while she took phone calls. Man, she sure got a lot of press coverage. It was hard to believe what she'd said about trying to discourage it. But why should she? She could use it as a way to get attention for the zoo and all the conservation causes she was trying to promote. There was nothing wrong with her tossing her head and getting everyone to look at her golden hair if it was going to save endangered species and get us wombat exhibits, right?

I flipped through the file and eavesdropped a little on her phone calls. They didn't seem very interesting. These articles were all about animals, the animals she'd had when she was a kid, the animals she was working on saving in the rainforest, the animals we were getting at the zoo. The phone calls were all about money, it seemed. Money someone might give us, how much money something would cost, where else we could look for money. Boring. What an awful job.

I gave up listening to her and turned my attention to the press clippings. Okay, so here was her life story from when she was a child and she used to bring animals home. I skimmed it. They didn't seem like very interesting animals. Just cats and dogs and baby squirrels—she hadn't lived where there were stray capybaras wandering the streets or anything. Her dad was a pharmacist, she was an only child, no brothers to compete with, he taught her sciencey stuff . . . all the clichés to make you think, oh, naturally she'd turn out to be this self-confident, assertive woman.

Now here was an article from when she first started with the rainforest conservation project. I was getting a little tired of the rainforest. Weren't there some other habitats we needed to conserve? I skimmed it without enthusiasm. The reporter had trotted out all the same old clichés about how we might find valuable medicines and blah blah blah. Why wasn't it enough to argue that we shouldn't go around wiping out every other living thing on the planet?

Oh, this was interesting. I didn't know she had a middle name. Allison Regina Craine. That must have rolled sonorously off her mother's tongue when she scolded her. Or did no one have the nerve to scold her even when she was a tiny child?

Here were some letters from schools that she had visited to give lectures about careers in conservation, those letters the teacher makes the whole class write. With cute drawings. Oh, please. Couldn't I go pick up some poop now instead of reading this?

Oh, no, here was the list of products that we were using at the zoo that we were going to replace with versions that were sustainably harvested and recycled and otherwise politically correct. What it didn't mention, of course, was how we somehow never managed to get the new sources in place before we ran out of the old supplies. Chocolate, coffee, wood shavings . . . Wait, wood shavings? What were we going to use for bedding if we ran out of wood shavings? We couldn't—

I turned the page quickly. There was no point in driving myself crazy about any of these things in advance. There would be plenty of time for that later, I was unfortunately sure. Okay, so here was . . . no, this must be in the wrong file. It was another thing about drugs and rainforests, but then the rest of it sounded like all the phone calls I was half overhearing about money and boring stuff like that.

She couldn't mean for me to read this, right? I hoped not, because it looked unbearably dull. I'd even rather read more letters from schoolchildren. I put that sheet of paper aside to show to her, so she could have it filed in the right place. That was considerate of me, right? Also, in case she had meant me to read it, she'd know I hadn't so I wouldn't get, like, quizzed on it or anything. I had all my bases covered. I moved on to the next clipping in the file.

It was a magazine article with a lot of color pictures of her with animals. Now this was more like it. She had a reputation for getting up close with the animals even now that she was director and didn't work directly with them. Here was a photo of her in the elephant yard—a little creepy after the murder, but if you didn't think about that, it was a great picture. She was dressed elegantly, throwing her head back and laughing, with one hand resting on the elephant as comfortably as if you had your hand resting on a chair. Here was another that must have been taken at Small Mammals before I got there, with an armadillo. There was a keeper I didn't recognize in the background, and I guessed he was George, the guy I'd replaced. I'd never met him, but he was one of my favorite people on earth, since I got my job because he left.

"That's a wonderful article, isn't it?"

Allison looked over my shoulder. I hadn't noticed her walk over to me.

"Yeah. These are great pictures." I picked up the boring piece of paper and handed it to her, still looking at the photos. "Here, I think this must have gotten in the wrong file?"

"Thanks, I'll put this where it belongs," she said, and swept-away into another room.

I looked after her. My moment of relief was immediately spoiled by wondering if now I'd gotten someone else in trouble for filing things wrong. I had been so busy trying to cover my own behind that I hadn't thought of that. I didn't hear her yelling at anyone through the walls, at least. But I suspected that she could make you feel awfully bad without needing to raise her voice.

Well, there was nothing I could do about it now. I kept going through the file. It was starting to get hard not to fall asleep reading basically the same stories over and over again. It didn't fool me that they were on different paper in different typefaces with different photographs. So I was relieved when Allison's secretary knocked on the door and told us the reporter was here.

She led me down the hall and opened the door to a conference room. At first I thought there was some mistake. Sitting at the table was a tall lanky woman with frizzy blond hair and her clothes a disheveled mess. It looked like she'd spilled coffee on her blazer not once, but every day for years, and there was an ink smudge on her cheek where she'd touched it with the pen behind her ear. I realized that she couldn't actually be a homeless person, because she'd never have made it into the director's office if she was. But she'd probably needed to show her press pass.

"Your sweater's buttoned wrong," I said, fascinated into thoughtless rudeness.

"Oh, thanks," she said, rebuttoning it and then extending her newsprint-stained hand. "I'm Beth Jackendoff. Great to meet you."

Usually I hesitate to shake people's hands because I'm afraid of what I might have on mine, but suddenly marmoset poop didn't seem so gross. I didn't put my hand out to reciprocate, and she dropped hers after a moment.

"There isn't really a zoo beat, but I always grab the zoo stories," she said, as if this was very clever. "I love animals. I have three cats and my dog, Buddy. You should meet Buddy. She's the greatest. You'd love her."

"You have a girl dog named Buddy?" I said, getting drawn into this irrelevancy in spite of myself.

"That was her name at the shelter and we didn't change it, she is such a good buddy. But we're not here to talk about my dog," she said, beaming.

"Yeah, right." You could say that again. I was beginning to wonder if I could fake a sudden illness. But no, I was getting a wombat. I had to pay the price.

"Hey, do you think there's a coffee machine around here? I've been running around all morning and haven't had a spare minute . . . I'd kill for a doughnut," she said longingly, like she was wishing for world peace.

"I don't know," I said stiffly. I was losing patience already. "I don't usually work in this building, as you know."

"Do you think you could ask?" she wheedled. "They'd probably rather give it to you because you work here."

It was easier to just go along with her, like it was easier to just let yourself get swept away by a mudslide than try to hang on to the branches. I got up and went back to ask the secretary if there was any way she could get some coffee to shut the reporter up, although I didn't put it that way. She was perfectly nice about it. I'd forgotten that coffee for the boss and her visitors was another normal thing you had in offices, like clean carpet.

I went back to the conference room and sat down. Beth was humming to herself and looking through a stack of paper. "Hey," she said, "do you know anything about reptiles? My son caught a snake in Maine on vacation and we brought it home, but it's not eating. I'm afraid it's going to die and we can't just let it out around here, can we? It might become, like, an invasive species or something."

I was about to tell her that I didn't know anything about snakes and she should talk to my friend Ray, but I caught myself in time. I really couldn't send her around to bother him. I sighed. There was no such thing as a free wombat. First I was going to have to talk about all her pets, then I was going to have to have the interview we came here for in the first place, and who knew where it was going to end?

After only a moment of discussion, it became clear that she had no source of heat for the snake. I explained the concept of cold-bloodedness, told her there was a pet store right up the street that sold heat stones and heat lamps, and hoped for the best. I really didn't care, but I figured Ray wouldn't like it if he knew I hadn't helped a snake in need. I doubted he had the same charitable thoughts about small mammals when he fed his snakes a mouse. But we fed out mice, too, so that wasn't a fair comparison.

The undoubtedly bird-friendly coffee arrived. I watched, fascinated, as she emptied a pack of sugar into it and stirred it with her pen.

"Well, let's get started," she said. Her tone suggested that we were about to have the absolute best fun ever. I tried not to groan. I'd already been here for an hour, and she thought we were just getting started. I thought of Chris and Caleb doing all my work for me back at Small Mammals. I hoped they really liked wombats, too.

She took out her notebook, and, the non-coffee-coated end of her pen poised above it, said, "Okay, so Hannah Lilly. That's two Ls and two Ns?"

Who spelled Hannah with less than two Ns? "Yeah, right, and two Hs."

"Two—Oh!" she giggled. "Right. I get it. Okay, so, just to let you know what I'm after, I covered"—she lowered her voice to a whisper—"the recent murder."

She seemed to wait for a response, so I nodded.

She continued cheerfully. "But the story I'm working on now has nothing to do with that. It's a feature article about the director, just to give an idea of the kind of person she is, and talk about what interesting work she's done since she's taken over at the zoo. Like—"

I interrupted. "Why should I believe that? You guys seem to go out of your way to make us look bad in everything else you've ever written."

She looked hurt. "Why do you say that? I work on these stories because I'm interested in the zoo. Why do you think I make you look bad?"

I felt my blood pressure rising. "Like when you're reporting on a murder, you mention every crime that's happened here in living memory, even if it's just a purse snatching."

"But that's what we have to do as reporters. We have to report both sides. Just because I think the zoo is a cool place doesn't mean I can leave out the bad things that have happened here."

"But how is that reporting both sides? It's not another side of the same thing—it's totally unrelated," I said, trying not to raise my voice.

"It's background," she said confidently.

I opened my mouth to continue the argument, but then I stopped. This was not what Allison had had in mind when she asked me to talk to the reporter. But it was exactly what I had been afraid of. Allison was sure she could bend a conversation like this to her will. I wasn't sure I had the same ability. I didn't plan to say anything about Allison that wasn't nice, but I had no faith in how it was going to look once Beth got it down on paper surrounded by who knew what dirt she was going to dig up.

Okay, let's try a different approach, I thought. I was mostly worried that I was going to get in trouble. Surely Beth knew what it was like to get in trouble with her bosses. Maybe I could appeal to her better nature, if she had one. She liked animals. I had a hard time believing that anyone who liked animals was all bad.

"Look," I said. "How do I know you're not going to twist what I say to you?" I lowered my voice. "I want to keep my job here, you know?"

"Oh, I won't get you in trouble. I promise. I'm really not going to do any muckraking. Honestly, that would take more time than I have for this article. Anyway, it's totally not the idea. It's supposed to be just human interest, not news. I'm not supposed to put in anything negative any more than you want to say anything like that. Really. Okay?"

Okay, that made sense. She had bosses telling her what to do just like I did. They published articles like that all the time. Allison would be a good subject for one. I wasn't naive enough to think that this was a promise that extended to anything she'd write in the future, but that would have nothing to do with me.

"All right," I said. "Let's get it over with."

Chapter 6

We talked for about another twenty minutes by my watch. It only seemed like three hours. I knew she'd probably end up using two sentences. For the rest of it, she was going to write the same article as all the ones in the file, on different paper with a different typeface. But I would be more than adequately compensated for my efforts, I figured, so I lay back and thought of wombats as I did my duty.

Finally I escaped from her, from the director's office and from the nice upholstery I was afraid I'd ruined, and half ran all the way back to Small Mammals. I took a quick walk around the outside of my exhibits to see what kind of shape they were in. Caleb was doing something in exhibit 24—at least Chris had got help with that much. But what the heck was he up to?

The female sloth was on a low branch, and Caleb was holding out a green bean. But he was holding it just out of reach. The sloth blinked at him. I was sure she was confused. Not that I spoil the animals, but the sloths were used to having their grapes and oranges put right into their mouths. I loved hand feeding them. It was so cool how they looked at you like friendly aliens who were happy living on this planet where people fed them fruit instead of just leaves. They had a good time being with us while they waited for the mother ship to come and pick them up and take them back to their planet where the gravity was less, so they could move faster—they had to move so slowly here.

The sloth thought about it for a year, and then moved one arm and pulled herself just close enough to take the bean in her mouth. Caleb smiled and let her have it. Everyone reacted with great satisfaction—I swear they almost broke into applause. It was nice to see people enjoying themselves so much watching an animal, when usually they walk past the exhibits so fast that you wonder why they came in the building.

I went behind the exhibit to the keeper area and met Caleb coming out.

"Hey, are you teasing my sloth?" I joked.

"I'm wondering if we could train them a little. It would be easier to crate them up," he said.

Caleb was used to working with elephants, animals that you had to train. There was no alternative. We could get by in other ways, so we weren't as diligent about training. I felt bad about it, but time was always short, and something had to give. And often that something was training an animal that you knew you could manage another way if you had to.

"It takes at least four people to catch them up and crate them," I said, nodding at the sloth. "And they can hurt you with those claws if they want to. It would be better to be able to reason with them, for sure."

"You have dogs, right? Have you done training with them?"

"I have pugs," I said. "I've worked with them a lot. But I think that for centuries they've been actively selected for disobedience. Not on purpose. But you know you're in for trouble when you hear breeders use words like 'mischievous,' as though it's adorable."

"Well then, that's even better experience for training wild animals."

I hadn't thought about it that way, but he had a point. Not that I could picture my sloths on an agility course. But we could do more than we had.

"Which sloth is which again?" he asked. "I can tell one is smaller but I don't know about the other two."

"The female is the naturally blond one." She was really light tan or straw-colored, but that was how I thought of her. They weren't green-tinged like in the wild. I guess we don't have the right algae for them to pick up the spores of or whatever. "The male is the one who looks like he's way overdue to have his roots dyed. He's dark underneath and blond on top. Their faces are really different too, but the colors are easiest to start. And try grapes or oranges—they like those even better."

Caleb nodded. He told me he'd finished cleaning the exhibit, and I went downstairs to start making some food.

"How was your trip to the dragon's lair, hon?" Margo looked up from some paperwork as I came in.

"It was fine. The reporter was more annoying than the dragon."

She shook her head. "I don't know how you find her so tolerable."

I shrugged. "She acts like she likes me. Maybe it's an act, but it's not annoying, you know?"

"That's how she is," Margo said darkly. "If she likes you, you're a princess. If not, you're no better than shit on her shoes. There's no in-between."

"She likes Jeff. She thinks he's cute. I think she's going to ask for him to do the tours when she's trying to get rich women to donate." I laughed.

"Let's hope that's all she has in mind," said Margo. She scowled. "Maybe we should keep an eye on him."

Before I could ask what she meant by that, Chris walked out of his office. "Did she really say that?" His tone sounded calm but unnatural, like he was trying to control himself.

Oh, bother. I'd just been making small talk. I hadn't realized this was going to cause such an uproar. I wouldn't have talked about her at all if I'd known he was listening.

"Um, yeah, roughly, I guess," I said.

"She's not doing that. I'll do the tours myself if I have to."

He walked out the basement door without saying anything else. That was what he did when he was angry. Usually he pretended he had a meeting to go to—at least I think he was only pretending part of the time. This time it looked like he was too upset to even pretend.

"What is all this about?" I said, bewildered.

Without looking up from the report she was working on, Margo said, "She has a bit of a history with junior keepers. She's pretty much had to give it up since she's been promoted so far up. Big sacrifice to make for her career, I'm sure, but she's done fine looking elsewhere."

"A history of what?"

Margo looked at me impatiently. "Hon, you're being awfully dense. Look at her now. She still goes through men like we go through bags of leafeater diet, for goodness' sake."

Oh. Well, of course this was what Margo would be talking about; she was Margo, after all. But was this what Chris thought, too? And did they really think it was likely that Allison was going to seduce Jeff? Come on, this was going a little far, wasn't it? Not that it wouldn't make me just as angry as the idea seemed to be making Margo and Chris. But she was director of the zoo now. He was way too young for her. She could seduce one of the people on the board of directors, right? Surely that would be more appropriate.

"Hm," was all I said, and I wandered out of the room into the kitchen, taking my embarrassment at seeming naive with me. Distractedly wondering if there was anything I needed to do to protect sweet little Jeff from this evil temptress or whether the whole idea was silly, I walked into a box of kale.

"Ouch," I yelled. "Why is this here? Who has kitchen duty today anyway?"

"I'm afraid it's you," Margo called from the other room.

"Oh, no. I'm sorry, I forgot." I was supposed to have checked in the food order and put it away. Who had done the rest of it already, then? Other people were really doing a lot of work for this wombat of mine.

Feeling guilty, I bagged the kale and tossed it in the fridge, then went out the kitchen door and started up the outside stairs to throw away the wooden box. Now distracted by how neglectful of my work I was being, I almost tripped over Chris, who was sitting at the top of the stairs.

"Oh! I'm sorry!" I sat down abruptly next to him in an attempt to conceal the fact that I had been about to fall over. "What are you doing out here? Are you okay?"

He avoided my gaze. His blue eyes looked dark, like the sky when a thunderstorm is approaching. He ignored my question.

"Did you find out when the wombat exhibit is going to open?"

"Oh! I'm sorry," I said again, feeling stupid. "I can't believe I didn't tell you. It's a week from Wednesday. It's, um, the only day Allison can do it," I said, apologetic for even mentioning her name again.

"Crazy," he said, but flatly, as if it were only to be expected. "What's the rush?"

"She wants to make a big deal so the newspaper will write about something other than Victor. And right after that she's leaving the country for a while. She's going to that Smithsonian place in Panama for her rainforest thing."

"She is?" he said, his voice rising. "What's she doing there?"

"Um, I don't know exactly," I said, startled. Why did these innocent remarks keep blowing up on me?

He looked at me. His expression softened. "I'm sorry. I shouldn't be taking it out on you."

I didn't know what to say. I just gazed stupidly into his eyes, which were looking less stormy and making my brain turn to armadillo gruel, as usual.

He turned away and put his head in his hands, resting his elbows on his knees, avoiding my eyes again, and said, "I hate her going there. I have good memories there. I don't want to have to think of her there."

I'd never seen him talk or act like this before. He was the one who was always calm and centered in the midst of chaos. I was the one who was always venting some kind of emotion, and he was the one who knew how to smooth things over. This was backward. I didn't know how to react.

But after a moment, curiosity took over. "What did you do there?"

"Everything. The agouti project that I told you about. All those summers when I was in college. And the research I did on tapirs."

I didn't realize that was where all those things had happened. I'd never thought to ask about the specifics. It wasn't like I was ever going to go to the places he talked about—they were clearly too far away from cappuccino bars and Thai restaurants. As far as I was concerned, it was like there was a mythical forest that Chris told me fairy stories about. I hadn't even thought about it being a particular real place.

"She wants to ruin whatever she can." He seemed to be talking to himself. He shook his head and stared at the ground.

I didn't know what to say. So what I blurted out was, "But she's getting us a wombat."

What a moron I am, I thought, staring at him. Right. A wombat is such a comforting thought that it should solve all his problems, when I don't even know what they are, really. Could I possibly be more self-centered without a special permit?

But he looked up at me, and after a moment, he smiled.

"Hannah." Margo's head popped out the door. "Telephone."

We both jumped. Damn Margo, didn't she know how to use the radio? No, Margo didn't need any electronic assistance to be on the prowl whenever Chris and I were within ten feet of each other.

"It's Supplies, about your new uniforms," she said, lingering.

I jumped up. Then I looked back and forth between downstairs and Chris, feeling torn. He was looking more like his usual serene self, and he nodded that I should go.

"I'm coming," I said.

This was why you shouldn't get involved with someone at work, I thought as I walked down the stairs. You shouldn't be sitting out on the back stairs having emotional conversations during work hours. And you shouldn't be walking around confused by heart-wrenching feelings when you're supposed to be thinking about your job.

The person on the phone said that my new uniform shirts had arrived. This was the end result of a long and annoying process that involved arguing about whether my current shirts were genuinely decrepit enough to be replaced. I thought that my standards for attire were low enough that they should just believe me, but I had to go through the same routine as everyone else.

I went into the office to sign out the keys for the scooter to ride down to Supplies. They were gone. I turned to Chris, who had come back inside and was sitting at his desk looking completely normal.

"Who has the scooter?" I asked.

"Bad news. It's gone. We're going to get electric ones instead of gas."

"What? Why?" We hardly had money to replace things that were actually broken. Why were we getting rid of scooters that functioned perfectly well?

"Part of the rainforest conservation project."

I plopped down in the chair opposite Chris. "Couldn't we keep the old one till we got the new one?" I shook my head. "You know, I bet they didn't wait till Allison's secretary ran out of file folders before they ordered the recycled ones."

"I think they didn't want some newspaper to find out how much pollution the old scooters produced," he said, shrugging. "No point in getting in trouble for something that we were about to get rid of anyway."

Well, it was true. And we should have seen this coming. The scooters were awful, with those little engines that had no emissions controls or anything. But it wasn't like we ever drove ours for more than a couple of hours a day. Some days we didn't use it at all. And we felt guilty when we did. Surely that should count for something, for a few more months, at least?

"This would all be so much easier to deal with if I could afford some more coffee," I said to no one in particular.

"We did talk at the curators meeting about trying to buy carbon offsets so we could use the scooters for a little longer," Chris added.

This was, unfortunately, obviously a joke. I put my head down on the desk and laughed weakly. "See, I don't have a car. We could have just traded carbon allowances with me to keep the Small Mammals one."

Chris smiled. "I'm sorry I didn't think of that."

"Stupid idea, anyway, carbon trading," I muttered. "Like buying medieval indulgences so you can go ahead and keep sinning." I sat up. "Oh well. Do I at least get to tie my uniform order to the back of a camel instead? That's a pretty nonpolluting form of transport. Better than horses, even, since they hardly use any water."

Now he grinned. "Nope. You have to use a pack animal from

within your own unit. Another one of those small mammal problems."

Suddenly I cheered up. "Oh great," I said, getting into the spirit of it. "Now don't you wish we'd gotten those hand-raised maras I tried to talk you into? They already knew how to wear harnesses. We'd be halfway there to hitching them up to a cart." I had a mental image of my deerlike rodents in harness pulling a sled like tiny rodent-reindeer. They'd at least be able to haul small branches, right? The idea made me grin back.

"My fault, then," Chris said. "So we can use my car instead. I'll come with you."

Oh. That was a good deal. Maybe this rainforest conservation thing was going to work out after all. He got up and we both headed back out the door.

Sitting on the couch in the keeper room, I took the new shirts out of the bag and looked at them. "These are different," I said, feeling the cloth. Even someone as uninterested in clothing as I was could tell the shirts were made from a different fabric.

Margo came over and picked one up. "They found out that the old manufacturer was part of a big multinational that owned some company or other that was cutting down acres of rainforest." She smirked at me. "You probably slept through that part of the meeting." She felt the cloth. "I like this better, actually. Nice when virtue is rewarded for a change."

"Yeah, for a change," I said, again wishing I could afford another cup of the virtuous coffee. I'd resisted buying a can of cheap, entirely nonvirtuous, mega-international-corporation cola from the soda machine as a substitute, but I wasn't sure how long I could hold out. Good intentions always had these unintended consequences, it seemed.

"At least they have shirts," she said. "We've run out of heat lamp bulbs, and now they're only ordering some fancy energy-efficient kind. But they're twice as expensive, and they don't have any in stock, because they're too cheap to order enough at once."

The heat lamps were used to provide supplemental heat in the animal enclosures. Sometimes it was just for a little extra comfort, but some animals, like the mole rats, absolutely needed them. They didn't really regulate their own body temperature like most mammals—they were practically cold-blooded—and they'd die if it got too cold. We would end up switching heat lamp bulbs around to whichever animals needed them most, and then finally breaking down and buying them with our own money. It wouldn't be the first time.

"I don't get it," I said. "How can they make heat lamps more efficient, anyway? Don't you make other bulbs more efficient by making sure they don't waste energy making heat?"

"Don't ask me, hon. Maybe they're expensive because they have to order them from another dimension with different laws of physics."

"That would sure explain a lot about why it always takes so long to get stuff from Supplies." At least it was a more interesting answer than that there was a lot of paperwork and that somewhere along the line, some crucial person was sitting around drinking their bird-friendly coffee and surfing the Web instead of working. "Anyway, wouldn't it save a lot more energy to replace the lighting in the public areas with compact fluorescents?"

"Don't get me started," Margo said. "I think there's some environmental certification body that gives us extra points for things that inconvenience the keepers instead of other staff."

"Tell me about it," I said.

I threw my new shirts in my locker and went upstairs to my line. Radar the fennec fox heard me walk in and ran into his holding, hoping for crickets. I took some out of the can. "Radar.

Poor little dumpling. Do you feel bad that you don't come from the rainforest? You would get so much more attention. Here you go, puppyhead," I said, tossing the crickets into his exhibit.

When I logged on to the computer to do my daily report, I was reminded by the mess of files I'd left all over my desktop that I'd been trying to do research on sloth reproduction. The female sloth, and the juvenile male, that we had in exhibit 24 were fairly recent acquisitions. We were supposed to be allowed to breed them, and I desperately wanted a baby sloth. I hadn't found anything useful, though. "I can't find a darn thing that tells us what I could do to get these sloths to mate," I said crossly.

"Slow music might put them in the mood," said Margo, who was putting away her radio, getting ready to leave.

"Veeeery slow music," said Chris as he passed by, headed up the stairs. You could hear the grin in his voice.

I snorted. "You guys are a lot of help."

Margo looked at me with an expression of complete innocence and said, "You should know all about very slow mating rituals." I scowled at her fiercely, but she just smiled. "Oh, I forgot, we haven't figured out how to get that one to happen yet either."

I turned back to the computer, hoping she didn't see me blushing. I had walked right into that one. She used to at least save those remarks for more discreet moments, but now she didn't care if Chris was within earshot. She was getting frustrated and hoped to move things along on his end, I figured. Like he was going to take her hints about his love life. I liked Margo, but I wished for a second that she'd find out whether Jeff was gay or not so she could start working on him instead. Then I felt bad. I didn't really wish that on him. I could take it.

"See you tomorrow," she said.

"Yeah," I muttered.

It was time to go home, but I got distracted by looking through my sloth files again. I should email them home, I thought. Then I could at least feed the pugs while—

The radio crackled. "Chris to Hannah in Small Mammals."

"Go for Hannah," I said, whipping my radio off my belt faster than I usually did. He was the boss, right? No other reason.

"Can you come upstairs behind thirty-five?"

"Ten-four," I answered, already halfway up the stairs.

"The roller's out," Chris said when I got there. "Everyone else has gone home. It's just you and me."

"Oh, no." The roller was a bird, the lilac-breasted roller. She was an escape artist. Probably she took advantage of us mammal keepers. We were used to little monkeys soaring through the trees, but at least they needed somewhere to land. They couldn't really fly. How were we supposed to compete with that?

"Did you call a Code Orange?" I hadn't heard anything on the radio before he'd called me. We were supposed to make a general radio announcement when an animal got loose. Yeah, sometimes you just grabbed the mole rat or chinchilla and threw it back in the exhibit and didn't say anything. It wasn't like it was a rampaging tiger. But you'd at least get a reprimand if you were caught.

"We can handle it," Chris said, calmly. "She's right up there."

I followed his gaze. The roller was flying back and forth over the top of the exhibit.

"I guess I'll go try to chase it out of there so you can net it?" I looked at the ladder that went to the top of the exhibit. I didn't want to climb up there. But I knew Chris was better with a net than I was.

"Last time the only thing that worked was to hose her down," he said.

I looked at him uncertainly. "Are you sure?"

"It rains where they live."

It seemed a little mean to get the bird wet. But Chris knew what he was doing. He had many years more experience than I did. It wasn't just that I didn't want to climb the ladder and crawl around on top of the exhibit that made it seem like a good idea. Really.

Chris got a net, and I unrolled the hose. I climbed partway up the ladder and turned the hose on, the stream of water as gentle as it could be and still reach the top of the exhibit.

It definitely rained where they lived, I thought, watching the roller continue flying through the artificial shower like it was no big deal. But after a while, she got tired of it. She didn't really want to get nearer to us, but now she wanted more to get away from the rain. She came out from the top of the exhibit and started to fly in circles around the keeper area.

I moved the hose to rain gently on her. Unfortunately, now it was also raining gently on me. I was used to getting wet in my job, but not usually from head to toe. Birds. Why did we even have birds? This was a mammal building. Right, naturalistic mixed-species exhibits. Sounds nice till you're standing in the keeper hallway drenched in ice cold water chasing a stupid bird around.

"That's enough," said Chris. "Take this. Herd her into the corner."

I dropped the hose gratefully and grabbed the net he'd been holding. I saw that the roller was wet enough that it was having trouble flying. You could see that it was beating its wings hard, but it couldn't get up near the ceiling anymore. I stretched my net out toward it.

Just then the bird sank quickly like a plane hitting an air pocket, and Chris reached out and grabbed it.

Oh, I thought dreamily, look at that. He caught a bird with

his bare hands. For a moment I gazed at the two of them in fascination.

I shook myself back to reality and tried to be helpful. He put the bird into the net I was holding, and I held it closed around his arm. The bird struggled. "Ouch," he said. I guess the bird was a little more critical of his performance than I was. But it finally let go, and he pulled his arm out and took the bird-filled net from me.

He smiled at me. "Good job," he said, and opened the exhibit door and climbed in.

I stared after him with dopey adoration. He could catch birds with his bare hands. I knew he was good with animals but . . .

But it was a good thing Margo wasn't here to see me with this look on my face, I thought, coming to my senses. My senses, which told me that now I was extremely damp and rather chilly. And which reminded me that while I had all those new shirts, I didn't have any extra pants in my locker at the moment.

I had a different look on my face when Chris emerged from the exhibit, I guess.

"You're going to have a little trouble flying home, too," he said.

"I'm fine," I lied. I was a tough little zookeeping woman. It was just a little water. I tried to keep my teeth from chattering.

"I could take you somewhere to warm up."

"Where?" I said, a little dubious. I was cold, but what was the mischievous look on his face about?

"It's very close. Come on."

He dug out his key ring and started back down the stairs. I followed, of course. What else could I do? He's the senior keeper. I'm supposed to do what I'm told.

To my surprise, he went to the door next to the sink in the kitchen—the one I thought we didn't have the keys for—and unlocked it. That door was only used when the shop guys had to look at the HVAC equipment. Or get into the steam tunnels. Once I'd asked if I could go with them and see the steam tunnels, which sounded mysterious and intriguing. They said sure. But when they said it was 120 degrees in there, I declined—it was August at the time. Now, though, that didn't sound so bad.

I looked at Chris. "I thought we didn't have keys to this door."

He smiled the mischievous smile again. He shook his head. "We don't," he said, obviously pleased.

He opened the door and motioned me in.

"No, you first," I said, a little nervous.

He shrugged and went ahead, and I followed.

"Does the door lock behind us?" I asked.

He showed me that his key worked from the inside too. I left the door wide open anyway. I wasn't taking any chances.

We walked through a long room full of roaring machines. I had no idea we needed such huge equipment to heat and cool this building. Space was tight, and I was afraid to even brush up against the machines. They might explode or something. Or suck me in to their unnervingly toothy-looking vents.

I thought the ventilation equipment was pretty creepy till we got to the back of the room, and then I saw what was really creepy. A wooden staircase led up into a dirt-floored basement. I peered into it. Why was the dirt-floored basement higher up than the concrete-floored basement we were standing in? Why did it have such a low ceiling that even I wouldn't be able to stand upright? Actually, the ceiling itself was okay—it was all the dripping pipes hanging down all over the place that caused the problem. And why was it so dimly lit? Either have lights or not, already, unless you were deliberately building a set for a horror movie.

I turned, meaning to head back, but Chris was standing behind me, looking expectant.

"Go ahead," he said, motioning toward the stairs.

"You've got to be kidding. I'm not going in there."

"Scared?" he said.

"No," I said, flailing around for an excuse. I couldn't think of one, so I started up the stairs.

"That way." He gestured to a far corner. I crouched and started to walk awkwardly in the direction he pointed.

At the far end of the room, a long dark tunnel headed off into the distance. A sign said in capital letters that entry was prohibited. The tunnel was mostly full of pipes along the top and sides, dripping to make puddles on the floor, with only a tight space to walk. It was lined overhead with bare light bulbs, which somehow made very little impact on the darkness.

Even just standing at the entrance to the tunnel it was very, very warm. I felt my fingers warming up already.

"Where does it go?" I asked.

"Where do you want to go?" he said.

"Nowhere," I said quickly.

"They go almost everywhere. Come on, you can go a little farther in," he teased.

I took a few steps into the dimness and suddenly something scurried across the floor in front of me. I was used to having mice run around the building, but this was a strange place, and that was awfully big for a mouse.

I stumbled backward, right into Chris, who was following close behind. He put his hands on my upper arms to steady me.

"Just a small mammal," he said.

I felt his hands on my arms, and I told myself I was only breathing that way because I was surprised by the rat.

We stood like that for a rather long moment, and I looked ahead into the tunnel and thought that this was what it would feel like to be a naked mole rat, in those long tunnels in their exhibit kept warm by the heat lamps and humid from all the little naked mole rat bodies. Then I decided that thinking of anything naked right at this moment was definitely the wrong way to go.

I pulled away and turned around. "That's far enough. I'm nice and warm. Let's go back."

"Up to you," he said, and we made our way back into the kitchen. I went to my locker and changed into a dry, rainforest friendly uniform shirt. At least Margo had already gone home, and I didn't have to argue about whether it was really the heat in the steam tunnels that made my face red.

The phone was ringing as I walked in the door, calling "Hi, piggies!" to the pugs. I picked it up.

"Small Mammals," I said distractedly. "I mean, sorry, hello."

The pugs' heads popped up from the couch. They saw that I wasn't going to pay attention to them just yet, so they lay back down. I never have figured out what they are always so carefully conserving their energy for, but if it ever happens, they'll be ready.

"Hannah? This is Beth. Do you have a minute?"

I sighed. I had thought I was done with her. But talking to the reporter was a favor to Allison. And there was no such thing as a free wombat.

"Sure," I said without enthusiasm.

"I don't want you to take this the wrong way, like we're trying to dig up dirt or anything."

Uh oh, that obviously meant that she was trying to dig up dirt. I should have figured this was going to happen. I'd thought we had an agreement. But an agreement with a reporter was like having an agreement with a snake not to bite me. Stupid to think it meant anything.

"What," I sighed. And how had she gotten my home phone number anyway? Damn.

"It's just my editors, really. I'd be perfectly happy with what I've already got, but they're really on my case to follow up on Allison's financial situation. Not that we think anything's wrong, but they think people can't help being curious. After all, her salary is a matter of public record, and it's taxpayer dollars, you know"—this was always their excuse for all their nosiness about the zoo—"and it's clear that can't be her only means of support. And you know the story goes into her childhood and all those things, which makes it clear it's not family money. She doesn't come from that kind of background. I mean, just looking at her lifestyle and the house she lives in and everything, probably people would think it wasn't appropriate for the zoo to be paying her that much, right? So it's better if we're clear on the situation. Anyway, it might not even get into the story, you know? Once I find out what they want to know, the editors might decide it's too boring to publish, really."

God, did she ever stop talking? "Why don't you ask me the question before you work on talking me into answering it?" I said, trying not to sound any more impatient than absolutely necessary.

"Well, I've been trying to look into her investments and that sort of thing. I know that isn't necessarily something you'd know anything about. It's not any of your business, really. But maybe she's said something casually about something interesting she's involved with. Maybe it's something to do with science or animals that would make an interesting side story, you know? You might not even realize that you know something interesting, but just tell me what comes to mind, and I'll follow up on it, see?"

"Have you asked her about this?"

"Oh, sure, and she's given me a few things, but you know how busy she is, and anyway, you know us reporters. I just want to make sure I've covered all the bases. It's good to get all kinds of different perspectives and all that."

Okay, so I could try to tell her I didn't know anything, which I really didn't, and then have to sit here for another ten minutes listening to her try to convince me to think harder. Or I could hang up, but she'd just keep calling back. It would just be less trouble in the long run to try to come up with some scrap of information so she'd go away and leave me alone.

"Let me think a minute," I said.

"Oh sure," she said, cheerfully.

I remembered that when I'd been in her office before Beth interviewed me, Allison had been making all those boring phone calls about money. But they must not have involved anything that sounded like animals or science or I would have paid more attention to them. I thought about the donors she'd brought to Small Mammals for tours. Maybe they were people she knew because she already had some outside connection to their business? She always explained who they were, as if I would care, but I always forgot immediately. Now I was sorry. Maybe I really didn't have even a scrap of information to offer.

But then a vague memory popped into my head. "There's something about a drug and the rainforest."

"Oh, that would be so perfect. I wonder why she wouldn't have mentioned that. That would make a great story, one of those things about how we have to conserve the forest because all these valuable things might be in it." She sounded like I'd given her a wonderful present. "What was it called?"

I couldn't even really remember how I knew this. "God, I really don't know. Oh, wait."

I'd seen it written down on something in her office. I dredged up a visual image of a syllable or two. "That's all I can remember," I insisted. If she was such a good reporter, she could figure it out from that. Anyway, why didn't she just go ask Allison about it? I was just a lowly poop shoveler. This was way above my head.

"Look, I really have to take my dogs out now," I said, as patiently as I could manage.

"Oh, sure. Sorry. What you've given me is great, thanks." Obviously I'd made her day. Whatever.

"Sorry for the delay, puglets," I said as I hung up and got the pugs' leashes to take them out. "I guess there's no such thing as a free wombat."

As we went down in the elevator, I thought about what Beth had said. I thought she was wasting her time. Allison's salary was so mind-bogglingly huge compared to mine, it was hard to imagine what you couldn't afford on it. Chinese takeout every day. Buying books without waiting for them to come out in paperback. Cookies from the expensive dog bakery . . .

I had a tiny apartment around the corner from the back entrance of the zoo that I could just barely afford. Allison's house was in the other direction from the back entrance. A long walk, but not too long for those short puggy legs. I'd go take a look at it again. It would be nice to have the pugs all sacked out and not get nagged to entertain them.

It was getting cold, so we walked quickly. November could still have beautiful fall weather that made me want to spend hours sweeping leaves out of the pools in the mara yard just for an excuse to be outside. But today had turned into the kind of day that let you know in no uncertain terms that winter was next on the agenda. The pugs were invigorated by this weather—they didn't think about how soon they would have to search for places to pee in snowdrifts taller than they were. But I remembered, and I wasn't looking forward to getting up before dawn and shoveling out spots for them. I walked along feeling thankful for bare sidewalks.

It was easy to remember which was Allison's house. It was the one with the tiger statue in the front yard. It was big for a single person. Maybe she had to have a lot of parties for donors and that sort of thing. Maybe she could take a tax deduction for the house if she did that? I had no idea. That sort of thing was beyond me—all I knew about tax law was that they didn't let you deduct your dogs as dependents. If I could pay the rent and balance the checkbook, my financial life was in order.

I stood looking into her yard while the pugs sniffed the iron fence. The garden was immaculate. I thought uncomfortably that the plants in my exhibits didn't look that good, despite being indoors, protected from the elements, and completely under my control. Although of course, she didn't have sloths in her yard chowing down on everything. Thinking about this, I realized that I didn't know if she had any pets. None were mentioned in all those press clippings I'd read. I peered over the fence, trying to identify the plants. Were they native? Did she garden organically? Or was it nice to come home and toss a few handfuls of pesticide in the yard as a break from worrying about conservation and sustainability all day? Yeah, it was kind of a nasty thought, but it was hard not to feel cynical when you were running as low on caffeine as I was. There was a bird label on the coffee cups, but no one could tell just by looking what kind of fertilizer you used in your garden. Were we picking the most important projects or just the most conspicuous ones?

Finally it occurred to me that I'd stood there long enough that it was starting to get weird. A person with two pugs is conspicuous. I didn't want to get mentioned across the back fence next time she ran into a neighbor. So I crossed the street and started back toward my apartment.

As I turned the corner, I looked back and saw that someone vaguely familiar was heading toward her house. I watched him walk into the yard, go up the steps, and ring the bell. I didn't have a good enough view to be sure who it was in the twilight, but I saw Allison come to the door and let him in. Then I turned away and kept walking.

Too bad I couldn't figure out who it was. I might have a nice piece of gossip for Margo. Oh, well, for all I knew it could be some kind of repairman or something. Although his self-confident air, like he belonged there, didn't go with that. And he wasn't carrying any tools.

None of my business, I thought. My life was complicated enough without thinking about who was going in and out of Allison's house after work. I headed home.

Chapter 7

It turned out to rather badly spoil my morning coffee break to spend it reading the article that Beth had written. In which I came off sounding just a tiny little bit like a sycophantic idiot. Ugh. Beth had promised not to give the impression that I was saying anything bad about Allison, but she'd gone a little overboard. Maybe I should lie low and hope that by tomorrow, everyone would have forgotten about it. I felt sort of like I was afraid I was going to get beaten up in the schoolyard for being teacher's pet.

And Margo was going to torment me for sounding so excited about the wombat. Okay, maybe I should have a little more professional detachment. But jeez, what was the point of working here if it was going to be weird that I was crazy about some particular animals? I might as well have gotten some nice clean office job where people thought I was a nut because I had more than one pug. Still, did Beth have to make me sound so much like a fawning fan of a rock star or something?

It was a good article when I wasn't in it, though, I had to admit. Some of it was routine, sure. There was the usual stuff about Allison's background, the animals she'd had as a child and the cool places she had visited. But there were all kinds of tidbits of information I hadn't known. Like how in school everyone thought she'd become a vet, but instead she decided to do some behavioral research on elephants. I couldn't tell exactly what it was about—Beth had garbled it in the usual way of journalists confronted with anything vaguely scientific, and I hoped she'd gotten more out of my instructions on snake care than she'd gotten out of Allison's description of her project. Although it was clear that she'd chosen a topic she could work on in zoos. None of that messy field research in places without running water, I thought, feeling superior for a second till I remembered that I didn't like those places either. But you sure couldn't see her sitting on the jungle floor in her high heels waiting for agoutis to come by, like Chris had done for so many summers.

Beth had even tracked down some keepers who had worked at Small Mammals back when Allison had been curator. But Chris was conspicuously absent. I was sure she must have asked him for an interview, and I would have loved to have heard that conversation. But obviously the immovable object had won over the irresistible force. The others talked about how hands-on she'd been, always hanging around the building doing something with the animals. If the staff back then were annoyed about her being one of those people who'd waltzed in with the right pieces of paper and been promoted over their heads, no one was talking.

But then of course there was the rainforest stuff. My eyes glazed over at the description of all the conferences she'd talked at and the projects she was directing. And I was a little annoyed that there was nothing here about the drug Beth had asked me about. Why had she bothered me at home and then not used the information? Oh, well, maybe she hadn't managed to find out enough in time. I'd been awfully vague.

The radio interrupted just as I got to the last paragraph of the story.

"This is the zoo police. There is a raccoon in the trash behind the restaurant. Can any keepers assist?"

There were raccoons in the trash all summer. Why shouldn't

there be? The trash cans were full of food scraps and were nice shelters from the rain, and no one ever responded to the work orders to have them fitted with lids that closed properly to keep the raccoons out. If we were going to provide raccoon hotel rooms and room service for free, you'd think we couldn't very well complain when they attracted guests.

I went into the kitchen and said, "Ready to spring into action, guys?"

Jeff was setting up a new box of mealworms. They come all tangled up in crushed newspaper, and we have to shake them out of the newspaper and put them into a bin with food to keep them alive until we feed them out. I always took a long time to do this job because I was distracted by the articles in the newspaper, which were hard to read with all the mealworm-bitten holes in them. Jeff looked up from the lost-pet ads from some town in Ohio and said, "Oh, yeah!"

"It's not Small Mammals' job to respond to every raccoon in the trash," Chris said mildly from where he was standing at the sink, for the four thousandth time, knowing it wouldn't do any good.

The radio squawked again, and someone was requesting a crate and gloves.

"But we're better at it," I insisted.

Of course, we were the only ones who had the right size crates and the bite gloves. A raccoon was a small mammal, so we had the stuff to deal with it. It didn't matter how many times it was suggested that all the other buildings could have a crate and bite gloves. It was easier for everyone else if we came to the rescue every time. And Jeff and I couldn't see any reason to object to this, because we thought it was kind of fun. It was like getting interrupted in school for a fire drill, except it counted as work. Where was the downside?

I looked at Chris. "This might be the last one of the season."

"Go ahead," he said, "but I'm not coming."

I ran to get the crate and gloves and nets, and we trotted off toward the restaurant.

"What's wrong with Chris?" I fussed. "He usually knows what counts as a good time around here."

Jeff just shrugged. This was obviously another one of those things where we'd come in in the middle of some long argument that we didn't know anything about. Jeff was the new kid, but when it came to some of these things, I was just as new as he was. There was a ton of history that had happened before we came on the scene. You never knew what trivial thing would turn out to be part of some years-long argument.

"We need a drill to train everyone else," I continued. "I wonder if Chris would climb into one of those disgusting Dumpsters to play the raccoon. Maybe we'd finally find out where he draws the line."

We had zoo-wide drills to practice procedures for recapturing escaped large animals. Some person on the staff would play the escaped animal, and it was frequently Chris. He was famous for climbing trees, jumping into ponds and luring supervisors into the mud, resisting fake anesthesia darts, hiding in animal enclosures, and in general making life as difficult as possible. He'd tell you it was to make the training a challenge, but a large part of it was really mischievous impulses. Blowing off steam from sitting in too many meetings, I figured.

"It would be hard to catch Chris in a net," Jeff said. "I don't think we have one that's big enough."

"Maybe that's why we don't do them." It would be easier to find a net that I'd fit in. But no way was I going to volunteer to jump in a filthy Dumpster and make raccoon noises.

As we approached the scene of the commotion, a blond guy with a striking profile was leaning into an enormous trash bin, waving a net around.

"Who's that?" asked Jeff.

I couldn't answer, because I was in too much of a hurry to run up to Matthew and yell at him.

"Hey," I said, "what are you doing? You're supposed to be catching it, not knocking it out."

"I've almost got it," he growled.

Jeff looked at me in alarm. Matthew did something that made the raccoon squeal. I grabbed his arm.

"Just a minute," I hissed.

He jerked his arm away from me. We glared at each other. Taking advantage of our distraction, the raccoon ran to the other side of the bin.

We broke off our little stare-down and lunged with our nets, but Jeff had already gotten it. Matthew the raccoon-beating, excessively-coifed elephant guy dropped his net and reached out. I elbowed him aside. "I'm wearing gloves," I said as I grabbed the net and helped Jeff twist it shut.

We lifted the raccoon-filled net out of the trash and transferred the raccoon to the crate without getting bitten. Then we stepped back to enjoy the aftereffects of the adrenaline rush. I forgot all about Matthew, and we went into our usual silly routine.

"Fine job," said Jeff, shaking my hand.

"All in a day's work for Small Mammals," I proclaimed, and we slapped each other's backs.

When we finished goofing around I noticed Mr. Matthew Stuck-Up Elephant Guy striding off, looking superior. What a jerk, I thought crossly. He needed to find an animal more his own size to take out his frustrations on.

Then he turned a corner, and I had a sudden flash of recognition. Seeing him from that angle, I realized he was the person I'd seen going into Allison's house last night. Oh my God. Could it be that—no, it was none of my business. I tried not to think about it. She sure spent enough time hanging around the Elephant House to get to know people, and he sure would look good in pictures with Victor gone . . . None of my business, I thought. Right.

I ran into Margo in the hallway in front of the big sloth exhibit. The building was mercifully quiet and empty. As I stopped to look at my sloths, I said to her, "You missed the raccoon."

"Must have had my radio turned down," she said with a satisfied smile.

"Matthew almost beat it to death with his net."

"Violent tendencies," she said. "I told you he was the one who killed Victor."

"You know, I wish he was. But I really don't think so," I said, gazing into the exhibit.

"Why?"

"Because I saw him going into her house after work last night."

She turned to stare at me, almost salivating. "You. Don't. Say."

"I say," I said.

"Hmm. But don't count him out. Maybe Allison wanted to be rid of Victor. Maybe she needed help."

Now I was staring. Allison? Margo had to be crazy. But she was ignoring me, muttering to herself. "Interesting. Another elephant keeper already. Repeating herself. And I was sure she'd sworn off the tall blond ones. Unpleasant reminder."

"What does that mean?" I said.

She looked at me in surprise, as if she'd forgotten I was there, and then said dismissively, "Never mind, hon. You've already made it clear you don't want to know. Hmm," she muttered to herself again, "I suppose it makes sense. Victor was too pretty. And an office worker, really. She needed someone macho like an elephant man to make up for it."

I felt a flash of anger on Victor's behalf. "That's awful, Margo."

She narrowed her eyes at me. "Who are you defending? Her or Victor?"

"Neither," I said, suddenly confused. Margo always had this effect on me. "I mean . . . I liked Victor. He liked animals."

"You are such a sucker for a pretty face, hon." She shook her head. "You need to settle down with someone, and you won't be so easily distracted by anything in pants."

"I am not—Wait a minute," I interrupted. "Look at those sloths."

Something very strange was happening. I got out my radio.

"Hannah to Chris," I said, trying not to sound excited. It was not cool to sound excited on the radio.

"Go ahead."

"Can you come up to the outside of 24?" I said, trying not to jump up and down. Were those sloths doing what I thought they were doing?

"Ten-four."

He arrived in a moment. He was walking quickly, obviously having been able to tell something was up. I was too excited to worry about my poor radio-acting skills, though. "What's up?"

I grabbed his arm. "Is that what I think it is?"

He followed my gaze and broke out into a smile. "What kind of music did you end up playing for them?"

I really did hop up and down a little. My sloths were mating! God, it was weird-looking. The female was still hanging on to the branch with all four limbs, and the male had somehow gotten between her and the branch. I'd read about it, and the description made it sound impossible, but there it was.

"Oh wow," I said. And then I calmed down enough to realize I was still standing there hanging on to Chris's arm, watching animals have sex, with Margo right here.

I felt myself turn red and pulled my hand away quickly. He didn't notice. He was watching the sloths. And then I forgot about myself and watched them too. I might have a baby sloth. I might have a wombat *and* a baby sloth. I couldn't believe what a glorious place the world was.

It was finally lunchtime. I flopped down on the couch. It had been another fascinating but exhausting morning. It was too bad I hadn't gotten my lunch out of the fridge first, because I felt like I was never going to get up off this couch again. I guessed I would just starve to death. It was too bad. I had really wanted to live to see the wombat.

Caleb came in. "Hannah, have you seen the baby rhino yet?"

"Yeah, how could I not?" Who would miss the baby rhino? I was over there the first day it went on exhibit. We had Indian rhinos, the ones that look like they have armor—not those boring African ones you always saw on television. It always seemed to me like practically all the animals you saw on television were African. Probably because you could film them out on the savanna from a distance, without getting close and endangering your expensive camera equipment.

"I mean from close up, from the keeper area," he said.

"No, why?" I said, sitting up.

"I have to go over to the Elephant House and get some things I left there. Do you want to come?"

Suddenly I felt a lot less tired. "Wow, yeah," I said, jumping up. "Let's go."

We walked down the stairs toward the keeper area door in the Elephants building. One of the hippos was in the indoor enclosure as we walked past, so we stopped and Caleb called it over. It was funny to hear big Caleb talking to this huge animal in a little baby-talk voice. Did all the keepers talk to them that way, or was Caleb always a small mammal guy in waiting? I didn't know.

The hippo came over, and Caleb patted its enormous snout. Even the whiskers were huge. It was a recognizable mammal-whiskery muzzle, but expanded to unbelievable proportions. I just wasn't used to things on this scale. I wondered how big the poop was. At least he was a herbivore, though, so it probably wasn't too awful.

"Want to touch him?" he said to me.

I looked at him in momentary panic, which I quickly covered up by nodding and smiling. There was a certain animal-person macho that I felt compelled to maintain in this situation, although more for myself than because I cared what Caleb thought.

I reached out and put my hand gently on the hippo's muzzle, far from the opening part where the teeth would be. It moved just its eyeballs to look at me. I felt encouraged. I guessed I had passed the animal-person macho test in the hippo's eyes, anyway.

I turned to follow Caleb as he opened the door to the keeper room. I hadn't heard him ring the bell, and then I noticed there was no one on the other side of the door and he was putting his keys in his pocket. He still had keys to the building? Shouldn't he have given them back? Someone needed to keep better track of the keys around here—he had elephant keys, Chris had steam tunnel keys . . . I was starting to feel left out, not having any illegal keys of my own. I'd have to work on getting some for the capybara exhibit.

Stephanie was in the keeper room alone. Caleb introduced me.

"Where is everyone?" he said.

"They're all out at lunch. I didn't go. I want to spend as much time as possible with Lucy as I can before she leaves. If she leaves," she said.

Caleb nodded and looked sympathetic. I wandered off to the other side of the room to look at a bulletin board with photographs on it. I figured they had a lot to catch up on. And that they'd probably feel freer to talk if I acted like I wasn't paying attention.

Anyway, although I didn't care that much about elephants, I loved looking at old black and white zoo photographs, especially if they had keepers in them. They were always men in those days. I liked to see how the outfits changed. I was glad we didn't have to wear those silly hats anymore or those awful pants. Blue jeans were exactly the right pants for the job. I was lucky to have a job where I got to wear blue jeans every day. But I kind of missed those khaki button shirts from what I thought of as the Marlin Perkins era. Our knit shirts were comfortable but didn't have that classic look. I guess however a zookeeper looked when you were a tiny kid, that's how you think a zookeeper should look.

"It must be tough dealing with the visitors these days," Caleb said to Stephanie.

"We're all just trying to stay out of the public area as much as we can and still do our jobs. Even if a conversation starts out about the elephants, it ends up about the murder. And if they ask me about the move, sometimes I just get too upset," she said.

"What's happening with the plans for Lucy now?" Caleb asked.

"I'm taking it to the animal welfare committee in a few days. And I'm trying to get the press interested. There have been a couple of little articles mentioning the move, but just rewritten from the press releases. Nothing that talks about the real issues. I'm supposed to talk to a reporter this afternoon, actually."

Aha, I thought. I bet I knew who. I bet she wouldn't just ask about the elephant move either.

"If only Victor—if only I'd had a little more time to convince him." Her voice sounded a little shaky.

Unfortunately, just when she had started to talk about Victor and things might have gotten interesting, Caleb finished gathering his things out of a locker and said, "Okay, I'm ready."

As we approached the door, it opened and Matthew came striding in. It was remarkable how annoying he was just walking into a room. His body language seemed to say that he was king of the universe. Maybe he needed to give that impression to work with elephants? Stephanie didn't act that way, though, and neither did Caleb.

He stopped when Caleb said hello. "This is Hannah, from Small Mammals," Caleb said. "Have you all met?"

I had the distinct impression Matthew looked down his nose at me, although granted, given the nose, and the height above me at which it was naturally placed, maybe he couldn't help it. "I believe we encountered one another earlier today," he said coldly.

"Yeah," I said, making the one syllable sound as rude as possible, which was pretty rude if I say so myself.

Caleb ignored our little altercation. Matthew and I stared at each other for another moment, and then he turned and walked away. I thought that meant I won the stare-down, but I suppose he thought he'd snubbed me, so we were both satisfied.

I looked after Matthew as he walked away, scowling. He'd be kind of good-looking, I thought, if only he got a brain transplant. Kind of a waste, really. I turned and followed Caleb and Stephanie out to the rhino exhibit.

The baby rhino and its mom were right up against the bars of the exhibit. We stood about a foot away so as not to get the mother agitated, since I was a stranger. The baby was so baby-like. How did all mammals manage to do that? No one would call a grownup rhino cute. But the baby was like a cartoon animal. I couldn't take my eyes off him. I could see the public looking at him from six feet farther away than I was. I was positive that waves of envy were billowing in my direction.

"Careful, Hannah," Stephanie said.

I had been leaning closer to the baby without realizing it—it was like a magnet. The mom was giving me the hairy eyeball. Don't you dare touch that baby, I felt her saying. These bars won't be strong enough to save you.

I stepped back. "Sorry," I said softly.

"It's okay," she said. "He's irresistible, isn't he?"

I could have stood there all day, but we all had work to do.

"Thank you so much," I said.

"No problem. I'm sure you'd do the same."

"I'll let you know if we have a baby sloth," I said, wistfully.

"That would be excellent," she said.

As we walked back to Small Mammals, I said to Caleb, "Do you think it's a bad idea too?" I asked. "Moving Lucy, I mean."

"Stephanie's the type who goes for the underdog. But maybe Lucy wouldn't be such an underdog in another group."

I thought about all the desperate rationalizations I could come up with if they wanted to ship out my favorite animal. Even if it wouldn't be so bad for the animal.

"Stephanie works with that cat rescue group with Robin, doesn't she?" I suddenly remembered.

"That neuter and release group for feral cats? Yes."

"Do all her cats have only one eye too?"

Robin was always taking home the cats they were planning to euthanize. She's got all these cats with one eye, or three legs, or that need to be on ten medications for the rest of their lives, and none of them even like people that much. I could never understand the point, really.

Caleb flashed a big smile. He was usually so lugubrious, I wasn't sure I'd ever seen him smile like that before. "It sounds like the two of them ought to start some kind of group home together."

We slowed down as we passed the camel yard. Caleb waved at the keeper, who was working on making a big pile of hay, and she waved back. I thought of the big piles of dung that that hay was going to be transformed into. I liked my job better.

"What was that about convincing Victor, anyway?" I said as we continued on, trying to sound casual.

"Victor was around a fair amount. She put a lot of time into trying to talk him over to her side."

Huh, I thought. That sounded, well, insane. Did she really think Victor was going to start telling the press that the zoo was wrong to move the elephant? Even if his relationship with Allison had been over, Victor had liked his job too much to risk it. It would have been hard for him to go back to writing about some boring corporation where he couldn't go out at lunchtime and visit all kinds of cool creatures. I didn't think I was just projecting. I'd seen his eyes light up when he talked to me about the tenrec. And suddenly I remembered I'd seen him at a regular afternoon demo I'd done a couple of weeks before that. He'd kept back so as not to get in the way of the public who wanted to see the naked mole rat I was holding. But he'd stayed for the whole thing, listening to me answer the same questions over and over as different people came and went. I felt sad thinking about it.

"Um, that sounds a little unrealistic," I said, trying to put it nicely, not knowing how good a friend of hers Caleb was.

Caleb shrugged. "Victor was good at listening politely. Stephanie wasn't entirely rational about Victor either."

That was interesting. Stephanie had some kind of a thing for

Victor? She'd probably thought all she had to do was wait, what with Allison's habit of discarding her lovers, and Stephanie's vague similarity to Allison in appearance, and Victor hanging around the Elephant House a lot . . . He'd been there to see the elephants, I was sure, but I knew how easy it could be to fool yourself about something you wanted badly.

I felt sorry for Stephanie. But it didn't make me like her any better. I wasn't the kind of person who adopted the sad one-eyed cats.

We turned down the path to walk around to the back door of Small Mammals. Was there anything else interesting I could get out of Caleb, about the elephant people? I had only another minute.

"Hey, um, is Matthew a friend of yours?"

"No."

Oh, good. "He was practically beating a raccoon to death just now. With a net. I know he's used to working with bigger animals, but still . . ."

"We don't beat elephants with nets," he said, without emphasis.

After a couple of beats of silence, he continued, "Elephant keepers can be difficult people. It's a lot less tense with you all. I'm enjoying the change."

Elephants killed more keepers than any other zoo animal, I knew. Maybe you might be a little tense all the time, living with that. Maybe it would make you want to beat raccoons. Like someone who has a bad day at work and comes home and kicks the dog.

"Well, thanks," I said as we headed down the stairs. "That was really cool. Thanks for taking me."

"My pleasure."

I opened the door to the keeper room and saw the couch, calling out to me, sad at my neglect. Five more minutes of lunch hour. Just five minutes, I thought, stretching out.

I was spot-cleaning an exhibit in my usual spaced out way. My brain was set in pattern recognition mode for spots of poop lying in substrate that was cleverly chosen so poop would be inconspicuous. I drifted along in poop-searching mode. As I bent over, I felt something muscular slink around my waist from behind. I realized that, bizarrely, I had no idea what animal was in this exhibit that I was cleaning. I pulled at it—it felt like a snake, but what would a snake be doing in an open outdoor yard like this? I couldn't pull it off, and it was starting to squeeze. I reached for my radio, but it was caught under the creature's arm or tentacle or whatever it was.

Starting to panic, I looked around. At the far side of the adjacent yard, someone was working with his back to me. Someone tall and blond—could it be Chris? I called out for help, and as he turned around, I saw it couldn't be. The profile looked like Ray, with his noble Greek nose, but that didn't make sense—Ray wasn't tall and blond. The person walked toward me, and I saw with relief it was Matthew. He was just who I needed, because I realized it wasn't a snake around me—it was an elephant trunk. But when Matthew saw my predicament, he just stopped and watched. The trunk squeezed me harder, and I couldn't breathe. Matthew laughed. Everything went black.

I sat bolt upright. For a second I wondered where the pugs were. Then I realized I was on the couch in the keeper room. Chris was sitting at the other end of the couch from where I'd been curled up. I was breathing hard in fear from the dream, and he looked at me with concern.

"Are you okay?" he said.

"Fine," I lied breathlessly.

I don't think he believed me, but it wasn't like him to pry. He looked at me closely for a moment and then went back to what he was reading.

I sat staring at him. I'd never realized that before about how Matthew looked. How if someone had wanted to make a demon who was a cross between two of my favorite people, they'd come up with something that looked a lot like Matthew.

Why hadn't Stephanie and Caleb said anything about who they thought was the murderer when they were talking? You'd think that they'd have more opinions than anyone and that the elephant people would talk about it endlessly. Except they wouldn't, if one of them had done it. Or if they thought Matthew had done it and that he might come striding into the room any minute.

I felt a little frightened of Chris sitting there, from the association and the lingering effects of the dream and the sudden feeling that I didn't really know any of these people, what they were capable of, what had gone on between them before I knew them. All the undercurrents. Undercurrents could sweep you away and kill you.

I took a deep breath. I sat and watched him reading until the feeling started to wear off, and he was just my Chris again, who would never leave me in trouble with an elephant trunk, who made me feel idiotically happy just to be in the same room with him

"Hey, what's that?" I said, scooting over on the couch and looking at the papers he was reading.

"It's the paperwork on the wombat." I thought that was what it looked like. He surrendered it to me before I even said anything. I grabbed it greedily.

I leafed through pages of medical records. There was supposed to be a sheet of information from his keeper. That was the interesting part, if the keeper had done a good job of filling it out. They would talk about the animal's personality and how it interacted with keepers and other animals.

I finally found it. "Oh, no. This says nothing at all." Most of the interesting sections were left blank: the questions about his interactions with his keepers, his favorite foods, whether they'd done any training.

"Well," he said, and then hesitated, casting about for an encouraging answer, "it was a rush job."

"You think it's really because the wombat has no personality to write about," I said, trying not to sound accusing.

"I never said that," he said, looking innocent.

Well, it didn't matter. The wombat would be cute. We had plenty of primates, and they had plenty of personality and it got tiring after a while. It wasn't like the wombat needed to be able write a good essay to get into a prestigious college, or entertain dinner guests. A nice simple nonprimate. I needed more of that in my life. We all did.

I handed the paperwork back to Chris. Unfortunately, Margo picked just that moment, as I was gazing after him walking back into his office, to come out of the ladies' room.

She didn't even have to say anything. She smirked, and I blushed. We'd had so much practice, we'd gotten quite efficient.

"I was just thinking about the *wombat,*" I lied, grasping at a less embarrassing thing for her to tease me about. Darn, why couldn't a person increase the entertainment value of her workday with just a little teeny tiny crush on a coworker in privacy around here?

"Oh, of course," she said, airily, waving her hand.

I got up slowly, like I didn't care, to go to the ladies' room and throw cold water on my face.

"And if I believe that, you've got a couple of pandas you want to sell me," she called after me as I pretended not to hear.

Chapter 8

I had just finished feeding out in the back room. I wandered out the door lost in mundane thoughts about what I had to do next in what order to get out of here at something resembling quitting time. So I didn't notice Ray standing there looking into the open door of Radar the fennec fox's exhibit until I nearly walked into him.

"Eek!" I squeaked. Ray grabbed the pile of dirty food pans I was about to drop. I noticed he looked as surprised to see me as I was to see him.

"Hey," I said, "did I leave that open?" Radar's was one of the few exhibits that were kept locked.

"Well . . . no."

I narrowed my eyes at him. "Someone let you in?"

"Nooo," he said, like he was looking for an escape, and then giving up. "You won't yell at me?"

I scowled. "What would be the point? Would it stop you from doing whatever you want?"

"No," he admitted cheerfully. "But it would be less fun if you were mad at me."

"Fine. I am not mad at you. I don't have the energy for pointless emotions today."

"I have the keys for this building. I thought you were off today."

"What is it with the keys around here?" I whined. "Wait. You visit Radar when I'm off?" I said, confused.

"Is that not okay?" he said plaintively. He was obviously afraid I'd ask him to stop, and then he'd have to be much more sneaky about it.

"I'm just surprised. He's not very herpetological. Except for eating lizards I guess. I didn't know you liked him that much."

"Something about the ears," he mused, tossing crickets.

"You can give him these little dog cookies, too." I showed him an unmarked container on a shelf. "Not too many, though. He'll get fat. Try not to have too much fun without me."

"I will," he said, in an uncharacteristically happy tone. "And how could I?" He closed the exhibit door.

"I thought you came here all the time to visit me, and just played with Radar on the side. Now I see it's the other way around, isn't it?"

"I'm not telling," he said, smiling secretively.

"You know what you ought to see? The baby rhino. It's kind of scaly, after all. Caleb took me to see it today. It was cool."

"How's he doing here?" I was surprised by the question. I didn't know he had any particular interest in Caleb.

"Fine, I guess. He doesn't talk much. I don't think I ever saw him smile before today."

He nodded. "He would have preferred not to leave Elephants, I think. Except that it meant seeing too much of Allison."

"Do you think he was jealous of Victor?"

He looked at me like the answer was stupidly obvious. "But would he have done something like that about it?" he said, making the connection immediately. He looked thoughtful. "He's just like the stereotype you'd imagine from his physical type. Slow to anger. Slow to let go of a grudge. Could he reach a limit and explode? I wouldn't rule it out."

His tone was analytical, but I knew he had some personal experience of this sort of thing. I was silent for a moment, just taking it in.

"I hope he didn't do it," I finally said. "I was kind of getting to like him. He was trying to target-train my sloth with a bean. We were talking about training them to get into their crates." I had to like anyone who liked my sloths. And it would really be great not to need four or five people to catch them up. It would be inconvenient if they took Caleb to jail and he couldn't help me train them.

"He has a tendency to get fixated on unattainable women," Ray said slyly. "Maybe you should be careful."

"What?" I said, irritated. He was being inexplicable again. Then I realized what he meant. "Maybe I'm only unattainable by you," I said, pleased with the chance to tease him for a change.

"Are you?" he said, giving me his most smoldering look. I blushed, damn it. I looked away. I shouldn't even have tried. He would always be better at this game than I was.

I changed the subject. "Hey, as long as you're here, could you be tall for me for a minute? I need to get a plant down out of this exhibit, and I screwed up by putting these new plants in first and they're in the way of where I need to put a ladder."

"I don't know. I think you'll have to talk to my illustrious Hellenic ancestors about that one, and I expect that if they'd had those genes to pass down, they would have done it already."

I looked at him, surprised. I'd never thought about it, because everyone was taller than I was. But it was possible that for a guy, he might not feel very tall.

"You'll always be tall to me, Ray," I said. He couldn't possibly be insecure about his appearance, could he? It seemed absurd.

"Flattery will get you everywhere. Although you could get there just as well without it, too."

"In here," I said, ignoring him and opening the exhibit door.

He climbed in. "Smells like mammals in here."

"Marmosets. Sorry, they're the stinkiest."

He reached easily for the dead plant I needed to take down. I watched while he did it, trying not to admire his back. I never used to like men with muscles, but I realized my tastes had changed since I'd started this job. I guess because now I knew how useful they were. He was just muscular enough to look like he could haul a bag of mulch around for me, without looking like he wasted a lot of mindless hours at the gym. I was perfectly able to haul my own mulch around, naturally. But I was never foolish enough to refuse a gentleman's offer to help, either.

He turned around and climbed out, and I slid the door closed. He handed me the dead plant with a flourish. "For you."

"Oh, thank you," I gushed. "Look, it's even got spines. How thoughtful."

"It's important to bring a lady surprise flowers sometimes."

"It's so nice someone still thinks of me as a lady when I'm covered in stinky marmoset poop all day."

"I like that in a woman," he said, grinning. Then he looked at his watch. "I'm afraid I have to get back and do a demo."

"Oh, you do actually do some work?" I teased. "Off with you then. The children won't want to miss the snake or whatever."

He went off down the hall, whistling. Radar stood looking out after him. I knew it was silly of me, but I thought he looked sort of disappointed as he watched Ray disappear.

It was time to go, but I had missed most of my lunchtime nap, making my walk home stretch to double its usual length in my mind. Five minutes, I thought. I went into the keeper room and took off my shoes and flopped down on the couch. I put a pillow over my head.

After a moment, I heard someone come out of the locker room.

"See you tomorrow, Sleeping Beauty," Caleb said.

"Bye," I said into the pillow. "Thanks for the rhino."

"Any time." I heard his footsteps disappear up the back stairs.

After a little while I heard someone walk very carefully and quietly past me to the locker room, and then very carefully and quietly back.

"Bye, Jeff," I said as I heard him start to very carefully and quietly open the door to the outside. Robin was on vacation, so I didn't have to try to distinguish the two sweet, considerate people by the sound of their footsteps.

"See you tomorrow," he said, sounding a little surprised.

After another little while the phone rang. I wasn't sure if anyone else was still around. Before I could start to feel guilty about not getting up to answer it, someone picked up.

"Hey," I heard after a couple of minutes.

I opened one eye and looked out from under the pillow. Chris was standing in the door of his office, leaning against the frame, looking at me with what was possibly amusement.

I thought he was a beautiful sight, as usual. But I was too tired to enjoy it. I closed my eye again.

"What are you doing after work?" he said.

"Sleeping," I said hopefully. I turned over onto my stomach. I thought briefly of what dirty pants must have sat on the cushions I was pressing my face into. But I didn't care. It was darker this way.

"That's too bad. So you won't want to come to the airport with me."

"No," I said into the couch cushion.

Normally I would accept pretty much any opportunity to spend time with him. But right now, nothing would get me off this couch short of an offer to go to his apartment and take all our clothes off. And I wasn't even sure I wouldn't take a rain check on that.

"Why are you going to the airport?" I mumbled into the

cushions, without real interest.

"To pick up the wombat," he said.

I sat up. "What?" I demanded. "It's not coming till tomorrow. Isn't it?"

"There's been a little misunderstanding."

"What?" I said again, shriller this time. This was a big deal, shipping an animal. You didn't make mistakes about basic things like the date.

"I got the date from the director's staff," he said. "But apparently she gave them the wrong information."

"How can you be so calm?" I said, jumping up. I guess I wondered this about him all the time. But really, in this situation? "When does it get here?"

"We'll be there in plenty of time if we leave now."

"Well, let's go," I said, heading for the door.

He didn't move. I looked back, and he was standing there looking like he was trying not to smile. I glared at him. What was his problem? I had an absurd vision of a wombat walking around and around on a luggage carousel with no one to claim it.

"I think you need shoes," he said.

I looked down at my feet. I felt myself turn red. I sat back down on the couch and started to put my shoes on without looking up. I was so flustered, I was having a hard time tying the laces. I hoped he wasn't watching, but I was afraid to check.

He sat next to me and leaned back on the couch like he had all the time in the world. "There's no rush," he said.

I didn't look at him. Every time we talked about the wombat lately, he got this look on his face, and I was sure he'd have it now. That look like it was really adorable how I felt about the wombat. I wasn't sure how I felt about that look. No, that was wrong. I knew how I felt about it. I just didn't know what to do about it.

"Okay, let's go," I said, jumping up again, this time fully shod. He stopped torturing me with his calmness and got right up off the couch. We locked up and headed out.

I stared out the window anxiously. Everyone on the road was a potential idiot who could do something stupid and get between me and my wombat. Every one of them was probably talking on a cell phone and eating a hamburger and combing their hair all at the same time instead of paying attention to driving, and they were going to cause a huge accident that blocked all the lanes of traffic and went down in Beltway history, and we would be stuck in it while the wombat walked around on the baggage carousel wearing its little paws down to the bone.

"How could she get this wrong?" I fumed. I resolved that I would walk all the way to the airport if we did get stuck behind a massive hamburger-eating pileup. I didn't know how far it was, but I was sure nothing would stop me.

Chris didn't say anything. He didn't say that it would be better if we followed the usual procedures to acquire new animals. He didn't say that this wouldn't have happened if he or our curator had arranged the shipment. He didn't curse and rave about how Allison was always micromanaging things that shouldn't be the zoo director's job. So I had to go on ranting on my own.

"I know we always have to drop everything for anything that has to do with her. But something like this?" I whined. "How could she make a mistake like this? It doesn't just inconvenience us. It could hurt the animal. What if we'd already gone home when that phone call came?"

I was angry. This was a serious mistake. What's more, I sometimes suspected she did things like this on purpose to keep us off balance. It kept her in control.

"It'll be okay," Chris said in a soothing tone. I recognized it as the same voice he used to talk to scared little animals that had some frightening thing happening to them. I tried not to succumb to it. There were so many things that could go wrong that I had to worry about. I glared out the window at the cell-phone-talking drivers, tapped my foot nervously, and considered taking up biting my nails again. Then I thought about what got under my nails every day and decided against it.

"How much farther is it?" I said, peering at the highway signs. I hadn't come out here often enough to be familiar with the route. We were somewhere in the most godforsaken suburbs of Virginia, and my wombat was right now flying around in the freaking *air,* and none of it seemed the least bit like a good idea.

Chris reached over and put his hand on my arm. I froze for a second. I always had a moment of panic at first when he touched me. I wondered if the animals felt this way when he caught them up in his hands. They would struggle at first, but then they would almost always quiet down. Like somehow they realized he would never hurt them.

I closed my eyes and let the tension drain out of me.

"We do this all the time," he said reassuringly. "We haven't lost one yet."

I giggled. I realized that was what I always told the children at the zoo who'd gotten separated from their parents. It was true. The zoo had been around over a hundred years, and we'd never yet had to find a new home for any kids who lost their parents permanently.

I gazed out the window. All of the clouds looked like wombats.

"Hey," I said, "wasn't that our exit? It said 'Cargo.' "

"No. He's coming as baggage."

"Baggage?" Suddenly my vision of the wombat going round and round on the luggage carousel didn't seem so ridiculous after all.

"Don't worry," he said, reading my mind, "they don't throw

him in with all the suitcases. It just means we have to pick him up at the main terminal."

I saw the main terminal now in the middle distance. It was just a big glassy modern box surrounded by parking lots, but today it looked magical. Today it was the Portal to Wombatland.

We parked and walked inside together without saying anything. We should be holding hands and skipping down the path to Wombatland, I thought nonsensically. I gazed around while Chris looked at the arrivals board and checked the flight number he had written down.

"We have plenty of time," he said, trying not to smile.

"I'm sorry I was in such a rush."

"No problem," he said, sounding perfectly content.

We walked to the baggage office and sat down outside it. Chris was completely relaxed. He had done this dozens of times. He didn't care about the wombat more than all the other animals he'd ever picked up at an airport, either. He sat with his long legs stretched out and his hands behind his neck, his elbows in the air, like he was at the beach or something. Like he had all the time in the world. How did he do this? It was so annoying. And why did he have to look so darned . . . well, attractive while he was doing it? I had to stop thinking of him that way. I wasn't looking for a relationship. I was happy with my pugs. I had to stop letting this get out of hand. *And where was my wombat?*

Just when I thought I couldn't stand it anymore, someone came out of the elevator with a large sky kennel on a cart. I almost jumped up in the air.

Chris got up, but I beat him to it. "Is that my wombat?"

"Yeah," said the guy, looking at the label on the crate. "What is that, anyway?"

Did some people not know what a wombat was? I stared at him in astonishment.

"It's an animal that comes from Australia. Related to the koala," said Chris, skillfully intervening before I could ask the guy what kind of an ignoramus he could possibly be.

The guy nodded. Yeah, everyone knew what a koala was. Koalas, pandas—give me a break. How do some of these animals manage to get all the press?

We crouched down, and Chris pulled away a corner of the fabric that was covering the wire mesh on the door of the crate. I saw the wombat sleeping contentedly inside.

"Oh my God," I said. "Look at that. Isn't he perfectly adorable? I can't believe it. Hi, pumpkin," I said to it in a squeaky little voice.

I turned to Chris, and he wasn't looking at the wombat. He had been looking at me instead. He was smiling at me as if I were, well, perfectly adorable.

I blushed furiously. You would have, too, if someone looked at you like that. But I wasn't sure I wanted him to think I was adorable. Maybe I wanted him to think I was mysteriously exotically attractive, or stunningly beautiful, while at the same time powerful and intellectually profound . . . but cute? Like a bunny? He was the small mammal guy, so okay, presumably he liked cute. But wait. What difference did it make what he liked? How did I keep going down these lines of thinking despite my intentions?

"Don't look at me like that," I said, glancing away. "You're supposed to be looking at the wombat."

Apparently that was a perfectly adorable thing to say, because he just smiled harder.

"It's your *job,*" I said desperately. "We're being paid right now. You're supposed to make sure he's okay after the flight. Shouldn't we wake him up?"

He looked in at the peacefully snoozing mound of fur. "No. He looks fine. I've looked at him all I need to."

"Then let's go."

I reached over decisively to pick up the crate. Which was heavier than I expected, so I couldn't lift it.

I was tired of feeling kind of silly, even if adorable, so without looking at Chris again, I just ordered, "Take it," waving at the crate, and started to march purposefully back in the direction of the truck. I took one sidelong glance to make sure he was following, which he was, trying very hard to not to laugh.

We took the still-sleeping wombat to the hospital quarantine building, and then Chris dropped me off at my apartment, and we did the sort of usual thing, where we stood around awkwardly for a couple of minutes, and I thought about how it was just about dinnertime and there was no reason we shouldn't both go get something to eat, but neither of us said anything about it, and finally he drove off, and we were both sorry. I went upstairs to get the pugs and thought about the wombat instead.

Chapter 9

I was standing in front of the big exhibit number 24 doing the morning check. I had found all the little animals, but I still hadn't seen all three sloths. This was unusual. The sloth was one of the biggest species in the building, so it was usually hard to lose track of one. Still, it was a huge exhibit, and it was surprising how small they could roll themselves up. So I wasn't particularly concerned.

Okay, one on the shelf and one in the tree. Was it possible there were two on the shelf all smushed up together? The ball of fur I saw didn't look that big, but that was one thing to check.

That would mean getting a ladder, though, which was a big pain, and making sure nothing got out of the exhibit while I was carrying the ladder in and out. Maybe I'd leave that to last. Where else?

The space under the waterfall was barely big enough. They'd never gone there before. Nope, no one there now. One of them liked to lie in a depression at the very top of the waterfall. Usually I could see it there from the ground. But what if it were sick and not lying in its usual position? I wasn't positive what kind of space was up there. I decided I had better get closer.

I climbed carefully up the slick rocks. I got about two-thirds of the way up and stopped. I had never gone any higher than this. It was stupid to think that a whole sloth could be curled up in the same place as always and not be visible, wasn't it? But I couldn't go whining for help and then have it end up that the animal was right there in its usual spot.

I wasn't really afraid of heights. Rapid deceleration from heights, now, that was a different matter. I took a deep breath and climbed higher. It wasn't too bad. The rocks were smaller up top, so spaces for a short-legged person to set her feet were closer together.

But it was futile. In fact, it was astonishing that a sloth usually curled up into this hole at all, I thought when I got up there. It sure couldn't do it and not have half of its body visible from the ground. I wished I known that before. I'd bet Chris could have told me that. But he probably would have climbed up here to check anyway, and rightfully so. So it was just as well I'd done it myself.

I sat there in the sloth's spot on top of the waterfall. So this is what this exhibit looks like from up here. Interesting. Kind of a nice tame rainforest canopy experience I was having. Now I just needed to be lowered down to the ground in some kind of sling, and everything would be cool.

I looked down the rockwork and remembered that climbing down was somehow always harder than climbing up. I was really, really sorry that I'd been too stubborn and independent to radio Chris first. It was ten times easier for him to climb up here. He would have called me if he needed someone to crawl into a tight spot. We were supposed to work as a team. People said that in lots of jobs, but it really mattered when you were doing stuff like trying to catch up an animal who was in the mood to bite your hand off.

But no. I had to be all self-reliant and worried about whether I looked like a helpless female, and now I was sitting on top of this damn pile of wet rocks trying not to whimper.

I started to climb down. What I needed was eyes on the ends of my toes. I cursed the extinct race of giants that had built this building. The waterfall would have looked just as natural with more footholds closer together. I reached a spot where I couldn't find a spot to put my foot and started to panic. I clung to the rock, feeling around with my toes. Damn, there was really nowhere—there. I let out a breath. Another couple of steps and now I was down to the level I usually stopped at. I knew I could get down from here.

But when I got down to level ground I still had my original problem. I hadn't found the sloth yet.

I checked the chutes to the holding. Had someone left the shift door open so the sloths could get into the large part of the holding that we didn't usually use? From inside the exhibit, I could see that the shift door was closed, but what if one had gotten in there and then someone closed the door behind it? I didn't know who'd be messing with my exhibit that way, but I was running out of things to try.

The shelf was more likely, so first I dragged the ladder in to check the sloth or sloths who were on it. I climbed up and poked the ball of shaggy fur so it would unroll. Very slowly it put its head up and turned to look at me with its alien eyes with their pinprick pupils. It was definitely only one sloth, the juvenile male. It opened its mouth, and when I didn't insert any food, reached out an arm, very slowly, and groped around with its awkward curved claw.

"I'm sorry, little guy, I didn't bring you anything," I said and stroked his fur. It's odd fur, coarse and wiry, but not unpleasant. After a moment he started to curl up again, and I climbed down.

I wrestled the ladder out of the exhibit and checked the holding area. Nope, nothing there.

I was starting to feel panicky. This didn't make sense. Was there any chance someone had moved a sloth out of the exhibit after I left? That would only have happened if one was sick, and I was positive that in that case Chris would have called me at home. Someone else would at least have written it on the exhibit checksheet, so I looked at that. Nope, no one but me had written anything there. No relief-inducing notes that Caleb had taken my sloth on a vacation to the Delaware shore so they could bond for his training attempts. I still had a problem.

I climbed back into the exhibit and tried to keep thinking straight despite my growing hysteria. I must have missed something. If a sloth was sick or, God forbid, dead, it could wind up on the ground. Were there any spots on the ground that I'd missed? I checked the corners of the exhibit and behind plant plots. Oh, no, what if it had fallen into the waterfall pool and drowned? You'd think it would be floating and obvious, but still. I went to check. You could see perfectly well that there was nothing in it, but I sank my arm in up to my shoulder and felt around anyway.

Either I was incredibly stupid or something was very wrong. I hoped it was the first. If so, it was time to get help figuring it out.

I radioed Chris. I couldn't keep the panic out of my voice. I hoped that all the usual static covered it up, but it looked like it hadn't from how quickly Chris arrived.

"What's up?" he said as he stepped into the exhibit. Then he looked at me. "Hannah, what's wrong?"

"I can't find the female sloth," I said, trying to control my voice. "I must be stupid. How could a sloth get out? I saw all three when I left yesterday. You didn't do anything with them, did you?"

"No. Where did you look?"

"Everywhere. I climbed up everything, and I looked on the ground in case it fell, and I looked in the holding in case anyone messed with the shift doors and underneath the waterfall and in the water."

Unfortunately Chris didn't think I was stupid, and I could

see he was growing increasingly concerned. Still, the first thing he had to do was recheck the exhibit in case I really had lost my mind.

"Are you positive which ones you have?"

"The juvenile male is on the shelf. I'll check the other one again."

He nodded and started to search. I climbed on a rock and tried to reach the sloth in the tree branch. I was pretty sure it was the male, but I couldn't reach it. I needed something to persuade it.

"I'm going to get an orange," I called.

I ran down to the kitchen and grabbed an orange and a knife and cut it into quarters and peeled it. My hands were trembling. Jeff came into the kitchen and took one look at me and asked what was wrong.

"My sloth's missing," I said, biting my lip to hold back tears. Getting hysterical wasn't going to improve the situation. It would not solve the problem that we were probably missing my female sloth who had just been mating with the male and might be pregnant.

"Missing?" he said, incredulous. "How could we lose a sloth?"

"I don't know. Maybe Chris will find it. Maybe I'm like the man who mistook his wife for a hat. I had a stroke, and now I'm the woman who mistook her sloth for . . . a ficus plant or something." I hoped so. That would be a problem for my career, but at least the sloth would be okay.

Jeff gave me a hug, which just made me want to cry more. "Don't worry. I'm sure everything will be fine."

I didn't trust myself to talk. I nodded and ran up the stairs.

Back in the exhibit I climbed up on the rock and poked the sloth with the piece of orange on the end of a stick. It was awfully uncomfortable. I had to stand on my toes on a slippery wet rock and stretch my arm out as far as it would go and just wait while the sloth thought about it for a year. Finally it slowly pulled its head out and looked at me. It was definitely the other male. He opened his mouth and waited for me to put the piece of orange right inside. Okay, they were a little spoiled. But their claws have two curved long nails that are very good for hanging from branches but not so good for holding food. It's just easier if you put it right in their mouths.

But I couldn't reach any farther. I had to wait till he figured that out, and stretched a little farther and took it awkwardly. He put his head back and chewed on the orange, sticky juice dripping out of his mouth onto his stomach. I always thought that the sloths looked happy somehow when they did this, even though they couldn't really change the expressions on their faces. The tamarins came leaping, squeaking, in a swarm like huge orange bees drawn to the sweetness. They wanted to sit on the sloth's stomach and get the juice, but I waved them away absently. I watched him blink and chew for a moment, and then I climbed back down.

I looked around. Chris was on top of the waterfall.

"I'm not finding anything," he said. "I'm going to get up on top of the exhibit and make sure there aren't any new holes in the mesh."

I nodded miserably. This was such a last resort that it was really bad news. The top of the exhibit was wire mesh that was strong enough to walk on. It was pretty much impossible that a hole big enough for a sloth to get through had suddenly appeared. But we had to check, and with all the foliage in the exhibit, we couldn't tell for sure from inside.

I held the ladder while he climbed up, trying not to feel useless. Then I went back into the exhibit and sat huddled up on the floor inside the door, as I watched him walking around over my head. Dead leaves floated down, and who knows what other kind of years-old debris. Some of it fell in my hair, and I didn't bother to brush it away. What was the point? The primates ran around making distress calls because of the oddness of someone being up there above their heads. I just sat in the dirt trying not to make any distressed noises of my own.

"There's nothing up here," he said after a while. No surprise. I went out and held the ladder, and he climbed down. He looked at me sympathetically and brushed some leaves out of my hair. "You saw them at the end of the day?"

"Yeah, I definitely saw all three on my way out." Not that we were expected to check every possibly hidden animal at the end of every day. But I liked to look at the sloths.

"You locked the door?"

"Yeah, for sure." It was hard to remember sometimes if I'd locked something, because it was so automatic. But the lock on this door didn't work well, and it was always a little bit of a struggle. So I remembered.

"Then the only explanation is that someone took it."

I stared at him. "Like someone stole it? That's crazy," I said, shaking my head. It would make more sense if we'd coincidentally both had strokes and were mistaking a sloth for a ficus plant.

He shrugged. "What's the alternative? She stole your keys and made a copy and escaped?"

Animals had been stolen from zoos before, it was true. We'd had some snakes stolen. Some kids had stolen a koala in Ohio a few years ago. But in both cases there was clear evidence of a break-in, like the hole the kids cut in the roof. Whoever did this had even been nice enough to lock up behind himself.

"I need to make some calls," he said.

I walked down the corridor with him, staring at the floor. I felt awful. This was almost worse than an animal dying. Could someone really have stolen my sloth? Was she okay? How did they get in? Was it someone else from the zoo?

"Hang on," I said when we got to the door to downstairs. "I'll be right down. I forgot to open the shift door to outside for the lemurs."

"I'll get it."

I was so miserable that walking that little way back down the hall sounded like a big effort, so I was grateful for the offer. I leaned against the wall and watched him walk back down the hall. Even in November it was often still warm enough to wear shorts in the building, and I couldn't believe that I was so incorrigible that I was thinking of how cute his butt was in those shorts. While my sloth had been kidnapped, for God's sake. Something needed to be done about me.

But it was a good thing I was staring at him, or I wouldn't have noticed what happened to the lemur chutes over his head as he began to pull on the lever. For a split second I froze in astonishment as the whole structure started to move, and then I was flying toward him and yelling as it all came crashing down.

I slammed into him and pushed him out of the way, and the metal structure missed us by an inch. His head hit the concrete floor with a sickening crack. The clanging of metal on concrete blended with the lemurs' alarm calls reverberating through the hall. Time stood still for a moment as I clamped my hands over my ears and pressed my eyes shut trying to keep my head from exploding.

I felt Chris tapping my arm. I opened my eyes. He looked dazed. I let out a little cry and made a move to see if he was injured, but he shook his head a little, wincing, and pointed up insistently. One of the lemurs in the holding was looking down at us through the hole where the chute used to be.

I jumped up. I couldn't tell what the lemur meant by his damn lemur look. He could have been searching for a spot to jump to, or he could have just been thinking, "Duh? What's this?" I loved them like crazy, but they were not the brightest bulbs in the heat lamp.

I looked around frantically for a net, which, as usual, was not where I thought I had left it, so I grabbed a broom and used it to gently convince him he wanted to jump back onto a branch. The shift door had fallen off with the chutes, so next I had to coax him into the lower part that I could still lock without spooking him so he bounded past me out the opening. All the time worrying about how Chris was.

I finally got the lemur locked in and ran back to Chris just as, above our heads, another lemur looked out of the indoor exhibit where he expected the chute to the outdoors and holding to be. He hardly hesitated—it wasn't a jump that a lemur would think twice about, as far as a lemur can think at all. He sailed over our heads and through the exit to the outside.

Chris tried to get up, but he was clearly still too lightheaded. "I'll do it," I said.

I didn't know where the third lemur was. I ran to the outside exhibit and got there just as it came leaping out to join me. Good—now I just had to block off one door and we'd be okay. I looked around and grabbed a potted plant. I climbed up the rockwork in the outdoor enclosure, barely able to hang on to the pot with one hand. I jammed it in so it mostly blocked the entrance. Then for a minute I clung to the rocks, breathless, thankful that for once when I was doing something awkward, there weren't a dozen members of the public staring at me. I didn't know how I'd even begin to explain.

I finally got my breath back and could climb down and go back inside. Chris was sitting on the floor where I'd left him with his head in his hands.

I knelt down and touched his shoulder. "Are you okay?" I said, finally able to worry about him instead of rampaging lemurs on the loose.

"I'll be all right."

We surveyed the damage. The chutes were old and rusty, with sticky doors that should have been replaced or repaired a long time ago. Finally would be, at least. Amazing what had to happen to get someone to pay attention to a work order around here sometimes.

I looked at the back of Chris's head. "It's going to be a bad lump."

He touched it and winced.

"I guess I could have been a little more careful," I said apologetically. Now that the adrenaline rush was dying down, I wondered if I had overreacted. Maybe I could have gotten him out of the way without slamming him onto the concrete floor?

He looked at me as if, in the nicest possible way, I was just slightly out of my mind. "Right," he said. "Next time save my life more politely."

I looked at where the shift door handle was, right where the full weight of the chutes had come down. Then I looked back at Chris and touched his hair, feeling thankful for his beautiful whole head in one piece and not smashed by falling metal or stomping elephants. Our faces were close enough that I could feel his breath.

I stood up quickly before I could do something I might regret later.

Chris got up carefully, and we started examining the wreckage. I couldn't understand how this could have happened. The building was old, but it wasn't that old. Lots of stuff—okay, everything—was a little bent or corroded or sticky or loose. But still, mostly we were only falling apart in small increments. How could all of the connections to the walls have failed at the same time?

"This is weird," I said. "It doesn't look that bad. Not more than anything else in the building."

"Look at this," he said, pointing.

It was a bolt with saw marks on it. It wasn't just broken. You could even see where someone had started cutting in one place and then reconsidered.

"Maybe that happened when they first installed it?" I said. He shook his head. And I knew it couldn't be true. It didn't have the layer of dirt and rust that was all over everything else in the vicinity. It was freshly cut.

We sorted through pieces of the wreckage. It looked like someone had cut the bolts so that the chute was just resting on their edges. The other thing holding it up, then, was the closed door. When the door was pulled away to the side, the delicate balance was upset, and the whole structure fell. The door must have been harder to open than usual. But Chris was strong and didn't work that door as often as I did, and half the doors in the building were rusty and bent and hard to open, so he didn't notice anything unusual.

So someone had stolen my sloth. And someone had done this, too, on purpose to hurt someone. The latter "someone" being probably the person who worked this shift door the vast majority of the time. Which was me.

It was too much to take in. And we didn't have time to talk about it. I looked up at the opening to the outside exhibit, with nothing but a potted plant keeping the lemurs in. We had to put the animals first.

"I'll find some wood to cover that better," I said. The lemurs weren't curious and troublesome like monkeys. They'd probably stare at the spot where the door used to be for a second and then give up. They wouldn't try to force their way around the plant. But I wasn't taking any chances. It was no day for a big lemur escape on top of everything else.

Chris nodded. "I'll radio if I need you on the phone." Once the animals were secure, his job was to report emergencies.

There were no boxes on a form to check off for this one, I thought.

I watched him walk down the hall to make sure nothing else happened to him on the way. Then I went to work on finding some wood.

My simple idea to cover the hole with some wood turned into a major project. The shed was empty, and I didn't find anything by rummaging around the building in increasingly more obscure places. I hated to ask the guys for help with this sort of thing. I didn't want to seem like I was too girly to do the tool-wielding parts of this job. What's more, they tended to take over, and then you didn't get to use the fun power saw and stuff. But finally I had to give up. If there was any wood to be had, they'd hidden it from me in the men's room, because I'd looked everywhere else.

I went downstairs and sat impatiently in front of Chris's office while he talked on the phone. After what seemed like forever he finally hung up.

"What's happened to all our wood?" I demanded.

He leaned his chin on his hands and looked tired. His head probably hurt, and he'd just had to talk to all kinds of annoying bosses about the missing sloth and chutes that fell down and tried to kill us. And then I storm in and want my minor problems to be the center of the known universe. I interrupted as he started to answer. "I'm sorry. Can I start over?"

I got up and walked away and came back while he sat there with his mouth open.

I sat down again. "Hey," I said. "Are you okay? How's your head?"

"I'll live." He shrugged a little.

"Are you sure you don't want to go home? I can cover for you."

"Thanks. But it won't feel any better at home." He smiled. "Okay, what's this about the wood?"

"I can't find anything but scraps. What about all the boards we used to get? There's nothing in the shed."

He looked pained again, but this was more a pain inside the head than outside. "We're having trouble ordering lumber because the director has decided that we can only use recycled or sustainably harvested wood. We're still working on identifying a vendor with a consistent supply at a price we can afford." He sounded like he was repeating exactly what someone had said, because he'd get too angry if he even tried to put it into his own words.

I groaned. "I thought this one was going to be easy—there's supposed to be a pretty good certification organization for wood. I could swear I was half awake at a meeting where they said it was all settled."

He smiled a little, then winced like it hurt. "Yes. But then they decided they were worried about potential conflicts of interest on the organization's board of directors. It slowed things down a bit."

"Right," I said, helplessly. "Look, I know that saving the planet isn't going to be easy. But we can't have lemurs running all over the place until we've solved that problem, you know?"

"I can call down to shops and see if they have anything," he said.

"No," I said. "I'll see if we have any metal sheets, and I'll call them myself if I need to."

"Also, they can't send anyone to pick up the debris until tomorrow."

I opened my mouth and then shut it again, cutting off my automatic impulse to rant about how impossible it would be to work if we couldn't use that hallway and how if something like this had happened up at pandas, they would have called out the

National Guard faster than you could say "charismatic megafauna."

"Do you think we can push it out of the way a little?" I said instead. "All of us together?"

We radioed Jeff and Margo and Caleb and went upstairs. Jeff gasped when he saw what had happened. "Someone could have been hurt. Were you nearby?"

"Um, we got out of the way," I said, not looking at Chris. I didn't see any reason for everyone to know the whole story.

"My word," Margo said, surveying the mess. "I knew this building was decrepit, but I had no idea it had gotten to this point."

I glanced over at Chris. He didn't say anything. He wasn't going to mention that it looked like it was done on purpose. Okay, neither was I. I noticed Caleb standing there, bearlike, just looking, having no reaction. We pushed what we could to the side and got back to work.

The rest of the afternoon seemed to last an eternity. Chris had gone out to a meeting, which made me restless and worried. I had the feeling that I should be watching him every minute to make sure something else didn't try to smash his head in. Then I got all weepy feeding the sloths, wondering where the missing one was. And I kept thinking about Caleb. It was really nice of him to offer to show me the baby rhino. Or was it? Did he have a reason for wanting to make me think he was a nice guy? And why had he seemed to have no reaction to Victor's murder at all?

When it was almost time to go home I decided there was only one thing to do. I picked up the phone and punched in a number.

"Reptiiilesss," said a familiar low voice.

"Ray."

"Miss Hannah. What a pleasure."

"What are you doing after work?" I demanded.

"Whatever you like, from the sound of it," he said.

"Can we talk?"

"Yes ma'am," he said. "I will report for duty immediately."

Chapter 10

On my way out the courtyard gate I met Chris, who was coming back in from his meeting. We stopped and stood in the doorway together.

"Heading home?" he said.

"Yeah." Well, sort of. "Are you feeling any better?"

"I'll be fine," he said, "don't worry about me."

I looked at him, thinking of the absurdity of the idea of not worrying about him.

"They're having zoo police guard the building starting tonight," he said.

I nodded. Better late than never, I guess.

We stood there a little awkwardly. I thought how if he were Jeff or Ray, at the end of such a long, frightening day I could give him a hug. But because he was the one I really wanted to put my arms around, I couldn't.

"Well, see you tomorrow then," I said, and left.

I pulled the courtyard gate shut and looked around for Ray. I didn't see him. I went and sat on the brick wall to wait.

Something fuzzy touched my neck. I jumped, startled, and turned around. It was a branch of butterfly bush, held by Ray, who was crouching behind the wall.

"I brought you flowers, your highness," he said, hopping over and sitting next to me.

"You stole those from Invertebrates." There was a butterfly

exhibit inside Invertebrates and also a butterfly garden outside.

"Because I know it's one of your favorite places. More than you like us upstairs in Reptiles," he said, mock-sadly.

I took the branch and held it out, wishing butterflies would come. "You even stole this from inside the building, didn't you? It wouldn't be in bloom outside at this time of year."

He just smiled his special trademarked evil smile.

"We need to talk about Caleb," I said. Enough beating around the butterfly bush.

"Your wish is always my command," he said, dramatically.

God, how was I going to get him to stop goofing around already? "You made all these remarks about how long he can hold a grudge and how his other relationships have turned out, and all this stuff like you're inside his head. But you don't even seem to be his friend," I complained. "How do you know so much about him anyway?"

He looked at me for a moment. "You don't want to know," he said as if it were obvious.

"Yes I do."

"I think you should trust me. You don't want to know."

"Why would I not want to know," I whined.

I was on the verge of threatening to hold my breath till I turned blue. Really, I couldn't handle Ray. It had gotten so that sometimes I could get stuff out of Chris with just that charming stubborn look that he couldn't resist. But I'd never be able to tame Ray even a little. That was probably because Ray liked me and maybe wanted to sleep with me and that was all, whereas Chris . . . I stopped and put the end of that sentence in a big locked box and quickly buried it in a deep hole at the back of my mind.

Wiping the dirt off my mental hands, I saw that Ray was waiting for me to pay attention. I paid attention.

"Are you positive you want to know?" His tone clearly implied he thought I was asking for trouble. But so what if I was? I had so much trouble already, how would I even notice a little more?

"Yes, I want to know," I said resentfully. "How many times do I have to say so?"

As if it were the most normal thing in the world he said, "We were in a drug program together."

Uh, okay, he was right. I hadn't wanted to know. So I immediately leapt to my own defense.

"Ray, you didn't want to tell me that because you think I'm such a naive goody-two-shoes that I would be shocked and appalled, right?"

He just gave me a look that invited me to answer my own question. Actually I kind of knew there was stuff like this in Ray's past—I hoped it was the past, anyway—but I mostly pretended it didn't exist so successfully that I was almost surprised whenever it came up. I can do denial with the best of them.

I looked away uncomfortably, and then immediately revealed myself to be a naive goody-two-shoes by saying, "Why would Allison get involved with someone with that kind of a problem? Wouldn't it be risky?"

"Perhaps that's exactly the thrill. Sometimes she goes for the dangerous types." He did the evil smile thing again. "Just for a change of pace. Maybe you should try it sometime."

"Yeah, in a coffin," I said, annoyed. "No thanks." I wasn't in the mood to be teased.

"Such a pity," he said. Then his expression turned serious. "Besides, don't you believe a person can change?"

I looked at him in surprise. Hmm, so he cared what Little Miss Naive Goody-Two-Shoes thought.

I had a momentary mean impulse to make some snarky remark. The way he was looking at me made the impulse disappear.

"Some people, I guess," I said, like it wasn't a big deal.

I didn't want to know more about Ray's past in this regard, either seriously or in jest. It wasn't something I could deal with. It was Caleb I was here to talk about. "Well, I see why you think he has self-destructive tendencies then," I said, trying to stick to the subject.

His serious mood didn't last. "But also, after all, he was involved with Allison. It's one thing to experiment with that one," he said, leering, "and quite another to become a regular user. I would never have made that mistake."

Now I regretted having passed up the chance to be snarky a minute ago, if he was going to keep this up. "Oh, cut it out," I said, irritably. "Why don't you stop taunting me and tell me whether you ever really slept with her?" I was tired of him having fun messing with my goody-two-shoes mind.

"I would never kiss and tell." He smiled at me. I realized he really was talking about something else. I felt my face getting red and looked away.

"He doesn't seem like her type," I said, desperately trying to return to the subject of Caleb again. I was thinking of Victor, who was much more suave and civilized, and Matthew, who spent too much time on his hair. Caleb was more the lumberjack-musk-oxen type. Although if it turned out you had to throw Ray into the set of examples, there wouldn't seem to be any generalization about her type at all.

"She has eclectic tastes," he said, shrugging. "You would have Thai for dinner one night and pizza the next, wouldn't you? It's not so different." He gave me one of those looks again.

I scowled. "And are you the Thai food or the pizza? Stop flirting with me. This is serious."

"Flirting with you is very serious."

"Listen," I said, stubbornly trying to keep control of the conversation, "some really weird stuff happened today."

I told him about the sloth going missing. I guess I should have started there, because now he stopped fooling around and listened.

Then I told the story about the chutes falling down.

"You could tell someone had done something to make them fall on purpose. There were other cuts in the bolts. Someone was trying to hurt us pretty bad," I concluded. "Or me, anyway—really I was the only one who should have been using that shift door today."

I had become so engrossed in telling the story that I wasn't really looking at how Ray was reacting. So I was surprised when he suddenly jumped up and grabbed me by the shoulders and said, "Are you all right?" as if it had all just happened. The look on his face was alarmingly intense.

"I'm fine—I'm more worried about my sloth now," I said, trying to suppress the weepy feeling I had every time I thought about her.

"Hannah, you're saying someone tried—" He stopped. "You think Caleb had something to do with this?"

Now his expression was really frightening. I shrank back a little from the violence of it. This was why Ray dressed up as Dracula really was a little scary, I realized. Because you knew this was somewhere inside of the real Ray even when he wasn't dressed up.

But then he seemed to take in my reaction, and he suddenly deflated like a balloon.

He put his arms around me gently. "I'm sorry. It won't happen again."

I wasn't sure he could keep that promise. But it was okay. I couldn't ask him not to be who he was. And I wouldn't want to.

He let go of me and rubbed his face for a moment. I just waited.

After a moment, in a calmer voice, he said, "Why do you

think he did it?"

"Ray," I said, "I don't want—"

He interrupted, "It makes me crazy that someone would try to hurt you. But don't worry, I'll wait till I'm sure I have the right one," he added, affecting a casual tone.

"Ray," I said again, warningly.

"Tell me," he said.

I wanted to tell him. I realized I wanted to tell him because he had those demons inside him, and he'd recognize them in someone else. It all came with the package. And that was the package I'd ordered myself when I called him on the phone.

"Okay, so I don't know what the sloth and the chutes could have to do with Victor's murder, but, like, how many criminals could be running around here? And if it was one person—obviously Caleb can do the stuff in our building. And see, I saw that he still has the key to Elephants, so he could have trained the elephants in secret and then . . . And he was training the sloth to follow a bean—so they'd be easier to crate, see? So one person would be able to catch them up."

It had all come out in a rush. But Ray barely had time to nod in understanding while I took a breath and then kept going.

"He has a motive for the murder: jealousy of Victor. But the rest of it doesn't make sense. Really, why would anyone take the sloth? No one's asked for ransom or anything. It's crazy."

"And the chutes falling down doesn't seem like a foolproof way to kill someone," he said. "Someone's trying to frighten you."

"Yeah, well, that's working out real well for whoever it is," I said, probably failing at making it sound like a joke.

"You know Caleb was a keeper at the hospital before he was at Elephants," Ray said.

"No. What about it?"

"Victor must have been drugged," he reminded me. "He must

have been unconscious, if he wasn't already dead."

Yeah. Not that there weren't lots of sources for drugs other than the animal hospital, but that was an interesting point. One that gave me the feeling of coming in late to a party that I often had around here. Everyone knew so much about everyone else's pasts that I didn't know. I wondered if Caleb still had the key to the hospital as well. Caleb was big and strong enough to carry an unconscious Victor, too—I hadn't thought about that part of it before.

I nodded. "So he could have killed Victor, sure. But the rest of it still doesn't make sense. I mean, we barely know each other. What could he have against me?"

That scary look flashed on Ray's face again for just a second. I momentarily regretted starting this whole conversation. I had definitely not intended to inspire him to go try and tear Caleb apart limb from limb. I hadn't realized he'd have such an impulse to protect me. I didn't think of myself as needing protection.

"I have to get home and walk the pugs," I said, thinking maybe it was time to end this conversation.

"I'll give you a ride," he said quickly.

"No thanks. I feel safer walking." I smiled. Ray had a red sports car with engines that sounded like a jet plane to me. He knew I thought riding in his car was nerve-racking. I was a city girl who felt safer on the sidewalk or in a subway station.

"I'll walk with you," he insisted.

"Ray, you don't walk anywhere," I said, rolling my eyes. "Look, you can't start following me around in case someone tries to kill me again."

He gave me a sidelong look that seemed to say, "Oh yeah?" But then he put his arm around my shoulders and kissed the top of my head. "I wouldn't think of it. I'm sure you can take care of yourself."

He only said that because he knew it was what I wanted to hear. "Liar," I said, fondly.

"You're a hard person to take care of."

"I don't need to be taken care of." I liked it that he cared about me. But I thought I was a tough little zookeeping woman. I didn't think I needed him threatening to disembowel anyone who might have tried to, say, dump a hundred pounds of metal chutework on my head.

He made a show of shaking his head sadly, as if I had deprived him of a special treat.

"Okay, how about if I let you drive me home after all?" I said.

He grinned. "It would be an honor," he said, and we got up and headed for the parking lot.

Ray dropped me off, and I took the pugs out right away since I was late. When I first started my job, sometimes I changed my clothes at work before I left the building if I'd gotten really dirty. That didn't last long, given the bother of carrying clothes back and forth from home. Still, for a while I wouldn't leave the house, even just to take the pugs for a quick pee in the rain, without changing into something clean. But by now I didn't care. If I didn't feel like changing and I wasn't literally covered in dung, I'd walk the dogs and even go to the supermarket in my work clothes. If people didn't like the way I smelled, no one had ever said anything.

I let the pugs drag me wherever they wanted while I thought about what Ray had told me. Now I understood how he'd seemed to know so much about the inside of Caleb's head when they didn't even appear to be friends. If they'd been in some kind of AA or group therapy thing, he could have heard all sorts of stuff. I doubted that Caleb had heard anything from Ray in return. He'd sit through something like that if he had to, but if he was going to conquer any of his inner demons he'd go off and do it by himself with no one watching.

But did any of it mean that I should be watching my back whenever Caleb was in the building? Fine, so Caleb had done dangerous things in the past, although the risk in doing drugs—and seeing Allison—was entirely to himself. Okay, he could have been nursing a jealous desire for revenge. Sure, he had once worked at the hospital. He could still have the keys, like his key for the Elephant House, and could have gotten drugs there to use on Victor.

But it could all be coincidence. Wasn't this the sort of thing they called circumstantial evidence? Which meant it didn't prove anything, right?

I'd been walking along with my head down, trying to keep the pugs from eating junk off the sidewalk. I looked up, and we were in front of Allison's house, across from the back entrance of the zoo. This was getting to be a habit. The pugs sniffed the front gate of her house vigorously, and I wondered who had been marking there. I still didn't know if Allison had any pets, I remembered. I was peering at the windows to see if there were any cats on the windowsills when someone called my name, and I looked around with a guilty start.

"Hannah," said Allison, walking up behind me. "It's a beautiful day to walk the pugs. Are we neighbors?"

I looked at the big houses on either side of hers. Not likely, I snorted to myself. Didn't she know what I got paid? But I just said, "Sort of. I live in a building in the opposite direction from the entrance."

"Would you like to come in and take a look around?"

I glanced at her. Had I been staring into her windows too obviously? But she just looked friendly, not like she was making some kind of oblique comment about my spying.

"Um . . ." I hesitated. "I don't know about the pugs . . ." Not that they weren't perfectly housebroken and all that. But I suspected she had much nicer things in her house than I did. I wasn't sure that any of the three of us were civilized enough. And oh, no, I hadn't changed my clothes. I thought I hadn't gotten that dirty today, but my standards were awfully low.

"Silly. You think it would be a problem to bring animals in my house? Come on in."

What could I do? I followed her up the steps, the pugs preceding me without any mixed feelings on their part at all. They are always pleased to be invited into someone's house. And their feet are the size of quarters, so they don't worry much about tracking mud in.

I stepped cautiously into the hallway. Her house was like your grandmother would have had if your grandmother was a lot richer than any of mine were. It was full of Oriental rugs and real furniture. She had not gotten down on the floor and put this furniture together with the little tool from an IKEA box. It had definitely come fully assembled.

I remembered the nasty thoughts I'd had about her garden last time I walked by. I supposed she didn't have to worry about buying furniture made of sustainable wood if it was all cut down a hundred years ago. It was nice and cool in here, too. Did she have to air-condition this whole big place? Or did these dark old row houses with thick brick walls stay naturally cool?

Gus put his head down and sniffed at a rug, snapping me out of my thoughts. "Do you have any pets?" I asked anxiously. Was there some scent already there that he needed to cover up? God, if he peed on her carpet I was going to die of embarrassment. Or if I didn't die of embarrassment I'd need to commit suicide. Or quit my job and move to Montana or someplace where they couldn't find me, and die of boredom. Oh, no, why had I agreed to come in? Damn my curiosity.

"In my house? No, I travel too much. But you see, I can just cross the street and visit all my animals. I know it doesn't seem fair—you all do all the work to take care of them for me, and I just get to enjoy them. But really, I do my share, too—it's just more indirect."

"Oh, sure." She was being ostentatiously modest, of course. If she wasn't out there raising money, probably none of the rest of us would have jobs.

"Isabel," she called to a figure in the next room, "would you mind making some tea for us?"

The woman nodded and disappeared. "Isabel is my housekeeper," Allison explained. "She's terribly shy, so I won't introduce you. Or the pugs—actually, I think she's actually rather afraid of animals. Isn't that funny? I didn't think to ask when I hired her. I'm not sure she's ever been inside the zoo."

That was hard to imagine. I was so completely surrounded by animal people that I was only occasionally reminded that not everyone was like us. Like sometimes when someone crossed the street to avoid my two tiny dogs. It happens more often than you would think.

Allison led us into a room off the hallway to the right. It appeared to be an actual drawing room like houses only had in old books. I was afraid to sit on any of the furniture. Why had I been in such a rush to come out that I hadn't changed my pants? Who knew what I'd sat in at work? Could I avoid sitting down for the whole visit?

I had an inspiration to go and look more closely at the pictures she had on the walls, which I had to do standing up. They were mostly pictures of herself and various famous people, either at the zoo or at places she had visited. Some were very recognizable, like Jane Goodall. Any animal person would know her immediately. Others were a little more obscure.

"Is that Desmond Morris?" I asked.

"Yes," she said, arranging a tray of tea and cookies that had magically appeared.

"Capybaras are his favorite rodent, you know." Okay, I know some odd things about capybaras. So sue me.

"Really," she said, as if that was quite fascinating.

"Do you know the painter Dante Gabriel Rosetti? He had a pet wombat." Honestly, it wasn't really that much of a non sequitur—it was another story about a famous person and my favorite animals, right?

"The pre-Raphaelite? Really. How interesting."

"He wrote poems about them," I began. There was one where he was waiting for a wombat to arrive, I remembered. It seemed so perfectly relevant. But I decided it would be better not to say anything about it. She was good at what she did, and feigning polite interest was part of her job.

"His wombat slept on the living room table," I said instead. "That would be a lot less work for the shops guys than the exhibit renovation we're doing."

She laughed. I moved along the wall of photographs. There was a picture of a chubby white-haired guy standing with Allison and one of the elephants. He was vaguely familiar, but it didn't quite make sense.

"Is this Newt Gingrich?" I said, trying to keep the disbelief out of my voice. I didn't know what her political leanings were, and I didn't want to insult her.

"Oh, yes," she said, coming over to look. "Whatever else you might say about him, he's a huge animal lover. I was hoping he might do us some good, budget-wise." She shook her head. "Too many troubles of his own, I'm afraid. But it was fun to show him around, anyway. He was the kind of person who could really appreciate it."

I wondered what kinds of animals he'd known some odd facts about. I always thought I couldn't really like someone who didn't like animals. But I guess I could dislike someone who did. It wasn't enough all by itself.

I turned and noticed that Gus was sniffing at the leg of an elegant little table that didn't seem to have any function aside from looking pretty. I hissed and yanked at his leash.

"Don't worry about the furniture." Allison waved her hand dismissively. "Most of it's not as fancy as it looks. I refinished it myself, back when I had more time . . . If you look at the back legs of that one, you'll see they don't match."

Hmm, I thought. See? Beth—or her editor—was wrong to think that Allison was living beyond her salary. She's just really good at appearances. And it's not like we didn't already know that.

"Come sit down and have some tea and cookies," Allison said, and the pugs started to hop up and down at the sound of the C word. She laughed. "We don't have any dog biscuits, I'm afraid."

"That doesn't matter. People food is better." I couldn't avoid it any longer, it looked like, so I sat on the chair that looked like it had the most cleanable upholstery.

"I'm a little cross at that reporter friend of ours," she said as she poured tea. "Did you see the article about the elephants?"

"Yeah." It had been a bit inflammatory, with quotes from Stephanie using phrases like "ripped from her family group" and comparisons to sending your children to live with strangers.

"It's getting so I can't believe anything I read in the paper anymore. If the coverage is so biased when it's something I know about, who knows what they're saying about things I have to trust them to explain to me?"

I nodded. I nervously watched the pugs as they eyed the table. I would never put food on such a low table at my house. One good thing about little dogs is that at least they can't steal food off the counter. There's no point in negating that advantage by putting food on the coffee table.

"The feature article about me was very nice, I have to admit. She kept her word about that. But I should have known that wasn't the only thing she was working on. They're all the same," she said regretfully. "Go ahead, have some tea."

I was much too nervous to eat or drink, but it would be rude to refuse. I took a tiny sip. "I'm afraid it's part of the problem with our location," she continued. "The reporters are part of this culture of digging up dirt, and they apply the same approach to everything else. Probably the reporter writing about the zoo is always trying to prove she's good enough to get promoted to a government beat."

"I'd rather have my job digging real dirt instead of the metaphorical kind," I said.

I hadn't really meant this as a joke, but she responded with a peal of laughter. "That's wonderful. Yes, you do an honest day's work, Hannah. Don't let any of those pencil-pushers make you feel any different. I know how people can be."

She picked up a cookie, and the pugs shifted their attention to her. She was usually the one focusing the laser beam on someone else, but they could give her a run for her money.

"Oh, may I give them some?" she said, as if it would be the rarest of treats to do so.

I looked at the cookie. No chocolate was all that mattered. They ate any other damned thing they wanted. "Sure." Like I was going to tell her not to feed my dogs in her own house.

"Pugs," she said, and they ran over to her. They knew that word—they turned their head when someone walked past on the street and said it, or when someone said "cute" or even "ooooh" in a high squeaky voice. It was all about them as far as they were concerned, and they didn't feel a bit guilty about it either.

"What are their names?" she said.

"The boy is Gus, and the girl is Rose."

"Oh, so you are both flowers, Rose and Ms. Lilly."

"But it's two Ls," I said reflexively, immediately wanting to kick myself.

"Oh, I forgot. Of course, that's totally different," she said, and I felt like an idiot, but then she smiled, like we were both in on a joke. She would never make someone feel bad by accident, I was sure. Only on purpose.

The pugs sat very hard, and then started throwing behaviors at her, trying to shake hands and wave bye-bye and stand on their back legs. I anxiously hoped she'd give them something before they decided to demonstrate their agility skills by jumping up on the table.

She laughed again, and broke the cookie in half and gave it to them. I was relieved that she seemed to have all her fingers left, but she just laughed and laughed, and when they had gulped the last crumbs they sat hard in front of her again.

I couldn't help relaxing a little. They really were being funny. And if she liked my pugs, how scary could she be? She could afford a new carpet if they ruined one, right?

"They'll keep this up all night," I warned. "You might want to put the cookies back in the kitchen eventually."

She wasn't feeding them fast enough, so Gus had moved on to using the heavy ammunition—the roo roo. He sat, popping up with just his front feet, rooing with all his might. This was Pug for "*Feed NOW.*"

She laughed and gave them each another cookie and said, "I see what you mean." She called her maid and met her at the door with the plate, not making her come into the room with the pugs.

They instantly settled down now that the food was gone. By the time Allison sat down again they were lying at my feet, and I had to push Gus with my toe to get him in a non-snoring position. They'd embarrassed me enough for one night.

"You know that not all the elephant keepers agree with Stephanie," she said, resuming our previous conversation, or her previous monologue. " 'Sources in the Elephant House' just means one person, in this case."

"It's a good story, is the problem," I offered. " 'Elephant moves and everyone's okay with it;' doesn't make an interesting headline."

"You are so right," she said, like it was the wisdom of the ages. "Good news is no news. I suppose a reporter can't help it that it's her job to look for trouble." She sighed.

"She says she loves animals."

"So many troublesome people do." Yeah, you could say that again. "People don't decide to work at zoos because they're good with other people. You understand, Hannah," she said, suddenly turning that laser beam on me again, "in my position, I can't help but make decisions that anger people. You can't please everyone. And I'm sure you know," she said, her tone was confiding now, "many people don't like strong women. Even other women. Clearly I would never have gotten to where I am now without being assertive, but it has its downside. Some people are going to dislike me no matter what I do."

I nodded. What she said made sense. Yeah, there was this thing about how everything she said made sense when you were in the same room with her. Probably being in her intimidating house intensified the effect. But none of these rational thoughts made any impression on my gut feeling that what she said was totally reasonable.

"The other keepers agree that Lucy might be better off in another situation. They're not so attached to one individual that they can't see reason. Not that you can avoid getting attached, naturally," she said. "But you can't put your own needs ahead of the animal's."

I wondered if that was what Stephanie was doing. I wondered

if I was unreasonably attached to my sloths, and if I would be less upset about the missing one if I weren't. I wondered if she and Matthew had talked about elephants when I saw him going into her house the other night, or if that was about something else.

"Matthew, for instance," she said. I jumped a little—it was as if she'd read my mind, although of course it was just a coincidence—we were both thinking of elephant keepers. "He's the senior keeper there, you know. I know not everyone finds him, well, a sympathetic character. But he has a lot of insight into those animals."

"Caleb seemed okay with it, too," I said distractedly, wanting to change the subject from Matthew, but then realizing I'd brought up yet another problematic man. God, who could you talk about that she hadn't either slept with or made angry or both?

"You see, then, Stephanie's is a minority opinion."

I was relieved that I had brought up Caleb without getting in any kind of trouble, but I needed to get out of here before I put my poop-encrusted foot in my mouth again. This was just too damn complicated.

I looked at my watch. "Um," I said.

"It's late. I know you get up early. And those pugs look like they need to go to bed." She smiled at the sluglike forms snoring lightly on her expensive rug.

She stood up, and so did I. I thanked her, and she walked me to the door. It closed behind me, and I felt like I was exhaling for the first time in an hour. I was sure I'd look back on that as an interesting experience. But now I needed a good night's sleep to recover from it. We walked home.

Chapter 11

The two sloths were in their usual places, on the shelf and in the tree branch. I wished I could enjoy the fact that at least I still had two, but they just reminded me of the one that had disappeared.

I had to get yesterday's sloth pan out of the chute in back of the exhibit. Like everything else in the damn building, it was hard for me to reach. I stood on the top of a skinny protruding rock and stretched my arm as far as it would go and groped around, hoping there were only ants in the pan and not cockroaches. If I felt a cockroach on my hand I was going to fall down and break my—

And then I felt wiry fur instead of the metal pan I was expecting. My heart almost stopped. It felt like a sloth. But it couldn't be—I had just seen the two of them.

I got down and walked back to where I'd seen them. They can move pretty fast when they want to. They do seem a lot like alien beings, with their strange calm faces and their slow movements, as if they evolved with a different level of gravity. But I was pretty sure they didn't have any cloak of invisibility powers that I didn't know about. They couldn't have gotten into the chute without my seeing them in between when I counted them and then walked directly over to get the pan.

But I checked anyway. They were still there.

I went back and got up on the rock and stretched myself dangerously out over the edge and tried to peer into the chute. I could just see something sloth-colored. My heart started racing. Okay, calm down. It could be something else. One of those burlap bags that are always around. Someone put some meal-worms in a bag for the primates to have for enrichment. It just looks like a sloth to me because I want so badly to see a sloth. My sloth-detection receptors are set too sensitively.

I climbed down and ran out of the exhibit. I got the ladder and climbed up to the chute. Oh my God. It really was a sloth.

I started to cry, with happiness and relief. I unlocked the door and climbed halfway into the chute, then reached out and prodded the sloth gently. "Oh sweetie, come and see me," I said, shakily.

She uncurled slowly and looked at me calmly. Their faces always looked the same, but I was so happy that even the bits of discarded ant-covered food on the floor of the chute looked radiant with joy. So to me, she looked happy to be back.

I lay there for a while, idiotically, flat on my stomach with my legs sticking out the entrance to the chute, dangling over the ladder. I remembered that this was the wrong ladder to use if I actually wanted to climb all the way into the chute like this. It was not really tall enough for me to be able to get back down safely. I remembered that the precisely parallel chute for the lemur exhibit had recently come crashing down with near-fatal effects. But I didn't care about any of that at the moment. I had my sloth. My sloth that might be pregnant with a sloth baby. I wept and swore that I was going to sleep right here in this exhibit to guard her till the baby was born. So what if the gestation period was what, four or five months? Okay, so I was a little bit excited.

Finally it occurred to me that I should stop bawling and let everyone else know. I squirmed around to get my radio, called Chris, and told him that the sloth was back. I probably shouldn't have announced this over the radio, but I was too worked up to think straight.

There was a long pause that could have been the radio not working as usual, or it could have been astonishment. Then he asked for my location and said he'd be right up.

I dragged myself farther into the chute and rested my chin on the floor so my cheek was leaning against the sloth's fur. I didn't care about the ants and the marmoset poop.

"That does look like a sloth." I looked down and saw Chris looking up at us. I nodded, sniffing happily. "Is she okay?" he said.

"I think so."

"Can I take a look?"

I didn't really want to share, but for him I'd make an exception. I started to wriggle back out of the chute. I waved my legs around looking for the top of the ladder. Uh-oh. This was a problem.

I wriggled around and looked at Chris. He looked suspiciously like he was trying not to smile.

"Um," I said.

I hesitated. I hated to ask for help, and it was going to be awkwardly intimate if he climbed up here and helped me. Aside from the fact that now he was definitely trying not to laugh.

Okay, this was no big deal, I thought. He just needed to get the other ladder for me.

"I got the wrong ladder," I said, trying to sound nonchalant. "Could you go get the other one?"

"I can help you down. It would be quicker." His tone was bland, but he had that mischievous look in his eyes. He knew exactly what I was trying to avoid.

Right. It would be quicker. What could I say? I closed my eyes and braced myself while he climbed up. He didn't even have to stand at the top of the ladder to be perfectly comfortable practically lifting me out of the chute. Then he put his hands on my hips and guided me onto a step and steadied me by leaning against me a little. I told myself that the faint feeling was just because I'd been lying awkwardly on my stomach for so long.

"Okay?" he said.

"Fine," I said, a little breathlessly.

He climbed down and let me get off the ladder, then climbed back up again to look at the sloth. I sat down on the floor and leaned against the wall, staring up at him. He was still wearing those shorts that made his butt look so cute. Sure, I'd probably saved his life because I wouldn't have noticed the chute starting to fall if I hadn't been staring. But that didn't mean it was okay. I should stop. Just in case that was what the dizzy feeling came from after all. I looked down the hallway instead.

He locked the chute door and climbed back down. "She looks fine," he said, shrugging. "Any ideas?"

"No. She was just there. The doors were all locked. Nothing looked different."

He shook his head.

"There was a guard on the building all night, wasn't there?" I said, bewildered.

"There was supposed to be. I'll check to make sure."

We looked at each other speechlessly for a moment. There was nothing intelligent you could possibly say about the situation.

"This is kind of scary," I finally said.

"Yeah," he said, and I got up off the floor and got back to work.

Margo called my name on the radio. "Your reporter friend is here."

What? What now?

I went to the front door. It had started to rain. Beth was

rummaging through her enormous bag. She was wet and bedraggled, and her curly blond hair was going wild from the humidity. She was humming to herself. I stood beside her, saying nothing. I was proud of my maturity. I had managed not to blurt out "Oh, no, not you again."

Finally she noticed I was there and jumped a little. "Oh, hi," she said. "You startled me. Are you ready?"

"Um, ready for what?" I had a bad feeling about this.

Her face fell. "Didn't the director talk to you? We're supposed to run an article about the opening of the wombat exhibit, and I also wanted to write about what the keeper's job is like. So she said I should follow you around for a day."

I counted to ten slowly, thinking *there's no such thing as a free wombat.* I took a deep breath.

"It must have slipped her mind," I said as levelly as I could manage. I was just there at Allison's house last night. Why didn't she mention it then? She was a busy important person. It must have slipped her mind.

"I won't be any trouble, really. Just do what you normally do. Well, I will have to ask you some questions, and the photographer is coming later—I have to warn you, the photographers can be a little bit complicated—but I won't get in your way. I just want to see a normal day, really, so it shouldn't make any difference at all that I'm here, right?"

I stared at her and watched all my plans for the day slowly bubble down a marmoset-poop-clogged drain. It would have felt good to slap her, but I was just able to grasp the fact that assaulting a representative of the press was a bad idea.

"Yeah," was all I said. What choice did I have?

"Oh, thanks. This is really going to be fun. Wait, I need to find my notebook . . . I have a tape recorder so I can sit down and talk to you later, but first I just want to follow you around and take notes. Don't worry about me, just do whatever you normally do, right? Pretend I'm not here. I won't get in the way."

Right, I thought. Fat chance.

She pulled out a notebook triumphantly. "Ready? Just go ahead, and I'll just sit in the corner and watch and take notes. It'll be like I'm not there, you'll see. If I got in the way, then I wouldn't be observing a normal day, right? So it'll be no trouble at all."

I nodded. I wondered idly how long I'd have to go without saying anything before she'd stop talking and notice. Probably hours. I started to walk down the hall and she followed me. When we got to the stairs to the kitchen I said, "I need to go and let everyone know you're here. Just wait right here, okay? Don't move, don't touch anything, and I'll be right back."

I ran downstairs. I didn't trust Beth by herself for a minute, but I didn't trust my tone of voice if I tried to radio, with everyone at the zoo listening in. It might get back to Allison.

When I got to his office, Chris was on the phone. I stood in the doorway making a big despondent face and bouncing up and down impatiently. I made the face worse and worse until he was afraid he was going to laugh and had to ask the person on the other end to hold on.

"That reporter is here. Allison arranged for her to come and follow me around for an article today and forgot to tell us. I have to go. I don't trust her," I said as fast as I could and ran back upstairs before he could respond.

When I got to the top of the stairs Beth was trying to put her fingers into the lemur holding. Nike was looking at her with the lemur look. The lemur look is always pretty much the same, but I'm sure he was thinking that she was an idiot.

"*No,*" I yelled. She jumped back.

"Is it dangerous? It looks so cute," she said, bewildered.

I took a deep breath.

"We need to get a few things straight," I said. "First of all, I don't care if anything bites you, but you could hurt the animals, and I care about that. Even if you work here, you're not allowed contact with the primates unless you've had a TB test. It's for the animals' protection, not yours. No one is allowed contact with the animals without the explicit permission of my bosses, or I can get fired. Allison telling you to follow me around doesn't count as permission. If you get me fired, I will spend the rest of my life hunting you down to the ends of the earth and I will kill you with my bare hands. Are you with me so far?"

She peeped, "Yes," and looked forlorn.

"Okay," I continued, feeling my blood pressure rising. "I said I didn't care if you got bitten, but I do, because you might sue us or—now I don't know how this would happen—it might appear in the newspaper and look bad for us." I had to stop and take another deep breath. "You can't have contact with the animals because they might carry diseases. Even if you work here, you're not allowed in with some of these animals unless you've had a rabies vaccination. There are also lots of places you can trip and fall and lots of sharp rusty things and lots of dangerous cleaning chemicals. You need to not do anything or touch anything or go anywhere unless I say so. Is that clear?"

She nodded and looked very small. I was pretty sure it was an act. I wasn't going to be able to take my eyes off her all day.

"All right, let's get going," I said, trying not to sound as disgusted as I felt.

"Great. What are you going to do first?" she said cheerfully.

First I'm going to go look in the animal meds fridge and see if we have any tranquilizers I can take. Unfortunately, tranqs are not one of the things we ever give the animals. "I have to finish counting my animals." I had a vague hope this would bore her into leaving, although I knew that was probably futile. "We have to make sure they're all there every day. A lot of them are little, and they hide."

"Oh, that sounds like fun. Like a game. Can I help?"

"Sure." Well, at least here was one thing where it would be hard for her to actively make my job more difficult. Even I didn't think she was so annoying that animals would run away if she were on the other side of the glass.

I unlocked the door to 24 and picked up my food pans. "I'm going to go put out their food. That should make them come out. Then we'll go around to the front and watch for them."

I climbed up into the exhibit, and she started to follow me. "Whoa, you can't come in here," I said, stepping back out and closing the door again. "This will just take a minute. I can take you back out front so you can watch me if you want."

"Oh, come on," she wheedled. "Can't I come in just for a second? I won't touch anything."

"I'm really not supposed to let you. Anyway, I already told you, you're not supposed to go in with the primates unless you've had a TB test."

She looked around. "But look how big that exhibit is. I won't get anywhere near them. And I'll wear one of these masks," she said, grabbing a box of disposable face masks off a shelf.

I sighed. That was in fact what you were supposed to do if you needed to go in with the primates and hadn't had a TB test. I had carefully not mentioned that possibility. I thought I got up pretty early in the morning, but apparently not early enough to stay one step ahead of Beth Jackendoff, Intrepid Girl Reporter.

I gave up. "Okay, but you need to stand right inside the door and don't take another step, understand? And don't open the door and leave without me, either. Because if you accidentally let something out, it's going to be a big problem, understand?"

She nodded and smiled cheerfully.

I set out the food pans around the exhibit, all the time looking back at her suspiciously. I had to get into the far corner of the exhibit to check on the armadillo and pick up its pan, and I couldn't see her from there. I was sure I'd come back and find her climbing all over the place, but she was standing right where I'd left her, leaning against the door.

"So what would happen if I let something out?" she said in an innocent tone.

"*Don't* even think about it," I yelled. "We can talk about that later. But you don't need to see it happen to write about it. It would ruin your article if I got fired, wouldn't it? And remember the part where I kill you with my bare hands and feast on your still warm and steaming intestines?"

I wouldn't get fired if something got out. It was just a fact of life that it happened occasionally. Unless I did it constantly or it was the result of some flagrantly incompetent act, I wouldn't get in any particular trouble. But she didn't have to know that.

"Okay," she said.

I opened the door and gestured for her to climb out.

"Do you know anything about dogs?" she said, out of the blue.

"Um, like what?" I said suspiciously as we walked around to the public area.

"You know my dog Buddy I told you about, right? She's so great. But we can't figure out how to get her to stop chewing on the furniture."

"On the furniture?" I said in a shocked tone. Maybe I was spoiled having pugs, which didn't have big enough mouths to get around parts of furniture, but this seemed like a pretty extreme situation for her to sound so calm about.

"Just the legs of the tables," she said, like it wasn't that big a deal.

We came around to the front of exhibit 24, and I started to

try to count the birds while she talked. She peered into the exhibit and continued, "It's just that we want to get a new dining room table, and we'd rather she didn't chew on that." She sounded like she was kind of sorry about having to inconvenience Buddy with this unreasonable desire.

I sighed. "Does she have any chew toys of her own?"

"Chew toys?" she said uncertainly.

Oh, boy. We had a little talk about chew toys and how she ought to take Buddy to a basic obedience class. I wasn't that good at counting the birds, and multitasking it with a lecture on dog training was a little taxing, but at least I had no brain capacity left over to think about how annoying this all was.

"What's that?" She put her hand up to knock on the glass.

"*Don't* tap on the glass. Ever. It's an agouti." I pulled her hand away and pointed to the sign that explained what an agouti is.

"Do you guys have any coffee in this building?" I supposed I would eventually get used to the sudden changes of topic. "The coffee at the snack bar was so expensive," she whined. "What's the deal with that?"

"All we have here is instant. The coffee at the snack bars is special bird-friendly coffee that's good for the rainforest. It's one of the things the director is doing as part of her rainforest conservation initiative. You must have talked about it for your article about her?"

"Yeah, but not about how expensive it is." She sighed. "It's a great idea to conserve the rainforest. I just didn't realize it would be so, well, inconvenient," she said sadly.

"Tell me about it. Every time we turn around there's something we can't buy. It's really complicated." She'd mentioned all that stuff in her article in a way that made it sound like a great idea. But that was before she had to pull out her wallet. "But you can't expect these things to be easy. There's so much we do that has effects we don't realize. Buying stuff isn't the half of it."

I peered into the exhibit. Yeah, that was part of my frustration with this whole campaign. Making such a big publicity deal about our shopping habits, basically. Sure, some of these products really did have a good effect, both for the ecosystem and the farmers producing them. But were we just teaching people that buying more expensive stuff was all they had to do? When they were still driving three blocks in their SUVs to run into the store with the engine left running to grab their bird-friendly, shade-grown fair-trade organic latte?

So American to think we'd save the world by going shopping, I thought, as I saw the other two agoutis trot by in back of the exhibit. Good. That meant I was done with the count, and now I hoped to get rid of her for a while.

"I have to do some cleaning in there now," I said. "You don't want to get wet. You can watch from out here."

"Couldn't I wear some of those boots?" She pointed at my black rubber boots.

Unfortunately we had many pairs of the boots in many sizes, and surely she was going to come downstairs later and use the ladies' room and see them all sitting there. So there was no use in lying. Why couldn't she stop noticing so many damn things?

"Well, I guess so, if you wear the mask, too. But you still need to try not to get in my way, okay? I don't have time to worry about not getting you wet. I don't even waste time worrying about not getting myself wet, so don't be surprised."

Unfortunately, she seemed thrilled and undaunted by the whole thing. We went downstairs to get her some boots.

I filled a bucket with water and opened a jug of disinfectant. Beth, fascinated by the strangest things, bent close to the bucket.

"Hey, stand back, I have to pour some of this in there. You

don't want to get it in your eyes."

"Really?" She stood back, looking at the bottle quizzically. "But don't you have to use something that's safe around the animals?"

"We have to be careful, sure, but the whole idea of a disinfectant is that it kills living things, you know? If it does its job, it's never going to be something you want to splash in anyone's face."

"Huh." She nodded like she'd never quite thought of that before, and picked up the jug I'd just put down. "Clean Green," she read the name off the label. "And it smells so nice."

"Sure," I scoffed. "That's what they want you to think. But you get it to smell so nice with nice fragrance chemicals. And you can't be fooled by the names on these things. This uses the same ingredients as the stuff you buy at home."

"Hmm," she said, peering at the jug.

"Green, you know," I said. "It's the new black. It's the fashion, so they use it to convince you to buy things. I read somewhere that they found that putting the word 'natural' on the label of anything doubles sales. Even though there's no standard definition, or any agency that enforces it or anything. You can't trust this stuff, you know?"

Beth opened her mouth to say something, but for once I managed to interrupt. Continuing my lecture on corporate greenwashing wasn't going to get my exhibit cleaned. "Okay, let's go," I said, picking up the bucket.

Back in the exhibit, I squeezed her into a corner and started to hose. Sometimes when you turn the hoses on to a certain point, the pipes make a loud roaring noise. Usually I'd adjust the faucet to quiet it. But this time I made sure I left it at exactly the point that caused the loudest racket.

Beth made a few attempts to talk to me over the commotion and finally gave up. She seemed to be standing there humming to herself again, looking around the exhibit with interest. I honestly didn't get her wet on purpose, but you can't expect to stand in there while I'm hosing and not get splashed, really. She wanted to see what my day was like, well, my day was all about getting wet and dirty. There you are.

I hosed for as long as I could. The plants all got watered very thoroughly and carefully and the exhibit was cleaned to within an inch of its life. It was due for a good cleaning, really. I probably would have done it anyway. She said to just go ahead with what I normally did, right?

Finally I had to stop, or I'd never get my other work done.

"Okay, let's go so I can clean my stuff in the back room," I said. She followed me obediently.

Chapter 12

"What's this here?" Beth said as I climbed out of a marmoset exhibit that I'd mercifully managed to convince her wouldn't hold two people.

"That's a nest box I was repairing," I said, annoyed at the reminder. "I haven't finished it because we've run out of wood. That's another result of the rainforest thing. The director wants the zoo to only buy sustainably harvested wood, but first we have to find a regular supplier that we can afford. So that'll have to wait till we get more wood in, who knows when," I said in exasperation, leaving out the part where I wondered how much of the delay had to do with sustainability standards and how much it had to do with someone who had their feet up on the desk, drinking bird-friendly coffee, not dealing with the paperwork.

She nodded. "She told me about that. I mentioned it in the article. That you were only buying that kind of wood, I mean. Not that you were having trouble getting it. But it's great she's so committed, you know?" She looked thoughtful. "I wish she'd told me more about that. It would have been an interesting angle. Maybe I could work it into this article . . . But wait—I really need to write about the wombat, you know? Do you think we could sit down for a minute and talk about it? And could you show me the exhibit?"

Not exactly just going ahead with what I normally do, I thought helplessly.

"Fine," I said. There was no such thing as a free wombat. "Let's sit down over here."

There was a desk, although I used it to pile stuff on rather than in any deskly way, and there was a chair in front of it. I gave her the chair to sit on and sat on one of my stepstools. She started to write something in her notebook.

"Oh, wait," she said. "My pen's out of ink."

She rummaged through the huge bag again. The desk was already covered with nest boxes and cleaning supplies. She started to take things out of her bag one by one and find places to squeeze them in among the junk. I could have given her a pen, but why interrupt the entertainment? She took out a camera and a tape recorder and perched them precariously on top of a couple of nest boxes.

What if I just gave a little nudge—the pile would all fall down, and her equipment would break, and she couldn't do this story right now, right? I sighed. That was mean, and anyway, there was no point. She would just go and get new things and come back. She was like a pit bull. A cheerful, friendly, talkative pit bull, grinning pleasantly with its jaws locked on to my sleeve.

Now she was taking plastic containers out of her bag. She saw me watching her. "That's my lunch. It's leftover beef stew. Do you guys have a microwave? I know it doesn't look very nice right now, but it'll be great heated up. I have to carry stuff around. I never know when I'll get a chance to buy something to eat. I have some potato salad, too. I know it's a weird combination but it's really terrific potato salad. You should let me give you the recipe. Oh, here are my pens," she said enthusiastically, starting to gather all the rest of the stuff back into the bag.

I should be the one writing an article, I thought. I felt like a field researcher observing some strange new species.

"Here we go," she said triumphantly. "Now I hadn't thought

of this question before, but this rainforest project keeps coming up. Are wombats from the rainforest?"

"Well . . . no. They're from Australia, which does have rainforests. But that's not where they live, and anyway the project is concentrating on Brazil. The director thinks we can do more good by concentrating on a single area, like doing the adopt-an-acre program and getting really specific to a certain location."

"Oh," she said. "So why a wombat?"

"Well . . . She doesn't mean that everything in the zoo is going to be from the Brazilian rainforest. We wouldn't be able to have lions and stuff, you know? The Small Mammal House has things from all different habitats, and that isn't going to change."

"Okay, but still, why a wombat specifically? What's interesting about it? Why would my readers want to come and see it?"

I needed to think of some relatively educational answer to this question. This was my job. I knew that "because it's cute and one of my favorite animals" was not acceptable. "Because it is really good at sleeping all day" wasn't going to cut it either. I was starting to feel a little nervous about the attention this acquisition was getting.

"We don't have a lot of marsupials at the zoo," I said. "Or a lot of stuff from Australia. Which is kind of the same thing, since there are hardly any marsupials outside Australia. So, um, that's a whole big interesting category of mammals that we should have some representative of."

I wished we were talking about the tenrecs and convergent evolution. Or I could give a really good spiel on the xenarthrans, and how the sloth and anteater and armadillo were related to each other even though they didn't look at all similar, and yet other animals that looked similar weren't closely related. I didn't have a darned thing to say about wombats except that they were cute.

"Marsupials . . . that's like kangaroos, right?" she said. "The ones with pouches?"

"Yeah," I said, relieved that at least she knew that.

"So wombats have pouches. But they don't stand up straight like kangaroos. Do the pouches look the same? Why don't the babies fall out?" she said, furrowing her eyebrows.

"The pouch on a wombat faces backward, so it's different," I said, then desperately hoped she didn't follow up on this. I had the vague idea this was unusual in marsupials, but now I couldn't remember the details. Or was it the other way around, the kangaroo sort of pouch was unusual? Koalas were the most closely related marsupials, but if their pouches were backward too, wouldn't the babies fall out of the trees? I began to sweat. I really needed to study for this wombat better. I was spending too much time with the poop and not enough time hitting the books.

"Can I see the exhibit?" she said, standing up.

I exhaled. Maybe the zoology quiz part of the interview was over. I was going to get some research done soon, I resolved.

She walked beside me, still asking questions, bumping into things as she tried to write down the answers at the same time. I rushed her through the construction zone that the wombat exhibit still was. Then I dragged her down to the kitchen so I could start making my food. I was so behind schedule, there was no point in even thinking in terms of a schedule anymore.

When we came down the stairs, Margo, Jeff, and Caleb were standing around the table, finishing up making their diets. Margo and Jeff exchanged a look.

"Lunchtime, don't you think?" said Margo.

I dug in the drawer for my diet book, and when I looked up, they had vanished. Only Caleb was left behind, obliviously putting away some strawberries. They smelled amazing, or else I was really starving.

"We're getting strawberries now?" I said, trying not to

salivate. We really weren't supposed to eat the animals' food.

"No," he said, looking a little embarrassed. "I brought them from home."

"Hey, you're turning into a real small mammals keeper already, Caleb." We didn't spoil our animals, exactly. We just paid a lot of attention to what we each imagined to be their special needs. Even sometimes when it meant spending money out of our own not-very-full wallets.

Beth suddenly pulled her notebook out of her bag again and flipped through it purposefully. She stopped and peered at a page. "Caleb McMahon, right? You used to work at the Elephant House?"

"Yes."

His monosyllabicity didn't discourage her. "How does it feel to know that an animal you worked with killed a person? I know you don't work there anymore, but I didn't get a chance to talk to any of the keepers there, and I wonder. I mean, elephants, they're like the animal that kills the most keepers, right? And you really know them as individuals. It must be like knowing a murderer."

It was funny how easily you could tell the difference: Caleb being perfectly still because he was slow and lugubrious versus Caleb being perfectly still because he was suddenly extremely tense.

"We don't know which elephant did it, as far as I know," he said stiffly.

"Yeah, but that's kind of more interesting—like not knowing which of your friends—"

"Excuse me," Caleb interrupted. He stormed out the back door without another word.

I stared after him. Interesting.

"Could I heat up my lunch in the microwave?" Beth said, apparently having rapidly put the conversation behind her. I supposed that people reacted to her that way so often, she hardly saw the significance of how badly Caleb did not want to talk about that particular subject.

I waved her into the keeper lounge, relieved to get rid of her, but it didn't last long. Instead of sitting down in there to eat, she came back into the kitchen. She walked around carrying her beef stew and a fork and started to look at everything in the kitchen. The kitchen has a big metal food prep table in the middle. Around the outside are various refrigerators, and a wall lined with containers filled with different kinds of animal chow and ingredients. She walked along that side of the room, eating her lunch and looking at the containers. Fortunately, we had recently put new labels on all of them, so she was reading the labels. Otherwise I knew she'd be asking me what each and every thing was. I was thankful for small favors.

"Can I open these?" she said through a mouthful of stew.

"Sure, as long as you close them tight so the bugs don't get into them."

She opened a container of monkey chow biscuits and picked one out. She sniffed at it inquisitively and peered into the container. Then she put her lunch down and went back into the keeper room where she'd left her bag. She came back with her notebook and a pen and wrote some notes. This was how she spent the next ten minutes, opening containers, sniffing things, and taking notes. I just kept chopping up stuff and measuring it, making my food pans, grateful for the break from her attention.

But soon the break was over. She came and looked over my shoulder. "Tell me what you're doing."

"This is food for the lemurs. That notebook has all the diets in it. Mostly I have them memorized, but you can look at them. It's just like a recipe. It gives the ingredients and amounts, and sometimes what size pieces to cut the stuff into, what kind of pan, and that kind of thing. The sheet in front tells you who gets fed in the morning and who gets fed in the afternoon. Some get fed only one of those times, but the primates get fed twice a day."

"Recipes," she said thoughtfully, looking through the book. She took it and carried it around for a while, comparing it to the ingredients in the bins.

"So what happens if an animal gets out?" she said, as if suddenly bored with the food.

I was so unhappy that she had remembered this question. I really wouldn't put it past her to try to let something out of an exhibit so she could see what happened and write about it. It was true that it was one of the more exciting things that could happen in the course of a day, so it would make a good story. And I had to admit, there was that adrenaline rush when it happened, even though it was obviously a really bad thing. So I tried very hard to make it sound extremely dull and boring.

"We have a procedure to radio everyone and get the right people in place and cooperate to catch the animal and return it to its enclosure. When we recapture the animal and get it back in the exhibit, we have to radio to say it's done. Everyone needs to know, even if they're not involved, because you're not supposed to use the radio for anything else while an animal is loose. The curator has to file a report every time it happens. That's so they can keep track, because if it happens too often, someone's not doing their job right." Those were all the boring parts of the Code Orange protocol that I could remember. I left out everything that might help her construct an exciting mental image of people running around with nets and shouting at each other.

She finished her stew and went back into the keeper room. She returned with her potato salad.

"Do any of the animals you work with bite? Yuck," she said,

looking into the bin full of wriggling mealworms.

I realized I had never appreciated before how peaceful it was to make food all by ourselves, just the keepers, even if we were goofing around and playing the radio loud and dropping metal pans on the concrete floor.

"All the animals bite, except the ones with no teeth," I said. "It's my job to try not to get bit, and I do that by never forgetting they all can bite. You should think the same way about your dog, really."

"Buddy?" She looked startled, then recovered. "Oh, Buddy would never bite anyone," she said confidently, as I had known she would. "Can I taste this?"

She held up a primate biscuit. It was the nicest-smelling kind of biscuit we had, sort of a pleasant orange artificial flavor smell. I waved her to go ahead. She took a tiny bite and chewed it thoughtfully, then wrote some notes. Then she looked over at the table.

"Is that organic produce?" she asked.

"No," I said, trying to squelch my automatic reaction of panic at the thought. The one thing Allison's campaign hadn't touched was food supplies for the animals.

"Why not? Wouldn't that be better?"

"Well, on the one hand, it's good that lots of people know about the benefits of organic farming nowadays," I said as I opened a can of marmoset diet with our old hand-cranked opener. "But it can have unintended consequences, you know? It's not clear that it's better to eat an organic strawberry if it had to be flown here from halfway across the planet."

"Huh." She scribbled some more, then turned back to the food bins and lifted another lid—and suddenly shrieked and jumped backward.

I whipped around and grabbed the lid before it crashed to the floor. "Sorry. Was that one of those big cockroaches? I should have warned you."

"It's okay," she said, gathering her pen and notebook from the floor. We were so used to the big palmetto bugs that lived around the building, we automatically knew where to be careful of them. It was hard to remember to mention it to newcomers—really.

Anyway, it was clear by now that there would have been no point in hoping to scare her off. She just flipped back to the right page of her notebook and said, "So what else do you do for this rainforest thingy? You know, like the coffee and the wood you said you had trouble buying."

I tried not to sigh aloud. "You've read about most of it, really . . . Okay, maybe they haven't mentioned that our uniform shirts are different, because the company was owned by some other company that owned some other company that was cutting down rainforest. That's not a big deal, though. It hasn't really caused any problems."

I cut up some carrots very carefully, as if it took so much concentration that I couldn't talk at the same time. I couldn't decide. If I talked fast, would she eventually run out of questions and leave? Seemed unlikely. Seemed more likely she'd just stay forever, so that the best strategy to do less talking was to talk slowly and pause a lot.

"They're trying to do something about the hamburgers in the snack bar, but it's hard." I picked up a sweet potato and examined it as closely as the chef of a five-star French restaurant would. I slowly decided it was okay and started to carefully cut it up into extremely uniform little squares.

"They tried free-range beef bought in the U.S., but it was so expensive, everyone complained." I counted out the pieces of sweet potato precisely and put them in the pans. Never mind that I usually just eyeballed it and tossed in a small handful.

"Beef is such a disaster no matter how you do it, I guess," I continued. “You know, deforestation and water use and it has a terrible carbon footprint . . .” I stopped before I got myself into a monologue about cow farts. “But they tried not serving hamburgers at all, and it almost caused a riot.”

I glanced over and saw that Beth was looking at the piles of different size pans and dishes. She seemed so engrossed in this sight that I decided to see what would happen if I just cut up some apples without talking.

“What else?” she said after about ten seconds of silence.

Right. That was what would happen.

“You know, really,” I said, “I don’t know anything else that wouldn’t be in the press releases you’ve seen. I mean, I hate to sound cynical, but they’re not going to do this stuff and not get publicity for it, right?”

“Well, it can’t help educate people if it doesn’t get publicity. And isn’t that part of why you do it?”

“Yeah, I guess,” I said. “Part of it.”

“You know,” she said, “we just ran a story about the hybrid car market. One thing it said was that more people bought the Toyota Prius than the Honda hybrid. Because the Honda just looks like the nonhybrid version of the same model. But if you drive a Prius, everyone knows it.”

“Yeah, exactly,” I said, surprised. “See, that’s the thing. How much of it’s just that you want to look good?”

“Still, if looking good means they’re not polluting, isn’t that still less pollution?”

“Yeah . . .” I said, uncertainly.

She moved over to the small fridge, which was where we kept the animal meds. She opened it.

“Don’t mess with that stuff, okay?” I said. “Those are the medications. I don’t want them getting mixed up.”

“What kinds of medicine? Are there any sedatives?”

I did a double take. That was just what I’d been wondering

earlier. But she didn't look like she was reading my mind. She was just standing there peering in, bouncing on the balls of her feet, on the verge of humming.

"No, there aren't. Why do you ask?" I said.

"I was wondering if the murderer could have used something that was meant for one of the animals," she said vaguely.

I tried to not yell. "Used it for what?"

She looked at me, surprised. "He was drugged. You didn't know that? He had to be unconscious for the murderer to get him in the elephant yard like that. No one would lie down in there with a pumpkin on their head."

"How do you know that?" I tried not to sound excited. We'd suspected this, sure. But she sounded positive.

"The police," she said like it was no big deal.

"Was . . . was he still alive when it happened?" I wasn't sure I wanted to know the answer, or if I'd be sorry, like a visitor peering into a bag of frozen mice.

"Yeah," she said, closing the fridge and writing a bunch of stuff on her pad.

God. That was awful. I wondered what else she knew that we didn't. But I was stuck on the mental picture in my memory and couldn't think of what to ask.

Thankfully she shut up and spent a few moments writing on her little pad. I finally finished preparing my food and piled up the pans and put them in the refrigerator. Then I went and got my lunch from the people fridge.

"I'm going to eat lunch now," I said, heading into the keeper room.

"I need to use the ladies' room, is that okay?" she said, following me.

"It's right there. You don't need to ask," I said, pointing, and managing not to tell her to take her time, because I didn't trust what kind of tone I would say it in.

Margo and Jeff, by some remarkable coincidence, stood up just as we walked in. "Back to work," Margo said brightly.

I sat down on the couch and closed my eyes. "Thanks a lot, guys," I said glumly to their retreating backs. They hadn't wanted a wombat, I reminded myself. It was only fair that I was the one who had to pay the price.

I enjoyed a moment of peace before I remembered that I was starving. I opened my eyes. Chris was standing in the door of his office, leaning against the door frame. I tried not to stare. I didn't have time to be distracted by the sight of him standing there looking like that.

"How's it going?" he said.

"I feel like I'm being pecked to death by ducks." I tore into my sandwich like a pack of hyenas disemboweling a wildebeest, unsure how much time they had before some bigger predator tried to scare them away from it. I was vaguely embarrassed at being so crude while he was watching me, but I was too hungry to care.

Beth came out from the ladies' room before he could say anything in reply. He vanished back into his office so fast that he almost left his grin behind, like the Cheshire cat.

She sat down on the couch. "The director travels an awful lot promoting this rainforest conservation stuff," she said thoughtfully. "How does the zoo afford it?"

I gave her a quick, suspicious glance. This was off the topic of how I spent my day as a keeper. I didn't know what she had up her sleeve. And this was really a subject I knew nothing about. It had nothing to do with me.

"I don't know," I said, trying to sound uninterested. I didn't want to talk about Allison. All it could do was get me in trouble. "I'm not sure it's the zoo that pays for it. She works with foundations and stuff. You should ask her about that. You should ask me about wombats."

I was immediately sorry I'd said that, remembering that I hadn't had very good answers to her questions about wombats before. "Okay, back to work," I said, jumping up before she could follow my advice. My five minutes of lunch break for today were over, anyway.

She followed me around for another hour while I fed out and filled out my cage checksheets for the day. Again she found this more fascinating that I could have believed was possible. I managed to talk her out of taking some of the checksheets downstairs and making photocopies of them by explaining that all we had to make copies was a really slow old fax machine. She was surprised, as if she still hadn't caught on that I didn't have an office job.

At two o'clock she finally said, "This is great. I think I have enough now."

I was overcome with relief. I could go sit down and do the rest of my paperwork. and it would feel like I'd stopped hitting my head against the wall.

"Now we just have to wait for the photographer," she said. "He's supposed to come at three."

Oh, God. I'd forgotten she mentioned a photographer.

"Beth, you never said anything about the time," I said, no longer able to control my annoyance. "I go home at three. He has to come earlier than that."

Okay, it was true that I went home at three o'clock only in a purely theoretical sense. I stopped getting paid at three, but I couldn't remember the last time I'd walked out of the building promptly at that hour. But that didn't mean I wanted to be here then, or at any time, messing around with some stupid newspaper photographer.

She looked distressed. "I forgot. I can call and see if we can reschedule, but I don't know. You know what these photographers are like. They think they're artists. They don't like to be messed with. Oh, well—" she said, starting to dig in her bag for a phone.

I interrupted. "Never mind, that's fine." It would be just as well that he came after hours and wasn't in everyone else's way, too. "Look, please just go walk around the zoo, or sit down outside, or get yourself a soda, and come back at three, okay? I just need some time alone to get some things done. Please?"

"Sure," she said cheerfully. "I'll see you later."

I watched her walk away and thought that if I liked my job any less I would leave right now and call the witness protection program and get a new identity and life. Then I went and lay down on the couch.

"He thinks a picture of you feeding that sloth would be good. Will it take food from your hand?" The male sloth was curled up in one of his favorite spots, on a branch where I could just barely reach him.

"Yes," I said reluctantly. It would have made life easier if I had lied. But how could I lie about sloths?

I told her I'd wait inside the exhibit and she could wave when they were ready. That way at least she wouldn't be able to talk to me the whole time.

I went around back, climbed into the exhibit and sat on a rock and watched them. It looked like it was going to take a while. Beth's huge bag was nothing compared to this camera guy's load of equipment. I supposed it made him feel manly and technological. I'd gotten plenty of pictures inside these exhibits that looked good enough for the newspapers to me with my little pocket digital camera. On the other hand, I sure didn't want him to start nagging me to come inside the exhibits, so I hoped all that technology would let him take good pictures through the glass. And I hoped it would happen before my bedtime tonight.

People weaved their way around the equipment he was spreading out, and Beth was talking to them, trying to keep them away. The photographer had clearly decided that he owned the place, and it didn't matter if anyone else wanted to look at the animals. He seemed to exude a force field of self-importance. Everyone meekly gave him a wide berth.

Finally he said something to Beth and she waved and beamed at me like Miss America. I stood up, and as soon as the sloth saw me, he opened his mouth wide. Maybe they are a little spoiled. I put the piece of orange into his mouth, and he started to chew. I looked into the sloth's strange alien eyes with the tiniest pinprick pupils, the eyes that drew me in to his sloth world. My blood pressure suddenly plummeted, and I forgot all about Beth and the photographer and Allison and even the wombat. The sloth chewed slowly on the orange. It was so good, he had to close his eyes. Sticky orange juice dripped out of his mouth onto his stomach. The tamarins came in a swarm like they always did, trying to steal the dripping juice, but I waved them away. We were as alone as if he'd taken me home to the sloth planet with him.

I had a few moments of peace before I was disturbed from my sloth trance by seeing a frantic movement in the corner of my eye. Beth was waving and saying something. At least she'd remembered not to tap on the glass. But my lip-reading skills were not that good. I had no idea why people always thought I'd be able to understand what they were saying through the glass. I took a last reluctant look at the sloth and climbed down and out of the exhibit, then went out the door to the public area.

"I need more light," the photographer said crossly. "I can't possibly work with this situation. Or else the animal needs to be closer to the ceiling where the lights are. Can you make it move?"

I stared at him in disbelief. "No," I said, not bothering to try to conceal my disgust. "I can't just make the animal move. What do you think this is, a circus?"

"Can't you pick it up?" he insisted

I was trying very hard not to hit him. I was concentrating so hard on that that I forgot to answer the question. After a moment Beth said to him, "Just a minute," and took me aside.

"Look," she confided, "I know, the photographers are so difficult. They think they are artists, and their whole art is manipulating reality and all that. He's used to always being able to tell people where to stand and what to do, he doesn't get it that you can't do that with animals. Honestly, I think he doesn't like animals all that much. He never wants to hear about Buddy."

Oh, I couldn't imagine why that would be.

"But he's really good," she wheedled. "We just have to try to be patient with him. I'll explain to him about the animals. Just wait."

They had a conversation out of my earshot, in which I assumed that she was telling him that zookeepers were very difficult and temperamental when it came to their animals, and he would have to be patient. It was becoming clearer and clearer that this whole ditzy thing was at least partly an act, and that we were all her puppets. I closed my eyes and envisioned the wombat. I wondered what it would like me to feed it for treats. If it was ever awake during working hours, that is.

Beth walked back over to me. "Okay, here's an idea. Can we put one of his lights on top of the exhibit, next to the lights that are already up there? Can he get up there on top?"

Oh man, another of my most favorite jobs. But if it would get rid of him sooner . . . "No. He can't go up there, but I can. If he'll tell me how to work the light, I'll put it up there for him."

I was only a little afraid of heights and of falling through the wire mesh on top of the exhibit. Chris had walked around up there when we were looking for the sloth when it went missing.

If the mesh could hold him, it could certainly hold me, right? Unless there were any weak old spots he hadn't happened to step on. Spots that were old and corroded like half the stuff in this building was. Spots that looked perfectly normal until I put my foot on them and then . . . Oh, dear.

We walked around back to the keeper area. I checked that I had my radio and took a deep breath. I tried not to think about rusty old wire mesh as I climbed the ladder, awkwardly holding the light unit. Every time I bumped it a little on the ladder or the wall, the photographer made little panicky noises and fluttery gestures. He was starting to need a sedative as badly as I did. Which only seemed fair, I thought, trying not to look down from the top of the ladder.

I climbed onto the top of the exhibit and pulled the light up after me. I put it down a little hard. I swear it was an accident. I was sure that all this commotion was going to make the sloth move, and this would all be pointless. I closed my eyes for a moment and thought of wombats, and then started to crawl to the spot above where the sloth was hanging.

I was surprised to find a wooden crate on top of the exhibit, almost in the exact spot I needed to put the light.

"Hey," I called down. "I'm not sure we need this light after all. There's this thing up here that's casting a shadow. I'll move it, and you can go around and see if that helps."

I moved the crate to the edge, near the ladder, so I could get it down more easily if I needed to. Chris was always reminding us we weren't supposed to store stuff on top of exhibits. But how could he have not seen it when he was up here? I wondered why he had left it.

I waited, blissfully alone, while Beth and the reporter went around to the public area to check the lighting. I was so enchanted by the solitude that I'd forgotten all about my fear of falling through the top of the exhibit. I'd also forgotten to toss my keys down to them, so they'd have to come back the long way. I swear, really, I forgot.

"That's fine now," Beth said cheerfully when they returned, as the photographer muttered darkly about endangering his equipment for no reason.

I climbed down the ladder and smiled sweetly as I handed him back his light.

It was 4:30 when they were finally done. I showed them out and then came back through the public area, taking a last look at my exhibits. Chris was in with the lemurs, feeding them pieces of mango. I waved at him as I went by. When I got around to the back he was coming out of the exhibit door.

"You're still here?" I said.

"I thought you might need some help with those newspaper people."

"You didn't have to do that," I said. "Although maybe someone needed to be here to call nine-one-one when I finally lost it and beat them with a shovel."

Probably I shouldn't be making a joke like that with what had been going on around here, I realized too late. But he just said smiled and said, "Yeah, like that."

"I did okay though," I said. "No casualties."

"You got a wombat," he said.

"Yeah."

"Expensive wombat, so far," he mused.

"Kind of," I admitted. "Hey, I found a weird crate on top of 24, did you see it when you were up there the other day? I thought we weren't supposed to store stuff up there."

"What were you doing on top of 24?" he said, sounding surprised.

"The photographer . . . oh never mind, it's a long story."

"I'd have gone up there for you. You should have radioed."

I was torn between thinking that was nice of him and hating that he knew I was afraid of doing it. It hurt my zookeeper macho pride.

"It was okay," I lied. "But thanks."

"There wasn't anything up there before. Can I see it?"

"Yeah, I left it on the edge by the ladder." We walked down the back hallway, and I started to climb the ladder.

He caught hold of my arm. "I'll get it," he said firmly.

I opened my mouth and then shut it and stepped aside.

I watched him climb down the ladder carrying what I now realized was a rather large and heavy wooden crate. It was a good thing that he knew how to deal with stubborn creatures.

"I remember these," he said when he got to the bottom of the ladder. "We used to use them for the sloths. See the bar for them to hang on inside? We changed to using the plastic crates because they're lighter. But these are not so wide. You can get them into holding and leave them there, and sometimes the sloths would go into them by themselves overnight. The crates don't fit into holding, so we have to catch them up the hard way every time now."

"Used to when? And what was it doing up there?"

"I haven't seen one for . . . ten years maybe? And I have no idea. I didn't think they were still around."

I looked down at the crate sitting between us on the floor. We both had the same thought at the same time and looked at each other.

"That must be how . . ." I trailed off.

We both sat there looking at the crate without saying anything.

"Let's go home," he said after a while. "It's late. We'll think about it tomorrow."

The phone rang. I felt so perfect in my total immobility. I had given the pugs each a disgusting slow-roasted bull penis, ordered from a special dog supply website that was really much too expensive for someone on a keeper's salary, and I was so exhausted that I lay motionless for half an hour staring at their enthusiastic chewing. It was a rare state for me, who had so much trouble sitting still. I hated to disturb the moment. But curiosity got the better of me.

"Hannah. Are you busy?"

Allison never said who she was on the phone. She just expected you to know. Of course, you always did.

"Um, not really." What else could I say? I had meant to be very busy lying on the couch for the rest of the evening. With the pugs as my role models, I was intending to concentrate very hard on doing it to the very best of my ability. But it would be rude to say so.

"If you can meet me at the back gate in a few minutes, you can come and watch something interesting."

I opened my mouth to say that the back gate would be closed by now, but fortunately I realized how stupid that was before any sound came out. Of course she would know that, and obviously she'd have a key. Could you imagine that the lowly zoo police would be able to unlock the gates and she wouldn't?

"Sure," I said, and we hung up.

It wasn't till I was putting my coat on that I realized how weird this was, her calling me at home and out of the blue inviting me somewhere. But how could I resist some neat animal thing, no matter what it turned out to be, and going to the zoo when no one else could get in? Being in the Small Mammal House when no one else could get in was half of the thrill of my job.

She was already inside when I got there. Her hair glowed oddly in the moonlight. It was one of those huge bright autumn moons. It probably had some kind of name, like the harvest moon, which made me think of harvest mouse, which made me wonder if there was a spiny moon or a striped grass moon. She unlocked the pedestrian gate and let me in, then locked the gate again behind us.

"I heard about your sloth." I tensed up at her words. I had been trying not to think about it, dammit. Why did she have to bring it up? "It's wonderful that she's back, but the situation is still extremely disturbing. I promise you, we'll get to the bottom of this," she said sternly. "But for now, I don't want you to worry. I called because I thought maybe I could help take your mind off it."

Oh. Now I felt guilty for being momentarily angry. She always kept me just a little bit off balance. But I got good stuff by putting up with it, so on the whole it seemed like it was worth it.

So where were we going? I wondered. Was there some animal that did some interesting behavior that you could only see at night? It would be like her to know exactly when some nocturnal animal put on a show that no one else ever saw.

She answered the question before I'd even come up with a theory. "Lucy is getting shipped out tonight. I know you're interested in training. It's always educational to see them work the elephants in a new situation."

"Tonight?" I said, surprised. Usually, we'd all know in advance the exact date of something like this, a large and popular animal getting shipped out. No one cared if we at Small Mammals shipped out a mongoose or the like, even if it was the only one of its species in captivity or something. But an elephant—that would be an event everyone would know about.

Of course she understood my reaction. "I know. But the situation is unusual," she said confidingly. "After all the press coverage . . . This is hard enough to do without also having a lot of extra people here."

Cool, I thought. She was trying to keep too many people from coming. And I got to be there.

But I was still no one, really. So when we got to the Elephant House, Allison went to talk to important people, vets and curators and the assistant director, leaving me to look around at everyone else who was standing and waiting and looking around. And to try not to think of the last special elephant training event that someone had pulled off. I supposed the elephant wouldn't have known it was killing someone. But it wouldn't be easy to get one to do it anyway. Sure, they were used to stomping pumpkins. But they'd hardly miss the fact that there was a body attached, and the difference would matter. After all, even making an elephant walk into a truck it had never seen before was a little bit tricky, despite it being already trained to follow commands to walk in a certain direction. That was why people were interested in being here tonight: because this wasn't a trivial exercise.

But Stephanie was conspicuously absent, I noticed. Was she so upset she couldn't show her face? I doubted it. She'd want to be here. I suspected they'd made sure she didn't know it was happening tonight. I thought about how I would feel if they shipped out one of my animals without telling me when. It would feel a lot like how I felt when the sloth was kidnapped, I was sure. If someone had done this because they thought they were being kind to Stephanie, they were wrong.

"Isn't it past your bedtime?"

I turned. "Margo? What are you doing here?"

She just smiled mysteriously. Which I should have expected. Margo knew everyone and could call in favors to get whatever she wanted. But no way was she going to reveal her sources.

"And how did you get invited?" she said.

I wasn't good at being mysterious. And I was too tired to think of a plausible cover story.

"Um. Allison."

"Really." Her tone was disapproving. No surprise there.

"Who's going to work the elephant, do you know?" I said, wanting to change the subject. This was the kind of job people fought for—a way of proving that you were special and showing how good you were—and so just the kind of thing Margo would know.

"Who do you think," she said, slyly, nodding toward where Allison and Matthew were standing together.

I watched Margo watching the two of them. That was why she was here, I realized. She didn't care about elephant handling. This was her thing—observing people like they were her study troop of baboons and she was sitting on the savanna, piecing together their relationships. Sometimes it didn't seem fair that she never got a journal article out of it just because her subjects were humans.

"She's too prominent to mess with a keeper now," Margo mused. "I'm thinking she's going to have to find a way to promote him."

"I thought he was already—"

"Not senior keeper," she scoffed. "I wouldn't put it past her to create a position to move Bruce up. Then Matthew could be curator. What's another level of management added here or there, after all."

Just then, Allison said something to Matthew, and he walked toward Lucy's stall.

I couldn't help admiring how smoothly it went. I thought again of my nightmare where I'd mistaken him for Chris. I hated to think that he was also as good with animals. It would be nice to believe that the animals could tell if someone was a jerk. But that was foolishness. If your technique was good enough, it didn't matter. They could hear the clicker and taste the treat, but they couldn't look into your soul. It was stupid to think that they could.

Lucy walked through the stall on Matthew's command,

walked up to the truck with him beside her. She started up the ramp. Then she looked at him. I thought I saw his hand move—anyway, something somewhere must have startled her, because she stamped her foot.

The clang of the metal ramp reverberated though the building, and as it faded away you could feel the hush and tension while everyone waited to see what happened next. But it was nothing. He gave another command, she walked the rest of the way into the truck, and he closed the truck behind her quietly so as not to startle her again.

The show was over. Everything was still for a moment. Then it was like everyone let out their collective breath, and people started to mill around and get ready to close up and leave.

I watched people walking by Matthew, congratulating him, giving a thumbs-up. Much as I hated to admit it, seeing him stand there looking full of himself, he was good. Except for that one false move that startled Lucy into stomping her foot—

Wait a minute. Someone had needed to train an elephant to stomp a foot on command. To do it even though the situation was strange and unfamiliar.

Had it been Matthew? But then, he would have been careful not to use that command accidentally, wouldn't he? But on the other hand, if she had learned the command from one person, she probably wouldn't automatically understand it coming from someone else. Trained behaviors didn't always transfer easily to a new trainer. My dog Gus would only lie down for me, no matter how precisely someone else seemed to be imitating my command. And I thought of a friend's dog that I had trained to shake hands. Now whenever she saw me, she tried to shake before I even asked. She knew I was the person who liked the shaking thing.

Lucy was poised to see the stomp command from Matthew perhaps, even if he only made a motion that was sort of like it by accident. She knew he was the person who liked the stomping thing.

And that made me think—was this why Allison was so determined to send Lucy away? Sure, she had lots of explanations. Sure, the plan had been in motion for a while. But so might the plan to kill Victor have been on her mind for a long time. Hers and Matthew's.

"Here comes your friend," Margo said.

I turned, surprised at her tone. It wasn't the usual teasing. But before I could say anything, Allison was beside me and Margo was walking pointedly away.

"You must need to get home," Allison said, smiling.

"Yeah, I guess so." I tried to sound normal. Not like she'd caught me thinking how she might have helped conceal the huge, conspicuous murder weapon that Matthew had used by shipping it out to another zoo.

"Let's go, then. I hope it was worth the loss of sleep?"

She smiled at me, and I thought, no, it's insane. Zoo directors don't go around murdering people, or conspiring to murder them. I wouldn't put it past Matthew. But Allison had plenty of power. She didn't need to do anything so crude, so risky. Sure, it was convenient that Lucy was being sent away. But Matthew had known about the plan as long as anyone had. Of course he'd choose the elephant that was going to be shipped out. It didn't mean Allison had anything to do with the murder.

"Yes. Thanks for letting me watch." At least it wasn't hard to sound sincere about that. Whatever all these people might be up to, it didn't make the elephants any less cool. It wasn't their fault. Lucy hadn't murdered anyone. She'd only been a tool. You couldn't blame her any more than you could blame a gun or a knife. She can't have understood what she was doing.

Allison had one of her staff drive us to the back gate in a scooter. I closed my eyes, hoping she'd think I fell asleep. I noticed that she'd already gotten one of those electric scooters that the rest of us were waiting for. The rainforest must be happy. But I was even happier not having to walk back.

A little bump woke me up, and we were at the back gate. The moon looked smaller. I said goodbye to Allison and thanked her again and walked home.

Chapter 13

"Hey, you're still here?" I said to Caleb.

"Just one last bit of paperwork," he said, sitting down at the computer.

Caleb was going to Philadelphia to pick up a tree shrew. We hoped it would mate with the one we already had. They'd get some of the offspring too, so we could both have more of these little brown thingies that didn't impress the public, no matter how many times we said that we were the only two zoos in North America to have this species in captivity. He was going to miss the opening of the wombat exhibit. He said it was too bad, but I thought he'd volunteered to go on purpose so he'd be away when Allison was around. Chris probably would have done the same, I suspected, but he couldn't get away with it.

I wandered into the kitchen to get my food pans. I should be in a bigger rush, I thought sleepily. I'd said I would go to a meeting of the animal welfare committee today in Robin's place, since she was on vacation. I hated meetings, but I figured I ought to see one of these at least once. I should hurry up and get upstairs and do the nastiest of the cleaning jobs so stuff wouldn't be festering while I sat in a nice clean conference room.

The phone rang, but before my drowsy morning self could move to the wall, Caleb had picked up the extension in the office. That'll just waste more of his time, I thought, feeling vaguely guilty and then immediately forgetting about it as I tried to balance the stack of pans while I walked up the stairs.

I loaded the stack onto a rolling cart when I got to the vestibule, and then I picked up the mara pans and headed out the side door. Caleb was coming up the outside back stairs, leaving, I assumed, on his trip to pick up the shrew.

To my surprise, when he got to the top of the stairs, he grabbed one of the logs that were sitting around for us to use in exhibits, and out of nowhere, he heaved it across the courtyard. It hit the ground with a crash that made me jump. But he didn't seem to notice I was watching. He continued to have a perfectly terrifying tantrum of some kind, kicking at the pile of branches that he'd removed the log from. I'd had plans for some of those branches, but I was so astonished by what I was seeing, it didn't occur to me till later to realize he was breaking them and I'd have to go out and cut more. I watched him, frozen in place. After a minute he stopped and just stood there, breathing heavily. Then he stormed out the gate, pulling it shut behind him with a crash.

I stood there in shock. Caleb seemed so mild-mannered, but now I thought of what a big guy he was. I went and pushed at the log with my foot. For the World's Smallest Zookeeper, I was pretty good at lugging those bags of mulch around, but I'd have had a hard time dragging this log inside, and he had thrown it across the courtyard. I shivered a little. And I had no idea how you'd get that gate to close hard enough to make a slamming noise like he had—it was hard to just get it to close all the way.

I looked back toward the door and saw Jeff standing there, staring, kind of wide-eyed, like I supposed I looked too.

"I heard something and came out here . . ." he said. "What the heck was that about?"

"I don't know."

There didn't seem to be anything to say. We kind of shrugged at each other, and Jeff went back in the building.

I picked up my mara pans. Then I put them down again and went back downstairs and poked my head into Chris's office.

"Hey?" I said.

"Hey," he said back.

"Caleb . . ." I said.

He waited.

"I just saw him do something . . . weird," I said.

He glanced over at me. As usual, he just waited. He didn't press me. He didn't have to. He knew I'd eventually come out with it, didn't he? I realized I was that predictable in not being able to keep anything from him.

Oh, well. So I was. I explained what I'd seen Caleb doing.

Chris's expression turned angry. "I'm sorry you had to see that. I'll talk to him when he gets back."

"No, don't," I said. I'm not sure why. Was I afraid he'd beat Chris up? Was I afraid he'd find out I was the one who complained? Or did I not want to get him in trouble?

Maybe all of those things. But anyway, that wasn't the point.

"Do you know what he was so mad about?" I asked, not sure if I expected to get an answer.

Chris didn't say anything. I looked at him. Yeah, he knew, but he didn't think he should tell me. As usual. I knew that look. And unlike when the tables were turned, I couldn't hope he'd eventually just come out with it.

"I won't tell anyone. I promise," I said.

He got up and closed his office door.

"He was speaking to the director on the phone just before he left," he said. "She was talking about transferring him again."

"Really? Why?" He'd practically just started working here—we were hardly finished training him on the whole building. Why mess us all up like that?

"I don't know why," he said, and I must have looked a little doubtful, because he insisted, "I really don't. It's between her and Larry, and I haven't talked to him yet. I don't know what she said."

I looked at him. "You have an idea." And he was too uncomfortable for it to be a normal sort of idea, like that there'd suddenly been an opening in another building that desperately needed some special skill of Caleb's. No, it was something more interesting than that.

He looked reluctant. I waited.

"Hannah, I know you like her, but . . ." He stopped.

"I don't like her that much. She's done stuff for me, is all."

We looked at each other. I had the funny feeling that a ghost of Allison was standing between us. That if I reached out to touch him, she'd push my hand away.

"She's messing with him," he finally said. "You know about their past. She's done this kind of thing before."

I didn't know what to say. He'd been here longer, known everyone longer, seen more than I had. He was sensible and right about everything else. This was bordering on gossip; he wouldn't say it if he didn't think it was important. But I didn't know what to believe. Sure, she could be manipulative. But jerking Caleb around to different jobs just for the hell of it? It was a real abuse of power.

I just looked back at him blankly, not knowing what to say or think.

"I hope I'm wrong," he said, shrugging.

"Me, too," I said. He turned to his computer, and I opened the door and left the office.

I hated to sit still, and Robin had seemed really sorry to have to ask me to go to this animal welfare committee meeting in her place. But it was turning out to be much more interesting and dramatic than I had expected.

Stephanie stormed into the room. She looked around and

saw that Allison had not arrived yet, so she had nowhere to direct her anger. She sat down, but you could see that she could hardly contain herself. I remembered how she'd momentarily seemed kind of sweet when she was showing me the baby rhino. But now she looked like the terrifying warrior woman again.

I knew Stephanie couldn't win this fight—it was clear to everyone but her. Lucy was gone. Allison had the upper hand in every possible way, including the fact that she was completely in control of whatever emotions she might have about the situation. But Stephanie wasn't going to let the battle end. Allison strode into the room precisely on time and distributed the agenda. The elephant issue was last. This would either give Stephanie time to calm down or time to work herself into a frenzy, so it was an interesting calculation on Allison's part.

The first few items were not fascinating or important enough to keep my brain from going into that Meeting Zone, which was a lot like being unconscious. I tried to pay enough attention to be able to tell Robin what had gone on, but she was probably just going to have to rely on the printed agenda that I brought back. Finally, though, we came to the interesting part.

"Everything about this was wrong," Stephanie began. She had gotten a partial hold on herself since she came in, and was clearly trying hard to be calm. "The decision itself and how it was carried out, both. Elephants form lifelong bonds with other elephants and with people. These are animals that mourn their dead! If Lucy's genetic material were so valuable, we could have bred her here. She may be so traumatized by this move that she won't be a good mother. And the zoo we sent her to—Boston's zoo is a disgrace for a major American city. There are small towns with zoos that size. It's ridiculous. And the climate is so much worse for elephants. I can't see how anything about the good of the entire species could outweigh the cost to this individual animal."

It was interesting to watch Allison throughout this speech. She gave every indication of patiently listening with genuine interest.

"And as for the execution—"

Allison interrupted, but quite politely. "Wait. You've raised some interesting points. Would you mind if I addressed them first before you went on?"

Stephanie seemed confused and disarmed, and nodded. She was no match, I thought, feeling kind of sad for her. She came assuming Allison would meet fire with fire, but of course that's exactly what she wouldn't do.

"You know I understand that elephants are social animals. But that's exactly why I thought that moving Lucy might work to her advantage. You know that I spend a great deal of time at the Elephant House, and I've observed these individuals closely for quite a few years. It's clear that Lucy is a little bit of an outsider. She might very well do better in another group, especially one with a normal family structure. So this move might actually be better for her, and I think the elephants left behind will feel her loss less strongly than they would one of the others."

This was the same kind of thing that Caleb had said. Caleb could make a sloth follow a bean, so I thought he was pretty good with animals, whatever else you could say about him. And Allison was, too, no matter what else you could say about her.

"As for the climate, I want you to know I looked at the health records of their elephants in very great detail. I was satisfied that there were no problems that could be attributed to the weather. In fact, studies have concluded that there's no reason not to keep elephants in northern zoos."

Stephanie was looking increasingly agitated. She clearly realized that this all sounded perfectly reasonable. I felt bad for her. I knew what it was like to lose a favorite animal. We had these terribly close relationships with them, and probably spent more hours with them than we spent with our own pets. But we didn't have any ultimate control over what happened to them. Even the decision whether to euthanize an animal rested finally with the curator. Larry consulted the keepers and took their views very seriously. But if he thought we were blinded by emotion and unable to decide rationally, or were just making the wrong call about the medical situation, we could be overruled in a second.

Stephanie changed tactics. "If you're so comfortable with your decision, why did you have her moved in the middle of the night? Without any advance notice?"

Allison looked sympathetic, and the first thing she did was answer the question Stephanie was really asking. "Stephanie, I know what it's like to lose a favorite. That's exactly why we all decided it would be better if you weren't there. I'm sure Lucy would have felt your distress, and it would have made it harder for her."

Now I really felt sorry for Stephanie. If she claimed that the whole thing was about being concerned with putting Lucy's needs first, there was no way she could argue with this.

"As for moving her at night, that was partly because the traffic would be lighter and the trip would be shorter," Allison added. "But also to avoid publicity. We didn't want the additional stress of reporters trying to force their way in. It was best for everyone. I'm sorry, I know it was hard on you, but it would have been hard any way we did it."

"She might have liked to say goodbye," Stephanie said, losing her battle to argue rationally about it, now on the verge of tears.

"Stephanie, if you want to take a trip up to Boston to see that she's doing well, I'd be perfectly happy to pay for it. We ought to do that kind of follow-up anyway."

Stephanie just nodded wordlessly. Allison wrapped up the

meeting. She had no hint of triumph in her voice as she gave her general sort of pep talk about a job well done. We all went our individual ways.

Walking around feeding out my afternoon food, I found myself still thinking about the meeting. When I was listening to her in person, Allison had definitely won the argument. But then when I thought about it afterward, I wasn't sure. There was something so unfairly overwhelming about Allison's stage presence, it almost didn't matter what anyone else said.

I stood and watched Radar running back and forth, taking pieces of kibble out of his bowl and carrying them into his exhibit to eat them. Stephanie had certainly looked murderous when she came into the meeting today. But if her anger about shipping out Lucy was the motive, why would she kill Victor instead of Allison? Maybe because the elephant move wouldn't stop just because Allison departed the scene. She had initiated it, but after that a whole bureaucracy took over. It would probably keep going from inertia without Allison there to reverse course.

So maybe instead Stephanie wanted to take away something that she thought Allison loved. She couldn't stop the move, but she could have revenge. Or so she thought, not knowing Allison had already shown Victor the much-used exit from her heart.

I turned away from Radar's holding and saw that Chris was leaning against the wall behind me, half smiling. I wondered how long he'd been there without my noticing. Great, someone could walk right in and steal my animals again while I was in some kind of dream world.

"Something wrong?" he said.

"No, why?"

"You look puzzled," he said. "How was the meeting?"

I knitted my eyebrows and, I supposed, looked puzzled. "I

don't know. This elephant thing. Allison has the power to cloud minds. Everything she said sounded so reasonable. But when I think back on it now, I wonder if I shouldn't believe Stephanie. I don't know what to think." I shook my head. "What do you think? You all must have had a hundred meetings about it."

"At least."

"So who do you think is right?" I insisted.

Chris usually paused before speaking instead of jumping in like all the rest of us talky monkeys. But this was more than a thoughtful pause—he was struggling with something. Finally he said, "It's hard for me to be objective about this one."

"Really? Why?" I was kind of startled. This was a surprising thing for him to say.

"It's a little too much like something that happened to me."

I put on that stubborn waiting look, the one I knew he had trouble resisting. He was good at keeping other people's secrets. But this was one of his own.

He sighed. "You know I'd rather talk about animals than people."

"So would I," I countered, "if only the people around here would stop acting so weird that they needed to be talked about."

He nodded in agreement. "It feels like when the tapirs got shipped out. It wasn't clear that there was a real need to move them, but it was also hard to make an argument that wasn't just that I wanted to have tapirs around."

Tapirs were his favorite animal, I knew. Even though they weren't small mammals.

Wait a minute—back up. "We had tapirs? When was this?"

"A while ago. Eight years? When she was promoted to associate curator. Just a couple of years after I started here."

"Were you their keeper?"

"No, I was always at Small Mammals," he said. "Robin was working with them, though." Robin had worked in Large Mammals when she'd started at the zoo, but I'd never known they had tapirs back then.

"What kind?" I said.

"Baird's. They were the species I'd done research on in Panama. I visited them a lot. They meant a lot to me," he said, in a funny tone, like he was telling me some kind of guilty secret.

I felt a fierce stab of anger. Anyone who would take Chris's tapirs away from him was a bad person.

"If they were going to ship the capybaras out," I said, "I'd raise a stink. Even though it's none of my business."

He nodded.

"What made it worse was . . ." He looked uncomfortable. "It was personal. She was angry at me."

I looked at him, startled. This was a pretty bizarre accusation. What kind of collection planning was that? Doesn't a curator have more appropriate ways to discipline her staff? I pictured her dangling a baby sloth out a window and threatening to drop it if I didn't behave.

"You think she'd ship a whole species out to get at one of the keepers? What was she angry at you for, anyway?"

He paused an even longer time this time. Finally he just said, "It was a long time ago."

It was that tone that I knew there was no point in arguing with. The one that said that my charming stubborn look had come to the end of its usefulness.

I looked away and rearranged my pile of dirty food pans in frustration. Surely he couldn't say a thing like that about her and not back up the story more? But, yeah, he could. God, he drove me crazy sometimes. Was this why he hated her so much? But he wasn't the type to hold a grudge for so long. There had to be more to it.

Then I thought of something. "Caleb said that Victor spent a lot of time visiting the elephants and talking to Stephanie. Could

Allison have thought something was going on between them? And been trying to get at Stephanie for that?"

He was silent for a moment.

"She might have thought I was spending too much time with the tapir keeper, too," he said, not looking at me.

I glanced at him sharply, remembering when I'd thought he liked Robin a little too much, too. He didn't seem to notice. Then I reminded myself it was none of my business who he liked now or, for Pete's sake, almost ten years ago.

Of course, why did Allison care either? If he was having trouble keeping his mind on his work for, um, personal reasons, taking away the tapirs wouldn't necessarily put an end to it. The keeper staff had all pretty much taken a vow of poverty, but you couldn't very well expect us to take a vow of chastity, too. At least I sure hoped not.

This whole conversation was making me very uncomfortable. "Well, I hope you're wrong. That would be pretty awful, using animals to manipulate people that way. It'd be a pretty sick way to run a zoo."

He looked at me without saying anything, and I knew he was thinking of the wombat. He was afraid she was using me for something. But what could she use a lowly small mammals keeper for? It was silly to think the whole wombat thing was about me. It was just a whim she had, and it had happened to be inspired by me.

"You have to be careful with her," he said. "She thinks she's above the rules."

"But so do you," I said. "You have the keys to the steam tunnels. You do all that crazy stuff at the Code Orange drills. All of you guys who've been here forever, it's like the place is your private playground."

I hadn't meant anything bad by this. I just so often felt like I'd come in on the middle of a long-running party—or a long-running argument—around here. There was so much history between the people, and between the people and the institution, that I wasn't a part of. I felt a little left out, sure. Still, it wasn't meant as an accusation.

But clearly I had pushed some button I hadn't meant to. His expression turned momentarily angry, and then it was like he'd closed up completely. I realized he'd been confiding in me and I'd blown it.

"I'd better get back to work," he said.

"I didn't mean . . ." I trailed off. I suddenly realized that the problem was that I'd compared him to Allison. He hated her so much, and I'd suggested they had something in common. But I couldn't figure out how to apologize for that, and then he was gone.

I felt sick and lonely and, as usual, distressed that I couldn't stop caring about him so much. But there was nothing I could do but bend down and pick up my bag of trash and go find more to put in it till the day was over.

Chapter 14

It was the day of the silly media event for opening the wombat exhibit. That was bad. But it also meant that it was the excellent day of actually putting the wombat in the exhibit.

We'd gone up to the hospital first thing to pick him up. For now, we were just going to release him into holding. Then, when people were ready to take pictures, we'd open the shift door and let him into the exhibit.

There was a little problem with this plan, though. We put the crate in holding and opened it. The ride on the bumpy back road from the hospital had woken him up for a change. But he was perfectly happy in his nice den-like crate. He looked at me when I opened the door. Then he closed his eyes and went back to sleep.

"Oh, no," I moaned. "Does he fall asleep in every possible circumstance?"

Chris looked away, smiling. "That reminds me of someone . . . I can't think of who."

I was pleased that he didn't seem to be mad at me after our disagreements yesterday. But I was too panicky to really enjoy the feeling.

"Don't joke around," I said frantically. "What if he doesn't come out into the exhibit?"

"We'll get him out," he said serenely.

"How?" I wailed.

"You never sleep through anything really important either,"

he said, grinning.

Suddenly I realized how funny it all was. I sat on the edge of the holding entrance and laughed so hard I felt sick. I leaned over and rested my head on the wall. "I guess I'm a little nervous," I said, gasping for breath.

He smiled at me like I was adorable about the wombat again, but I felt too weak to object. He motioned for me to move over and sat down next to me. We shouldn't be sitting here in the wide open holding door, I thought. But the idea that this wombat was suddenly going to try to push us aside and storm out of there was so laughable that I had to stop thinking about it before I got hysterical again.

"You weren't up there keeping him awake late last night, were you?" he teased.

"Oh, yeah. I brought some beer to celebrate . . . stupid of me," I said, starting to giggle again.

"This is why there are all those rules about quarantine," he said mock seriously. "I should give you a written reprimand."

"Will I get in so much trouble that I won't be allowed to represent the zoo in the newspaper?" I said hopefully.

"I'm afraid not," he said sadly.

I sighed and leaned my head on his shoulder for a moment. I knew it was a bad idea, but it felt so nice. Feeling much calmer, I stood up.

"Okay, time to seize the day," I said.

"Or the morning meeting," Chris said.

"Right." Today, I suddenly felt, I could even seize the morning meeting. "Let's go."

Robin was sitting at the computer printing something out.

"Hey," I said. "How was your vacation?"

"It was great." She smiled. Of course, being Robin, her time off had been spent at a pet sanctuary, volunteering to socialize and take care of cats and dogs that were so warped that they couldn't be placed for adoption. Not my idea of great, but it was her vacation.

"Look," she said, handing me a sheet from the printer. "I made these for the exhibit opening."

"Oh!" I exclaimed. They were wombat stickers. Robin was the crafty one, always spending her lunch knitting or embroidering, doing paint stencils on the back walls of her exhibits and even in the keeper area. I always felt so clunky next to her, with her delicate fingers doing needlework and her uncanny ability to still look clean and ladylike at the end of the day instead of being soaking wet and covered in unmentionable stains.

"You can hand them out to the kids," she said.

"These are great. It's a neat drawing." Nice and round on round stickers. They gave me a nice wombatty feeling. I would hand them out to adults, too, if they would take them. But there were some things you needed kids as an excuse for.

"I'm sorry it's not fancier, but I didn't have much time," she said.

"No, it's really nice of you to do this. You must have so much to catch up on."

"Yeah, and not just work," she said. "Margo tells me I missed quite a lot."

"Uh, yeah," I said. Getting promised a wombat, the murder, the sloths mating, the sloth disappearing, the chutes, the sloth coming back, Caleb rampaging around the courtyard . . .

"Chris to Hannah," the radio sputtered.

"Go," I said.

"Show time," Chris said.

"Uh-oh," I said, not into the radio, and then replied, "Ten-four."

"I'll be up in a couple of minutes," Robin called after me as I trotted up the stairs to face the media circus.

Naturally Beth led the parade. In a wombat t-shirt that she'd put on over what she was already wearing.

"Look," she said. "I got this at the shop on my way here."

"Are those our shirts?" I hadn't even seen them yet, and she already owned one? That wasn't fair.

"Yeah," she said, digging in her huge bag. "Here's another I got for my son. Want to see it?"

I took it from her. "Wow, it's really expensive," I said, looking at the price tag. I had wanted to buy a whole bunch of them, but if this was the price of the kid's shirt, no way. I was afraid to ask what the adult shirt had cost.

"Yeah. It's organic cotton. Hey, did you know how much pesticide is usually used in growing cotton? I have it in my notes here. One of your PR guys was at the gift shop . . ." She flipped through her reporter's notebook.

"Yeah, I get it." I wanted to weep. I'd known this was coming, that we were going to start having some organically grown cotton clothes in the gift shop. But why did this have to be the one thing they'd manage to get done so quickly? I had really wanted lots of wombat shirts, damn it.

"It's really nice fabric, too," she said.

"Yeah," I agreed, sadly. Oh well, I had a real wombat. Who needed shirts. I guess.

"There's my photographer," she said, "I better go talk to him right now. You know how he is."

I nodded as she walked away. Yeah, I knew how he was. He would probably ask if we could bring the wombat out on a leash. I hoped there'd be someone around to restrain me. I hadn't wanted my picture in the paper, but if it was going to be there, I'd rather it wasn't a police mug shot.

I looked at the rest of the reporters. It must be a slow news day. I saw someone setting a big camera up on a tripod. Wait a minute, I realized. That was a film camera. It was a TV camera. TV for a new Small Mammal exhibit? They had to be kidding. Oh, shit. I didn't want to be on TV. I really very badly didn't want to be on TV.

I looked around frantically for Chris, who had hung back when I started talking to Beth and then quietly vanished. I found him down the hall contemplating something in my pygmy marmoset exhibit.

"Help," I whined. "There are TV cameras. I don't want to be on TV. No one said there would be TV."

"There was TV at the pumpkin stomp," Chris said reasonably, watching the marmosets eating gum. Oh, for Pete's sake, I thought. Here I am about the face this media onslaught, and he's feeding the pygmies gum? Wasn't it his job to solve problems around here? I just managed to resist the impulse to grab him by the arms and shake him.

"Come *on*," I said. "Even I don't think a wombat is anything like a baby elephant pumpkin stomp. Who could imagine there'd be TV?"

Really, I did still have some tenuous grasp on reality. Who would have expected the TV stations to care about a new wombat? My stomach was starting to hurt.

"So they'll only use ten seconds of film at the end of the broadcast," he said.

Oh, sure. Easy for him to stand there perfectly serenely, looking at pygmy marmosets. He wasn't about to make a fool of himself in front of the entire local television viewing audience. He wasn't going to have to go around with a bag over his head for weeks, hoping no one would recognize him as the person who'd said that stupid thing about the wombat. No, he'd just be able to stand here every day watching the pygmies eat gum, secure in his anonymity. But what about *me?*

I tried not to whimper. "This is crazy. I mean, it's not like it's a panda cub or something," I was astonished to hear myself say. We always complained about the big animals getting all the attention. I hadn't known how lucky we were.

"Don't worry. You would be great on TV talking about the wombat."

Oh, right. I had a funny feeling that this wasn't a completely objective opinion. I knew how he looked at me when I was excited about the wombat.

"They're going to be disappointed." I had visions of a hysterical unhappy media mob attacking me, no doubt led by my old friend, Beth's photographer. "They're expecting something big and charismatic. We should have taught him to do tricks," I said nonsensically. "I know he mostly sleeps, but after all, you can clicker train a chicken, there must be something . . ."

He finally realized I really was in a total panic, ridiculous as it was. He turned to face me and put his hands on my shoulders. "Hannah," he began, in what I recognized even as I started to fall under its spell, as his best small-mammal-whisperer voice. The voice that calmed nervous little animals. I felt my blood pressure beginning to drop.

Just then we heard those footsteps behind us. We stepped away from each other like we'd been caught at something.

"Hannah, Chris, here I am," said Allison, in that way she had, as if her arrival meant that all was right with the world. "We should be ready to go in about ten minutes, but I wanted to get here early. Is everything set?"

There was a moment of awkwardness. "I don't have my wombat stickers," I blurted. "We were going to give them to the kids who come. Robin made them."

"I'll go look," said Chris, disappearing almost immediately. I should have realized he'd seize on the opportunity to get away from Allison. I wondered if I'd thought of the stickers for that very reason.

"Aren't you excited?" Allison said, beaming.

"I didn't know it would be on TV," I said, trying not to sound miserable. She'd gotten me a wombat, and I was whining about a few cameras? But no one had warned me that making a televised spectacle of myself was part of the deal.

She put her arm around my shoulders and did that thing where she focused her attention on me like I was the only person in the universe. "Hannah, don't worry. You'll be wonderful, I can tell. Look," she said confidingly, "I have to do this all the time. You'll get used to it. It's no big deal."

I looked back at her a little dubiously. But she seemed so confident. I wasn't convinced when Chris said I'd be great on TV. He thought I was adorable about the wombat. He maybe also thought other things about me that I didn't want to think about. His judgment couldn't be trusted.

But Allison did this all the time, and she thought I would be great. She knew what it was like. She thought I had what it took. That meant something.

Okay, I said to myself, I could do it. It was no big deal. It would be over before I knew it, and maybe I would be on TV for ten seconds. And then I'd have a wombat. Small price to pay.

"All right," I said.

"Excellent," she said, beaming like I was the Queen of Wombats and she had just crowned me and strewn the path with rose petals.

I stood there full of confidence, looking forward to my date with destiny, for about five seconds. Then it occurred to me that Chris had left, and that he wasn't going to come back if he could help it. He'd send someone else up with the stickers and find some important reason to leave the building or be stuck in his office until Allison left. And I would have to get the wombat out of his crate and into the exhibit all by myself.

And just then Robin walked up to us, holding out the stickers that Chris had gone to get.

"Here they are," she said, smiling.

"Thanks," I said, faking a smile back, overcome by another wave of panic. "I have to go downstairs a minute, I just thought of something else. Is that okay?" I said to Allison frantically.

"Certainly. I'll go talk to these people and make sure everything's going to go smoothly," she said, walking toward the assembled media like they were a waiting, adoring throng of admirers.

I dashed down the hall and almost crashed into Chris coming out the door into the public area.

"Please," I begged. "Don't leave me alone. What if the wombat won't come out of holding and the whole thing is spoiled? You can stay back in the keeper area. Please."

"I wasn't going to leave you alone," he said, looking serious.

I stopped dead.

"Of course you weren't," I said, feeling like an idiot.

He smiled that smile that made my guts turn to armadillo gruel.

"Well, let's go then," he said.

Beth came back from talking to the photographer. She said, "He said they want you standing next to the exhibit when the wombat comes out."

That was fine. That way Chris would have to worry about getting the wombat to come out. I was more worried about screwing that up than I was about having my picture taken, I realized. I wasn't supposed to be a good TV star, so the expectations weren't that high. But I was supposed to be good with animals.

I unlocked the door to the keeper area. Chris was half lying in the open holding, looking into the wombat's crate. I envied him not having to deal with all those people. Couldn't I just stay in here with the two of them? That was all the company I needed or wanted.

"Is he awake?" I said anxiously.

"Not at the moment," Chris replied, serene as ever.

Okay, but now it wasn't my problem. "They want me out there for the picture. Can you get him to come out? Now? I mean in a second, when I go out there." I was having a hard time not babbling.

"Sure," he said, getting up. I took a deep breath and went back out to confront my fate.

After the wombat came out and people clapped and pictures were taken, Allison had to give a speech. Another one of those things about conservation, except without so much rainforest in it. I stood there trying to look interested.

I heard the door of the keeper area behind me open and close quietly, and Chris appeared beside me.

"How did you get him out?" I whispered while Allison kept talking, thinking I'd learn one of his special animal secrets.

He just put on a mysterious look and didn't answer.

"Come on," I said, nudging him with my elbow.

"I can't reveal all my techniques. You'd be after my job next."

I rolled my eyes. "No way. Sitting in all those meetings. Come on, I need to know."

He put on a show of looking around for eavesdroppers. Then he whispered dramatically, "I tipped the crate."

I caught myself from bursting out laughing just in time, remembering that Allison was still lecturing to the assembled crowd. "I could have done that!" I whispered indignantly.

"But you would have thought it was too mean."

Okay, he had me there. But I saw that the wombat didn't

look any worse for the experience, so now I could do it the next time I had to. Maybe I could keep it a mysterious secret from Jeff, I thought, feeling old and experienced.

Finally Allison had finished speaking and the cameras were being packed away. The public was allowed to get close to the exhibit, and some of the reporters came to talk to me. I talked to someone from a high school paper who wanted to know all about how I became a zookeeper. A couple of others were doing papers for their college journalism classes. This was more what I'd expected, not real TV stations.

But I felt like an old hand now. When one of the TV guys came over and asked if he could film me answering a few questions, I said, "Sure," like I'd been doing this all my life. I was riding on a wave of adrenaline, I realized, watching myself enthusiastically explaining how wombats were related to koalas. Someone tie that girl down, part of my brain said, but my mouth just kept on going. I was the media darling. I was next in line for zoo director. Everyone out of Hannah's way.

CHAPTER 15

And then it was over. And as usual, poop had not miraculously disappeared, nor food pans flown into exhibits unaided while some special event interrupted our day.

Suddenly I was exhausted—drained from the nerves, crashing down from the excitement—and as if I didn't have enough work to do, people had to make my job harder. Some days I would hate kids, if it weren't that you really have to blame most of their behavior on their parents. First of all, who would think it was a good idea to give a tiny child yogurt in a squeezable tube? It's obviously a dangerous weapon. And then bring them into a building clearly posted "No Food or Drink," and then ignore them while they squirt the yogurt all over the window of my fennec fox exhibit. And then just drop the tube and leave without making any effort to clean up or to find anyone to clean it up before it starts to dry into dairy-product cement.

I hadn't seen any of this happen, but the circumstantial evidence was definitive. So much for my big moment in the media spotlight. I was back to cleaning up after primates. I'd have been better off if the kid had eaten the yogurt and vomited—then I would have had to call housekeeping to clean up, because they were trained in the correct treatment of biohazardous material. I supposed it was nice to know that the zoo thought that all the germs I dealt with every day were less serious than human cooties.

I was crouched down in front of the window scrubbing at the

yogurt when I heard someone saying my name from a little way down the hall. The voice was familiar, but I couldn't place it right away.

I looked up from my awkward position on the floor. He was walking quickly toward me, almost running. It was, what? almost two years since I'd seen him, and he still looked kind of like how you'd picture a barely grownup Harry Potter who'd finally traded his glasses for contact lenses. A little geeky, but in an adorable way, and with a hint of hidden depths. Although the only particular spell he used to be able to cast was the one where he got me to put the pugs in their crates for a while and take all my clothes off.

I fell back onto my rear end and sat on the floor looking up at him stupidly. "Tim?" As if there could be a question.

"Hannah," he said, sounding positively joyful. "Do you work here? That's so perfect. I can't believe I ran into you."

I couldn't believe it, either, except I did. What were the odds of running into your old boyfriend who you'd carefully lost touch with, who didn't even know you were working here? Hundreds of people walked through the building in a day. Most of the time I wasn't in the public area, so the chance of any one of them seeing me was minute. But it happened all the time. It always made me wonder how many other long-lost people I missed just walking past the other side of a closed door.

But I hadn't missed this one, I thought, stunned. "What are you doing here?" Not that I had any reason to be surprised he was here rather than anywhere else. I'd been so careful not to keep track.

"I'm here for a conference for a few days. I gave my paper yesterday, so I had time to come to the zoo today . . . Hey, can I help you up?" he said, putting out his hands.

I was still sitting on the floor. I was kind of afraid to touch him. And I could get up perfectly well by myself. But I took off my yogurt-coated rubber gloves and reached up.

He pulled me up and we held on for a minute, looking at each other. He looked thrilled. I don't know how I looked. But I knew how I felt, exactly how I was afraid I'd feel if I ever saw him again, this sick combination of longing and a terrible knot in my stomach.

"We used to go to the zoo all the time. How perfect that you should be working at one. What's your job?"

"I'm a keeper. I, um, feed and clean up after animals and stuff. I love it. I'm really happy," I said, although I wasn't exactly feeling really happy right at that moment.

"Wow, that's so cool. Oh my God, and how are the pugs?" he said, excited.

That was the last straw. I felt like I'd been kicked in the gut. I grabbed his hand and pulled him along behind me as I ran through the hall, through the employees' door to the vestibule, and out into the courtyard.

And then I sat on the concrete steps and wept hysterically. All the good memories I'd never properly mourned came flooding back. The pugs had loved him so much when they were puppies. We had taken them all over New York with us, hidden in our pockets when they were tiny, even in restaurants. We took them to Prospect Park, and they played with the big dogs like they didn't know they were little, and both of us laughed till our stomachs hurt at their minuscule fierceness. He'd stayed up all night one time when Gus was sick, even though he had exams the next day. If I kept thinking of those things, I'd never be able to stop.

And then when I said I was leaving to go to graduate school and Tim tried to talk me out of it, I accused him of all kinds of awful things: that he had no faith in my abilities and wanted to keep me down, and all of that. But he'd turned out to be right. He'd known me better than I'd known myself. And that just made me want to run and hide from him harder. When he tried to contact me through my old department, I ignored his message. I couldn't face him finding out he'd been right, couldn't face thinking about whether I'd lost him for no good reason.

Poor Tim. Of course he had no idea of any of this. All he knew was that he was thrilled to see me and suddenly I was bawling my eyes out like someone had just died. But I didn't even know how to begin to explain.

"Hannah, what's wrong? Are the pugs not okay?" He reached his hands out to touch me, and then hesitated awkwardly.

"No, they're fine," I said between sobs. "I'm just so sorry."

Now he got it. "Oh, Hannah. Never mind that. I'm so happy to see you, please don't cry."

He put his arms around me and pulled me against him. I closed my eyes and pressed my face into his shoulder. After all this time, the feeling was still familiar and comforting. How had I ever thought that anything else was more important?

"I'm sorry," I said again, trying to stop crying because he had asked me to, and it was the least I could do.

"You did what you had to," he said.

"I didn't have to be such an asshole about it." I sniffled.

He held me tighter. "Oh, Hannah . . . you know, breaking up with somebody—no one's invented an anesthetic that works for that. What can you do?"

My radio crackled.

"Chris to Hannah."

Oh, no. I pulled away from Tim and took a deep breath and then another. Chris tried again. The radios didn't work half the time, so we were used to people not answering on the first try. I took another breath and pushed the button.

"Hannah. Go ahead."

"What's your location?"

"Courtyard," I said, sentence-fragmentally.

"Can you pick up the phone?"

"Take a message?" I said, hoping my inability to form full utterances would sound like more radio malfunctions.

"Ten-four."

I put the radio away, and then I pushed my hair away from my face and looked back at Tim. I wondered for the first time what a mess I must look. I had no idea how much poop and yogurt were on my clothes, and now my face was probably all red from crying and God only knew what my hair looked like. But his expression was one of concern rather than like he was wondering what had become of my appearance since he'd seen me last.

"So enough about me," I said, trying to smile. "What about you? Are you still in school? Still living in Brooklyn?"

"Yeah. I'm about to finish my dissertation, and then I'm going to start a post-doc."

"Really? Where?"

I felt like I was holding my breath a little, waiting for the answer. What difference did it make where? We hadn't exchanged a word in two years.

"Hopkins," he said, trying to sound casual.

I stared at him. "That's really nearby."

I heard the door open behind us. Chris came out carrying a trash bag that wasn't very full and probably didn't need to be thrown away right this minute. He was a good analyst of radio voices. He put the trash in the trash can and then stopped and looked at us.

I introduced them. I just said Tim was an old friend. They shook hands. You had to know Chris to realize he was looking over Tim like he was trying to figure out whether he needed to be run out of town. He appeared to decide that he was harmless and went back inside.

I turned back to Tim and realized he'd been watching me as

I automatically watched Chris walk back into the building till he'd vanished from sight. I rubbed my face a little, as if doing so would make the blush go away.

"So how long have you been working here?" Tim asked.

"Um . . . a little over a year. I was volunteering, and I took a leave after the first semester when there was a temp job here, and, well, I never went back, I guess."

He nodded, like it was just interesting.

"You were right, I guess," I said. "About me and . . . more school. You know."

He shrugged. "You're happy here."

"Yeah. It's perfect."

"I'd love to hear more about it," he said, and then added a little hesitantly, "I don't really have to be back to conference till tomorrow."

There was a note in his voice, a tiny fear of rejection, that I'd never heard when I knew him before. I felt a little sick thinking that I was the one who'd put it there.

"That's great," I said quickly. "Could we have dinner? On the early side. I have to get to work really early in the morning."

"Sure," he said, sounding like his usual self again. It was always so simple to make him happy, and somehow I'd managed to screw everything up so badly. And yet he was glad to have found me again.

"So I'll look around the rest of the zoo and meet you later?" he continued.

"Okay—wait, no. First I should show you some animals here." How could I have almost forgotten this? Tim was the only person I'd known, before I worked here, who would come with me to the zoo as often as I wanted to go.

"What do you mean?"

"I mean take them out and let you touch them."

His eyes grew wide like a little boy's, increasing the Harry

Potter resemblance for a moment. "For real?"

"Yeah," I said, suddenly completely happy. "Let's go."

When I finally went downstairs and opened the fridge, I couldn't find my P.M. pans. I started to rummage around. All the food supplies had been put back in the fridge for the end of the day, so maybe the pans got pushed out of the way? I was so exhausted, maybe I just wasn't seeing them?

I'd never felt so thankful for strawberry yogurt in squirty tubes, for sure. But when I'd run into Tim, I hadn't even done my P.M. feeding yet. And I'd never finished cleaning the glass, either. I was barely going to be on time to meet him for dinner at this rate.

"Hey," I heard Chris behind me.

"Hey yourself," I replied from the depths of the fridge.

"I fed out for you."

I pulled my head out and looked at him. Then I let the door close and leaned against it.

"You didn't have to do that."

"Someone got yogurt all over Radar's glass," he said. "I took care of it."

"Oh. Thank you," I said, with an emotional intensity you don't normally expect in a conversation about strawberry yogurt.

"It looked like you were busy with something important."

I knew it was really a question.

"I need to lie down on the couch."

He knew that was really an invitation. We went into the keeper room. I lay down on the couch and he sat next to me, my head almost touching the side of his leg.

We were quiet for a while. Then I said, "I lived with Tim, in Brooklyn. I broke up with him to move here. I'm not proud of how I did it."

I didn't know how to explain any more. How sweet and

vulnerable he had been. How he would look at me like he couldn't believe his good fortune. And then how I wouldn't even answer his email when he was looking for me. Looking for me, after how horrible I had been.

I felt Chris put his hand on my back ever so gently, and I realized it didn't hurt because I wanted Tim back, or because I wished I hadn't left. If I hadn't left, I wouldn't have this job now, and this was where I belonged. It hurt because I had never resolved how I'd dealt with the end of our relationship.

"It was easier to leave angry at each other instead of sad," I said, half to myself.

Chris rubbed my back. "Anything that's in pain lashes out at what's nearest."

I don't want to ever do anything like that to you, I thought. Now I was the one who couldn't believe my good fortune. But I was so sure I was going to screw it up again. Wouldn't it be better not to try?

I must have fallen asleep for a minute. I woke up and felt him stroking my hair gently. I felt like I was in a cocoon of serenity. That was his magic spell.

"Who was on the phone?" I said, very belatedly.

"It'll keep till tomorrow." His tone was so soothing, I would have believed anything he said. "Ray came by," he added.

Another connoisseur of radio transmissions. "Did he say anything?"

"Just to let you know."

I couldn't decide whether to worry that I'd been obviously hysterical on the radio for the whole zoo to hear, or to be comforted that the two of them were looking out for me. I decided to stick with the latter for now. I wondered what their conversation had been like. I'd almost never seen the two of them talk to each other. Probably monosyllabic and full of implications. They could both be such guys sometimes, I thought, smiling as I drifted off to sleep again.

We were walking back from the Japanese restaurant, where we'd sat on the patio with the pugs, and where maybe I'd had a little too much sake. I thought I was so brave, finally getting up the nerve to approach the subject in a roundabout way.

"So, are you still in the old apartment?"

"Yeah. It doesn't seem as much too expensive for one anymore, with the way the rents are going up around it." And then he answered the question I was really asking. "I don't want a roommate. And there hasn't been anyone else I wanted to be there."

I felt that sick feeling again. I realized that I'd always made myself feel better by assuming that he'd get snapped up immediately. We were both getting to an age where you started to think all the good ones were taken. He was so sweet and gentle and funny—how could he be alone for this long?

He shrugged, seeming to read my mind. "I've been so busy . . . And who knew where I'd end up after I finished the degree, so what was the point?"

We walked slowly, letting the pugs sniff whatever they wanted. It could take all night to get back to my apartment if we let them be in charge, and right now I was in no rush.

"So how about you?" he said, like it was no big deal.

"There's no one," I said, a little uncertainly.

He looked at me like he was waiting for me to finish.

"Yet," I added.

He nodded. He reached out and took my hand as if he'd just been given permission and we walked, each with a pug leash in one hand and the other's hand in the other.

"So," he said after a while, "this Chris fellow. What's wrong with him, then, that he doesn't see what a catch you are?"

My eyes smarted with tears. "It's not him. It's me. After what a jerk I was . . ." I trailed off.

"Oh, Hannah," he said. "You know it probably would have happened eventually, one way or another. I'm probably going to end up going from post-doc to temporary jobs all over the country for who knows how long. Could you really have followed me around for years like that? You just cut to the chase, that's all."

"But I thought—" I began, and then I realized I hadn't thought. I'd been in the state I always envied in the animals. "I guess I was so totally in the moment . . . like it would always be that way." I looked at him, wondering, did I really not know him as well as I thought I had? "I thought you felt the same way."

He shrugged a little. "I was living in the moment just the same. But it was because I was pretty sure it was all that I would have."

I squeezed his hand so hard, I was afraid it would break. I couldn't believe how completely he had forgiven me. He was right, of course. I'd spend the last two years feeling I'd destroyed the love of my life. But the odds had always been against us.

We got to a block of row houses that, in the dark, could almost have been Brooklyn. I stopped abruptly, a feeling of déjà vu washing over me.

I turned to Tim, and I could see the same feeling on his face. The pugs snorted around in the grass obliviously. He put a hand on the back of my neck. "Hannah," he began questioningly, and I answered the question by pressing myself against him and kissing him.

We stood there doing that for a while, until he said, "We can't just stand here like this."

I looked around. "Why not?" I said. "People in this neighborhood do stranger things than kiss on the street all the time."

"But—"

"Come back to my apartment then."

He kissed me hard. "I thought you'd never ask." He grinned.

This might be stupid, I thought as we half ran down the street, the pugs actually keeping up with us, as if for the first time in their lives they'd finally had enough time to sniff one patch of sidewalk as thoroughly as they wanted.

"Are you sure this is a good idea?" he said.

"No. Do you want to think about it harder?"

"No," he admitted.

"Oh, God," I said, "We have to stop at a drugstore. I'm so embarrassed."

"Why?"

"Well, like, if I have no birth control devices around the house, doesn't that mean I'm so unattractive that one wants to sleep with me?"

"Silly," he said, stopping to kiss me again. The street was much more crowded than on the block that made us think we were in Brooklyn. But like I said, it was the kind of neighborhood where no one noticed.

I giggled a little. "What?" he said.

"I almost forgot, for a science geek you're really a good kisser."

"Well, for a zookeeper you smell pretty nice."

"Beast," I playfully pretended to knee him in the groin, but carefully. I had plans for those parts later.

"Good, you like beasts," he said. "Let's go already."

The pugs whined at the bedroom door.

"Where are the crates?" he said.

"I don't use them anymore—we could lock them in the kitchen. But they might learn to open the fridge if we take too long."

"Wait," he said.

He opened the door, blocking it with his foot so they couldn't come in. Through the crack in the door I could see them gazing up at him adoringly.

"Settle," he said firmly, and they both lay down on their sides.

He closed the door, and the quietness continued. I stared at the door in disbelief.

"Wow," I said. "I forgot about that."

He was the only one they'd ever do the "settle" command for. I'd forgotten he had two magic spells. Then he came back to the bed and got back to work on the other one, the one that made me take all my clothes off.

I woke up and watched Tim breathing evenly, as I had so many other nights what felt like such a long time ago. He opened his eyes and looked confused for a minute. Then he looked in my direction.

"Hannah," he said softly, remembering where he was. He was still half asleep. "Where are the pugs?"

I got up and opened the door, and the pugs came in and jumped on the bed. He smiled and closed his eyes and we all fell back to sleep.

Chapter 16

I was on time for a change, but I walked around like a zombie. Yesterday had been an emotional roller coaster, water slide, and bumper cars all rolled into one. And I'd been, well, a little too busy last night to get much sleep.

I stood at the kitchen table. Everyone else had gone off to their lines to start working. I stared at the little tiny syringe and the bottle of pink medicine.

It was okay now, I told myself. Although I still thought Tim was wrong that there was no way I could have done it better. It should have been, "I care about you, and leaving hurts, but leaving is what I need to do now." But the only way I could tear myself away from him was to convince myself I hated him. And to try to make him hate me, too, so I could leave with some stupid kind of clear conscience. I was so ashamed. But if he'd forgiven me, I could forgive myself. Couldn't I?

I shook my head. I needed to focus. This was how you ended up with tamarins running all over the building and everyone having to stop their work to chase them with nets. And grapes with the wrong amount of medicine in them. I couldn't even remember what this was, I thought, peering at the bottle. Would an overdose be serious?

Somehow Chris was standing at the table beside me.

"What's up?" he said.

"Nothing. Not enough sleep," I said, too tired for any extra words.

I didn't expect him to dignify this half-truth with a response. But he said, "Can I help?"

I thought, what would really help would be if you put your arms around me, and tell me that we were meant for each other, and that I was stupid to keep resisting it.

"Do you think you could make up these meds while I go check my line?" I said instead. "I'll come back for them later."

It was almost as stupid a request. If I couldn't do this part of my job, I should just go home. This was the easy stuff. This was the stuff where if you needed help with it, they started a personnel file so they could try to fire you someday.

"Sure," he said, like it was no big deal.

"Yeah. Thanks. Um, see you soon."

That didn't make any sense, I thought as I climbed the stairs, but at least it was more appropriate than blurting out something like, "I love you, and I hope you don't mind I slept with my old boyfriend last night."

I decided to go look for the sloths first. The sloths were the most soothing animals to look at. The wombat was wonderful, but because he was new, he still made me a little anxious about whether he was going to be okay. I didn't know whether I knew how to take care of a wombat. So the sloths would be good right now.

I could only see two sloths from the public area. I went around and checked the holding area chute from the back. No one. I climbed into the exhibit. My heart was starting to beat just a little bit faster, but I assured myself there was no way a sloth could have vanished again. The third one was surely just in some funny little place it was hard to see.

It wasn't unusual for it to take this long to find one of them, I told myself after a few minutes. I was just sleep-deprived and on edge because of all that had happened. I stood still for a minute, trying to calm my breathing. Jeff walked by in the public area, and I smiled and waved, trying to pretend nothing was wrong. The look on his face showed what a bad actress I was, and after a moment I heard the exhibit door open.

"You need some help?"

"I'm fine," I lied. "But could you look and see if there is a sloth in any of those high places?"

"Sure."

He checked the shelves and the top of the waterfall, and I watched his face, waiting nervously for it to open up into a smile.

"Not up here," he said.

My stomach started to churn.

"Thanks," I said, brightly, "I'll take it from here."

"Are you—"

"Really, now it's just all these low spots to check. Thanks."

He climbed back out of the exhibit. I pretended I didn't see the concern in his expression. So sweet of him to worry about me. But I was just so tired that I wasn't seeing the sloth right in front of my face. Right? I kept telling myself that for about ten more minutes, until I finally had to admit the truth.

I radioed Chris and asked him to meet me behind 24. I climbed out into the back hallway and leaned against the wall. My brain couldn't take in that this was happening again. All I could do was wait.

I heard him walking down the hall. I hadn't noticed before that I could recognize even his footsteps.

He took one look at me and said, "Not again."

I nodded. I must have been a sight, standing there with tears running down my face, covered in leaves and dirt from hysterically tearing the exhibit apart looking for the sloth. He climbed into the exhibit without another word. I sat down on the floor in the hallway and leaned against the wall. I thought about how nice it would be when he came out, smiling at how silly I was, and how wonderful it would be to feel like a complete idiot when he showed me where the sloth was hidden.

But I didn't really believe any of it. So I wasn't surprised when he came back out after I don't know how long, and just shook his head.

"Who would do this?" I wailed. "This is just crazy."

I looked at Chris and saw that look on his face. Like he had an answer to that question, but he couldn't decide whether to say anything. So I lost it.

"What?" I yelled. "Don't look at me that way! What do you know?" I ran over to him and was going to, I don't know, pound on his chest or grab his shirt and stare at him threateningly or some such foolish impulse. Instead I started to sob.

He put his arms around me, and I cried all over his shirt for a minute, against my better judgment. If he had some idea about this sloth-disappearing act that he wasn't telling me, I should be angry. I shouldn't be standing here wishing he'd hold me like this all day.

I pulled away. "Tell me. You can't have an idea about this and not tell me."

"You're not going to be happy," he said reluctantly.

"Like I'm happy now? What's the difference?" I wailed.

He put his hands in his hair in that way I thought was cute, and I wanted to cry again. I was such a jumble of emotions. Fear and anger about the sloth and not knowing who'd taken it, and this constant mess of affection, lust, and frustration at Chris for always having some damn secret or other. Why couldn't he trust me? I couldn't stand it anymore. I wanted to crawl under a rock and never come out again. I had wanted this job so I could work with animals. Why were so many of the complications about the people?

I shook my head. This was getting me nowhere. I tried to squash those feelings and just gave him my best look, the one he wasn't as good at resisting as he used to be, that said I wasn't going anywhere until he spilled the beans.

He sighed. "The person who could have done all these things is Allison."

My expression changed to one of dumbfoundedness. "You're crazy," I snapped. "You're just saying that because you hate her for some reason. Or no reason at all—how would I know?" I sat down on the floor, sure that if I didn't, I would storm away down the hall.

"Hannah," he said. He sounded sad. I tried to resist the way that made me feel. He sat down on the floor opposite me. "Please, just listen."

He looked at me pleadingly. I was so angry, but so unable to refuse him anything. I was so sure he was wrong, but so sure he was right about most things. Two parts of my brain had each other in a stare-down, and the contest was going nowhere.

"Fine," I said, reluctantly. I stared down the hall. Not looking at him, it was easier to fight against the urge to agree with everything he said and give him whatever he asked for. It wasn't just Chris I was angry with.

"It has to be someone who can get into the elephant yard," he began. "It has to be someone who knew enough about the routine here to come up with the idea of sabotaging the lemur chute—"

"Right. And that's more likely to be Caleb," I interrupted. "How would the director know about the chute and who works that exhibit?"

"You're forgetting she used to work here."

"Yeah, but that was a long time ago. Come on," I said skeptically. He was grasping at straws, I thought, because he wanted this to hang together; because he hated her.

He shook his head. "Things haven't changed that much. And she's been here a lot lately." He hesitated. "And she's spent a lot of time talking to you."

"What, so I helped her try to kill us?" This was stupid, and it was making me angry.

"Not on purpose. But she knows how to make a question sound innocent and interested. You'd never realize she was pumping you."

"You think I'm that naive," I said, getting angrier. Sure, I had mixed feelings about her. She was hard to deal with, and sometimes she made our lives more difficult instead of easier. But she'd gotten me a wombat. She'd thought of me when I was having troubles and taken me to see the elephant getting shipped out. She'd treated me like more than just a poop-shoveler—someone good enough to talk to newspapers, and sit with my pugs in her fancy parlor. If he was right, all that had been done to manipulate me.

But he couldn't be right. It didn't make sense. He only thought it did because he hated her. And I couldn't stand the idea that he could hate someone enough to be that wrong.

He put his head in his hands. "Hannah, please hear me out."

He looked sad and tired and it tugged at my heart.

I sighed. "I'm sorry. Go ahead. I'll try not to feel like you're explaining what an idiot I am."

"Hannah, I'm not—"

"Wait," I interrupted. "Let me try again." I took a deep breath. "Go ahead. I'm listening."

"There's only one way the sloth could disappear and reappear even after we posted a guard on the building. The steam tunnels."

"So it must have been you," I said peevishly. "Because we know you have a key to the steam tunnels that you aren't supposed to have, and you have the key to the exhibits. So where are you hiding my sloth? At least I know you're feeding it the right stuff." I scowled at him. The idea that Allison did it was just as silly as the idea that Chris had done it himself. What was this supposed to prove?

"Did you ever wonder how I got the key to the steam tunnels?"

That stopped me. I knew he wasn't really supposed to have that key. How could I have been so uncurious as not to consider that before?

"No. I guess I figured you had a good reason. Why does it matter?"

"Well," he said, "I've had it since Allison worked here."

"Oh." I stared at him. He'd copied her key. Or she'd copied his? No, she outranked him. She was more likely to have figured out a way to get it. But then Chris would have thought it was cool to have it, too. He was totally rule-abiding to all appearances, except when it came to doing something cool at the zoo that wouldn't hurt anyone anyway, like wandering around the steam tunnels and sneaking into other buildings. He'd gotten mad when I compared him to Allison, but both of them were above the rules sometimes.

"But look, how do we know the same person did all these things?" I said, conveniently ignoring the fact that that was my whole argument for suspecting Caleb. "Victor was murdered. He has nothing to do with Small Mammals. Someone tried to hurt us with the chute, but why? The sloth is stolen, but what does that have to do with murdering anyone? There's no connection."

"I know," he said. "The only connection is that Allison has something to do with all of them."

"Why would she want to kill Victor?" I demanded.

He looked uncomfortable. "I'm not sure you should believe her story about their breakup. And she can be . . . pretty hard on her exes."

"Like she goes around *killing* them? That's—"

I stopped dead and stared at him.

"Wait a minute," I said incredulously. Somehow it hadn't hit me before exactly what he was suggesting. It was just a puzzle: who had done it in the Small Mammal House with the metal saw. But suddenly I felt the reality of what he meant.

"I just realized," I said. "You think that Allison wanted to hurt *me*. With the thing that happened with the chutes."

He just looked at me.

"Why would she want to do that? She's been wonderful to me. She got me a wombat. She . . ." I was dumbfounded.

"I don't know why," he said very quietly. "But it scares me."

He looked at me in that way that turned my insides to armadillo gruel. I looked back and felt tears coming to my eyes.

Part of me wanted to throw myself into his arms, but before I could take a step, the part that hated to feel stupid rushed in and took over.

"No," I shouted. "You're wrong. You're just crazy with hate for her. I don't know why. You don't like her to do special things for me, or . . . I don't know. I don't know what your problem is, but I won't listen to any more of this."

I ran down the hallway without looking back, trying not to burst into tears. I ran through the hallway of the public area and managed to fumble my key into the door and stumble into the keeper area before I started to cry. I ran to my back room and closed the door and sat on the stepstool and took deep breaths until I stopped sobbing.

I sat with my head in my hands. I felt sick to my stomach. I was miserable, whether he was right or whether he was wrong. It was stupid to think it was her. Allison, who always got someone else to do all the dirty work and heavy lifting for her? She carried a drugged body into the elephant yard? And a heavy wooden crate through the wet, muddy steam tunnels? She didn't have the shoes for it. The mental picture would make me laugh if I wasn't so many millions of miles away from feeling like laughing.

I knew both Chris and I were having trouble being objective. He wanted it to be her because he hated her. I didn't, because she'd been nice to me, even if she was a lot of trouble, too. Or maybe because it was too bizarre for the director of the zoo to be a murderer. I'd gone along with everything she'd asked me to do, and she'd tried to kill me? How unjust. All those inconveniences, all that hard work I did, and now she wants to murder me. What kind of reward system is that for a workplace?

Chris had to be wrong. But if he was wrong, that was awful, too. How could he hate someone enough to make such a horrible, and wrong, accusation?

I just wanted to lie down and cry. But I had to go downstairs and get my food to feed out. I didn't want to go downstairs and risk seeing Chris again. But I had to feed my animals. And stupidly, I really had to pee. My bladder didn't care about the pain in my heart.

I went downstairs and tried to trot quickly through the kitchen and keeper area without looking to either side of me. Margo was doing something in the kitchen, and I just waved at her and trotted by. But when I walked past Chris's office my eyes refused my attempts at control, and I glanced to the side. He was sitting there, and I saw him look up and see me.

I spent a long time in the ladies' room. I wasn't sure what I wanted. Did I want him to say something when I went by again? Or ignore me? Or just have gone somewhere else by now?

My animals were hungry. It was very late. I had to do my job. I took a deep breath and pushed open the ladies' room door.

This time I didn't look as I passed his office. I grabbed my pans out of the fridge and pretty much ran.

I got upstairs and started to throw food pans into exhibits as fast as I could. And all of a sudden I realized that I recognized how I was feeling. The feeling that I needed really badly not to run into him. The feeling where every time you see something that reminds you of someone, you have to turn your head away so you don't think about it. Like after you break up. Oh, man, this was so unfair. Here I was telling myself I shouldn't sleep with him because of the risk that I'd eventually feel like this all the time at work, and now I was feeling the pain without ever having had the pleasure.

I went to the desk that I used to pile nest boxes and supplies on and cleaned off some space. I sat in the chair and put my head on the desk and immediately I was unconscious.

A noise woke me. I opened my eyes. From where I sat I could just see Ray sitting in the open doorway of the fennec exhibit. He was tossing crickets into it one by one. I was so glad to see him.

"Ray," I said sleepily, "you really do come to visit Radar, not me, even on the days I am here." I wondered how he'd gotten the crickets out of that noisy can without waking me up.

He got up and came over to where I was sitting. Like a cat, compact and muscular, he hopped on top of the desk and crossed his legs and sat there.

"Never," he said. "We were just comforting each other in our loneliness without you." Then he looked at me. "You look sad. You sounded sad on the radio."

"Oh, great," I moaned. So I was broadcasting my emotional state like a radio soap opera to the whole damn zoo. And that was just about the sloth. I'd really better stay off the air now.

"Only Ray could tell," he said soothingly. "Why so sad?"

"The sloth is gone again. I had a big fight with Chris about it. I don't want to talk about it."

I put my head back down on the desk with my forehead pressed against his leg. He stroked my hair with one finger. I wondered if I wanted him to take me in his arms and make me forget about Chris and his crazy ideas and his secrets and his blue eyes. I squeezed my eyes shut harder and just managed not to cry.

"Have you had lunch?" he said suddenly. "Not having lunch makes you sadder."

"What time is it?"

"Lunchtime. What do you want?"

"Nothing," I whimpered. "I don't want lunch. I just want to sleep."

He suggested all my favorite things, and they all turned my stomach.

"This is a serious case," he mused. He reached down and took my face in his hands and made me look at him. His hands felt cool, like a reptile, but soft and comforting.

He hopped off the desk and pulled me up out of the chair. "Come with me," he said. "You need French fries."

I stared at him. It sounded like the usual Ray non sequitur.

"Doctor's orders. Dr. Ray says, French fries and soda will revive you."

That might be okay. The only edible food the zoo stands sold was the French fries, but they were really good. I usually didn't have them because if a person got in the habit, it would really be a problem.

He took my hand and pulled me along behind him. "Fried things and sugar are Dr. Ray's prescription for troubles in love."

"It's not—" I denied automatically.

"Shh, okay, I know. Just come with me."

I sat on the grass and he handed me French fries one by one, like I was an invalid, maybe a fennec fox who was too sick to catch his own crickets. I started to feel a little better.

"He's not the person I thought he was if he can accuse her of something so horrible. On so little evidence. He just keeps insisting I should believe him that she's capable of terrible things. I don't want him to be right. How could she be so awful? She's been so wonderful to me. How could I be so wrong?"

"I know," he said soothingly.

"But," I said, starting to get teary again, "I don't want him to be wrong. Because then he's making up such a horrible thing. How could he . . ." I trailed off, trying not to whimper.

"Shh," he said, rubbing my back.

"I don't know what his problem with her is. The annoying things she does aren't all that different. She breaks the rules all the time, she thinks she's above the rules. We can quarantine the wombat on exhibit even if the vets don't like it if she says so. She can go around the procedures for adding species to the collection if she says so. But she's the director. Isn't that her privilege? He'll take a lemur out of its exhibit and walk it around the public area when the building is closed. He has keys he shouldn't have. He doesn't call a Code Orange if he doesn't feel like it. She's not the only one who breaks the rules . . ." I trailed off. "What should I do? I can't be caught between them anymore. I can't take it."

He stroked my hair and said, "You know, princess, I know how it feels. How your pride is hurt if it turns out that you're wrong about someone. But is that what's important?"

I nodded miserably. I didn't want to admit it, but it really was likely that everything she'd done had been a way of using me for something, somehow. That was just how she was. I'd been a fool to think I was any different from anyone else. It didn't help that it meant I'd been a fool in front of Chris, who'd been trying to make me realize this all along. I closed my eyes and sank deeper into the pit of misery.

"But I can't judge anymore. They both—I can't be objective about either of them anymore."

He put his hand on my forehead like he was checking to see

if I had a fever. For some reason this was a very comforting feeling.

"She does this thing where she turns her attention on you, and it's like a drug and you can't think straight," I said. "She got me a wombat. I would be friendly with the devil if he'd get me a wombat. And Chris . . ."

"Mmm-hmm?"

I wasn't sure how to say this to Ray, lying on the grass all cuddled up together with him, having my back rubbed. "I, um . . . I look at him and my brain turns to mush, sometimes."

He nodded like he understood. Like what I'd said was perfectly reasonable.

"Half the people at the zoo hate her," I continued. "More than half, maybe. Maybe that many people can't be wrong. But, Ray." I turned my head and looked at him. "Lots of people don't like successful women. Lots of people would be jealous of someone like her. And she has to make some decisions that make people mad, right?"

He looked back at me sympathetically and waited for me to draw the conclusion myself.

I flopped onto my stomach and closed my eyes. I was just making excuses, I realized. I didn't even really like her. She made me feel like I should roll over on my back and show her my unprotected belly and throat and hope she wouldn't hurt me. And then when she doesn't, it's a kind of high from the relief. That's all it was.

The answer was stupidly obvious. Allison wasn't important. We didn't have an equal relationship. She was superficial. She made me feel important when I had her attention. She could give me things I wanted. I was sucked into the feeling of being close to someone powerful. It really was just like a drug.

And I was such an idiot that I was letting her come between me and Chris. Who really mattered.

I sat up.

"I've been very stupid," I said. "I'm so glad we had this little talk."

"You're not stupid," he said with a sigh, "or if you are, you're in good company."

"This doesn't make her a murderer. It doesn't mean Chris is right about that."

"I know," he said.

"But he doesn't have to be right about anything. Even he isn't perfect."

Ray just smiled.

"Caleb could have done all those things, too," I continued. "That makes a lot more sense. He wouldn't have needed to use the steam tunnels. And can you imagine Allison carrying a body in her high-heeled shoes?"

"Not really," he admitted with an evil grin. It wasn't something you should laugh about, but it really was a funny picture.

I lay back down and closed my eyes. "I'm so tired," I moaned. "I can't think straight. I can hardly remember my name."

"Hannah," he said, in a sweet little voice I'd never heard him use before.

"Thanks," I said, almost giggling, but I was too tired to even giggle. I was so sleepy. "I should go apologize," I mumbled groggily. "Chris can think what he wants. It doesn't matter. I shouldn't be mad at him for it. What does it matter what he thinks about her? Why should I care? She's not important." I struggled to keep my eyes open.

"Kiss and make up," Ray said, nodding.

I sat back up, *"No,"* I began.

"Shhh. Okay. Lie down," he said, and I did.

"I'm so tired. The sloth and all this other stuff . . ." I mumbled. I wanted to tell him about Tim. I knew he'd understand, but I wasn't sure if I could do it. "And this whole stupid wombat thing with all the reporters again and no time to do any of my regular work. And then last night I ran into my old boyfriend," I said, speaking quickly, trying to get it out before I changed my mind, "and I didn't get any sleep really, and . . . oh, never mind . . ."

He was quiet for a moment. I remembered Chris telling me he'd come by yesterday afternoon, when I was showing Tim around. I wondered again what they'd said to each other.

"You wouldn't be the first person on earth to sleep with an ex, you know," Ray said.

It was a good time for him to have pulled one of his mind-reading tricks. "I guess I knew that, but thanks."

He got one of those evil smiles on his face. "Once you've been eating the pie, no one notices if you go back for another slice."

"Ooooh," I moaned.

He leaned down and gave me a quick peck on my forehead. "Couldn't help it."

"That's okay." It was. I couldn't be his friend if I couldn't deal with that sort of thing. "I guess it's true, anyway."

"Are you sorry?"

"No, I'm not sorry. It's just so . . . complicated."

"Well, then. You have enough problems right now. That's not one of them."

Okay, I thought. Let that go. I let out a deep breath and felt all the tension in my body disappear along with it. Funny, it wasn't usually Ray's job to make me calmer. But Chris couldn't help me with this one. It was too much about him.

I felt Ray put his cool hand on my forehead and thought how lucky I was to have him. The gibbons hooted in the distance, and I heard the noises of children walking along the paths, talking quickly, excited about being at the zoo. A breeze blew across my face, and briefly I felt like I imagined animals to be, alive in the moment with no past or future. I felt my strength come back.

"Okay," I said. "I'm ready."

I walked into the building feeling a little sick. I was determined to apologize to Chris, but I was afraid to, also. But I thought I had the nerve if I could just find him right away before I thought about it anymore.

I heard the phone start to ring as I walked down the stairs to look in his office. He wasn't there and no one else was picking up, so I did so, reluctantly.

"Hannah, oh good," said Allison. "I heard about the sloth. I've decided that we need to have a keeper on duty in the building overnight until we get to the bottom of this. Obviously the zoo police did not perform adequately." Her tone implied that heads would roll. It was a tone she was very good at.

"Yeah. I'll do it," I said, thinking, dammit, I wished she'd done this sooner. I was positive that if I'd been in the building last night, no one would have gotten their hands on my sloth.

"Good. You can't do it every night, certainly. You'll have to take turns, but I'm sure everyone will pitch in. But I thought you would want to go first."

"Yes, please." I knew they'd pay me overtime, which would just about cover the expensive coffee beverages I'd need to buy in order to stay awake all night. But I would have done it for free earlier if they'd have let me.

"Is Chris there? I should clear this with him," she said, as if it would matter what anyone else thought once she'd made up her mind.

I knew that more than anything he'd rather not talk to her, but I had to think fast to make up a reason not to radio him to pick up the phone. "He's, um, medicating the lemur for me.

This one's gotten really difficult and skittish. He wouldn't have his radio turned up while he was doing it. I'll tell him the plan, okay?"

"Have him call me if he has any questions." Right, if hell freezes over and pigs fly.

I hung up the phone and stood looking down at it, working up the nerve to radio Chris for his location. Now I not only had to apologize, which was hard enough, but I also had to give him this message from Allison. There was no way to keep her out of things even for a second, I thought, frustrated. I should go walk around until I found him, I suddenly realized, because I had just told Allison that I couldn't reach him on the radio, and sometimes she carried a radio. I was impressed with myself for finding this perfect rationalization to postpone the inevitable.

I went upstairs and dawdled in various places until I found him reading something off the checksheets in the back room of my line. He looked up. I plunged in.

"That was Allison. She wants us to have a keeper inside the building on watch instead of just zoo police. I said I'd do it tonight."

"No," he said immediately. "I won't let you."

I stared at him. He'd never reacted like this to anything. This was not how he managed. No, wait. He had been like this only once before, when he said he wouldn't let Jeff do any more tours for Allison.

But this was different. This was about my sloth. He never just flat out overruled a keeper on an animal issue. Sometimes there was negotiation and discussion, and it ended out coming out his way, sure. But never like this.

"You're just going to contradict the director's instructions then?" I said angrily. "Fine, you can talk to her." After I'd gone out of my way to make sure he didn't have to, I thought resentfully.

"I didn't say that. I just said you're not going to be the one to do it."

I couldn't believe what I was hearing. It was like he'd been replaced by his evil twin. Who was this person who was telling me what I could and couldn't do, after the director of the whole zoo had told me different?

I glared at him, speechless with fury.

"I'm only doing this because I don't want you to get hurt," he said. I'd never heard him use that angry tone before.

"I can take care of myself. I don't need to be protected." I tried not to shout. The last thing I wanted was for everyone in the building to hear this conversation.

We stared at each other. He looked like a stranger. Where had my Zen agouti monk gone? He was always the still center of the daily chaos of our lives. Now I didn't recognize him. I'd come in here ready to apologize, to be friends again, to tell him how much he meant to me. What had happened? It was like a nightmare.

And suddenly I thought of another tall blond guy who had seemed only vaguely familiar. Oh, my—

"Fine," I said breathlessly.

I turned and stormed out the keeper door and through the hallway, leaving small children tossing about in my wake. I continued out through the courtyard and didn't stop until I'd gotten to my hiding place out behind the lemurs. I collapsed into the grass, breathing heavily.

A tall blond guy walking into Allison's house. That dream I'd had, where it looked like Chris in the distance, but then it turned out to be Matthew. I'd decided the guy walking into Allison's house that night was Matthew. But if Matthew could look like Chris at a distance, then why not the other way around?

He'd tried to convince me that Allison had done the sloth-napping, the chute booby-trapping, the murder. It had been half a joke when I countered that he could have done all those things, too. But of course he could have. At Small Mammals certainly, and at the Elephant House? Who knew what he had illegal keys to, aside from the steam tunnels. And train an elephant to stomp a pumpkin with a body? He could catch birds with his bare hands. He could make an animal do anything.

He wouldn't let me stay in the building overnight. Not to protect me. To protect himself. So I didn't see something that was going to happen, or find something when left there alone with nothing to do all night.

But why would he have been at Allison's house? Maybe they'd done everything together. It made sense that she'd have an accomplice. It had seemed crazy to imagine Allison in the steam tunnels, doing the dirty work. And she was so good at getting other people to do it for her.

But then, why had he tried to convince me to suspect her? Maybe they'd had a falling out. He was smart. Maybe he'd figured out a way to make her take all the blame.

He had seemed to hate her, though. Why would he conspire with her to kill Victor? I didn't know. But the hating her . . . it was so out of character. He was so obviously emotional about it, for him anyway. He was never like that in public. Maybe he was putting on an act to fool people. So nobody'd ever figure out the two of them were in on the plot together.

It was a perfect way to keep my nose of their business, too. He seemed angry, sometimes even hurt, whenever her name was mentioned. He knew I wouldn't want to make him angry. And that I'd kill myself before I'd hurt him. So I wouldn't pry.

I curled up, hugging my stomach, feeling ill. And lately . . . I'd denied it to myself, but he had seemed so . . . so affectionate toward me. I had a crush on him, sure. It was totally unrealistic, but lately I could almost, almost, believe that he returned my feelings. But maybe he was playing with me. So I'd never suspect him. So I'd never think he had tried to kill me with the booby-trapped chutes.

But why? I had no idea why. But he had the means and the opportunity. I always said that around here, I felt like I'd come into a party late. Everyone else had been here for so long, I had no idea what undercurrents I might step into with the most innocent remark. Something I did, something I knew and didn't realize was dangerous to someone—who knew what it could be?

My instincts said that Chris being evil was impossible. But let's face it. My instincts had other things on their mind. What did I know about him really? Nothing. That he had blue eyes like my favorite flowers and shoulders that made me weak in the knees. That he was good with animals the way I longed to be good with animals. And that although I knew it was foolish, deep down I believed that the animals could tell who were good people and who were bad ones.

And yet . . . he'd grown up around dead animals. Dead animals in the freezer. Animals killed by hunters. It had just seemed normal, he said. Animals kill other animals, and so do we.

But Ray . . . Maybe I knew nothing, but Ray had been here forever, too. And he had convinced me to go and make up with Chris. Ray had made me see that I should choose Chris over Allison. Ray had no ulterior motives. No, more than that. If Ray had an ulterior motive, it was better served by me having a fight with Chris and never speaking to him again. Because it was clear who my second choice would be.

My breathing had slowed. This was crazy. Neither Allison nor Chris could have done these things, much less the two of them together. I was just so, so obsessed with both of them, I couldn't think straight, right? They both took up so much space in my mind, they had this huge gravitational force and everything had to revolve around them. If Chris wasn't the hero, he had to be the villain. I couldn't imagine him as a minor character. Which made my logic completely unreliable. Right?

I stumbled to my feet. I looked over at Small Mammals. I couldn't go back in there. I couldn't see him again. I rummaged in my pockets. I had my keys, thankfully. I'd just have to go home in my work shoes.

I started to walk down the path. I hesitated in front of Reptiles. But I couldn't make myself go inside. I'd never felt so entirely alone in the world. I moved on.

Chapter 17

I walked and walked and walked with the pugs, trying not to think, trying to get so tired that I'd be unconscious the moment I hit the bed. Suddenly I noticed a pug with its face against the ground doing something more than just sniffing. I jerked on Gus's leash and yelled *"No!"* uselessly. I grabbed his mouth, but it was too late, whatever it was had been chewed and swallowed.

"Damn," I said, tears of frustration and exhaustion springing to my eyes. "One day you're going to eat something poisonous. Stupid pug."

This happened all the time. There was nothing I could do. The pugs were closer to the ground than I was, and I would never be able to see everything before they did. The world was such a dangerous place already, and they had to make it worse by eating every damn thing they saw on the street.

I rubbed my eyes. I needed to go home and go to bed. I was at the end of my rope. We were walking past the gates of the zoo, almost back to my building. I stood there with the pugs and felt frustrated. Why couldn't I go in there with them? I knew why, but it was strange to have them cut off from such a big part of my life. I supposed it would be dangerous for them in there, though. If they got away from me, they could end up in a bear enclosure or something. Or some zookeeper would call a Code Orange and try to net them and break their necks.

Funny how most people probably thought the animals were

the dangerous thing about working at the zoo. Way more often, keepers got hurt lifting things or cutting themselves or falling. And lately, it was the people who were the most dangerous. And unpredictable. You knew a tiger would try to kill you. You knew to be careful. You weren't surprised. Not like with people.

I turned and dragged my weary dogs toward home.

As I was standing outside the door to my apartment, I heard the phone ringing. I dug in my pocket for my keys. I was still wearing my work jeans. I pulled out some string and some dead leaves and a few rubber gloves. I heard the machine pick up. I rummaged in the other pocket. I heard Beth's voice.

"Hannah, this is Beth. I'm so sorry to bother you at home. There's going to be a story of mine about the director in tomorrow's paper. You've helped me so much, I owe it to you not to let this story be a surprise to you. Please call me tonight." And she left her number.

By the time I'd figured out that the keys were in the other pocket with my pocket knife and my pen and a piece of tie wire and unlocked the door, she had hung up.

I played the message and wrote down the phone number crossly, almost poking the pen through the paper. It sounded like her promise not to do any muckraking hadn't gone very far. I didn't want to talk to her. I was exhausted, and I wasn't interested in listening to her excuses. I had bigger problems on my mind.

I crumpled up the phone number and stuck it in my pocket with all the other junk. I was in the bedroom kicking off my shoes when the phone rang again. I hesitated. But it wouldn't be Beth again so soon.

And it might be Chris. What if something had gone wrong and he needed help? What if something had gone right, and he'd found the sloth? What if something had gone even righter, and he'd found out who killed Victor and kidnapped the sloth? Which would be the best news of all because that would mean it hadn't been him.

I ran back down the hall. "Hello." It sounded like a croak, I was so tired.

"I found your sloth," said a familiar voice.

"Allison?" No matter what time it was, she expected you to know who she was on the phone. This was getting to be a habit, her calling me about stuff at night. What was going on now? It couldn't be another elephant move.

Whoa. I backed up my train of thought slowly. *Allison* had found my sloth?

"What?" I squeaked. "Is she okay? Where did you get her?"

"It's nothing you need to worry about. Everything is fine."

"Oh, wow." I was overwhelmed with relief. Chris couldn't have had anything to do with stealing the sloth. She'd never say everything was fine if he had. That was all that mattered for now.

"I'm going to call Chris now so he can come get her. But I wanted you to know first."

"No," I said. "Let me come get her and bring her over to Small Mammals. I live right next door, remember?"

She laughed a little. "What, don't you trust Chris?"

"Of course I do," I said, flailing around for an excuse. I couldn't admit that I wanted to spare him having to talk to her. "But I really want to see her. You know," I mumbled, trying to sound embarrassed at being such a sentimental bunny-hugger.

"Well, okay," she said, with a smile in her voice. "I'm in the offices at Big Cats. You can meet me here."

"I don't have the keys." The words came out automatically, despite the fact that I was too exhausted to think straight. The bosses always forgot we didn't have the keys to that hallway.

"That's no problem. I was going to suggest we meet in front

of the exhibit."

I nodded, forgetting I was on the phone. "Wait." I realized the keys to the office were hardly my biggest problem. "How will I get into the zoo? Can the police let me in?"

"There's no need to bother them. You know where my house is, right?"

"Yeah," I said uncertainly. This conversation was getting more incomprehensible every minute. What did her house have to do with anything?

"Cross the street and go to the section of the fence directly opposite my house. Go to the far right-hand side of it. It won't look any different, but if you pull at the bottom corner, it'll come away and you can crawl in. Make sure you put it back after you."

I shook my head. She not only had a key to the gate, she also had a secret entrance. Of course she would. You never knew when you might need a secret entrance, right? There were security cameras on the gates. They weren't meant to watch the director, surely.

"Got it?" she said. "I'll see you soon."

But I didn't run right out the door. I was excited, if bewildered, that my sloth was back. On the one hand, I wanted to see her right away. On the other hand, Chris was at Small Mammals overnight watching the building. So he was right there. It made a lot more sense for him to go and get her.

And also . . . I was kind of afraid to see him. What would he say? What would I say? Had I ruined everything between us? How could I just walk in and hand him a sloth like nothing had happened?

But Chris was already staying late watching the building when I should have been doing it. And he wouldn't want to see Allison. Seeing her always made him unhappy. Anyway, I wanted to be the sloth-returning hero. Well, as much as I could be, if it was really Allison who'd located her. He'd be so pleased and surprised when I brought the sloth back, I thought, wandering back to the bedroom to find my shoes.

I picked up a shoe and looked at it, my thoughts rambling on. I wondered if she'd found out who took the sloth when she got it back. But it was good news that she wasn't the slothnapper or the murderer. What a relief. Chris would think so, too, really. He would be glad to find out he'd been wrong about her, because it would be terrible for the zoo if the director had done such things. I could forgive him for thinking the way he did about her. He must have been made really upset by the tapir thing or whatever his problem with her was. He seemed to be able to forgive me for anything. We could just kiss and make up about the whole thing, I thought, sleepily. No, no, skip that kissing part. What was I thinking . . . ?

I pulled a shoe on and tied it. There was something wrong with the shoe. It didn't feel right. I looked at it. It took me a long moment to realize that it was on the wrong foot. I untied it laboriously, put it on the other foot, and tried again.

Maybe this is a bad idea, I thought. It was dangerous to work with animals when you were this tired. I couldn't let my feelings for Chris get in the way of my professional judgment. I shouldn't be doing this now.

I went back down the hall again and dialed the phone. I listened to it ring anxiously.

"Small Mammals, Chris."

"Chris?" My voice sounded tiny and timid, but he recognized it anyway.

"Hannah," he said, and he was glad to hear from me; I could hear it in his tone. My heart did a little dance. "Hey, everything's fine here. Go to bed."

"Everything's more than fine," I said. "Allison has the sloth. I was supposed to meet her at the tiger exhibit in half an hour to get it from her. I don't mind going, but, you know, you're already there. Maybe you might as well?"

There was a long silence. "Chris?" I said, wondering if we'd been cut off.

"She has the sloth? How did she get it?"

"I don't know where she got it. I figured she'd explain when I got there. She seemed like she was in a hurry on the phone."

He was silent again for a moment. I was a little surprised that he wasn't pleased by the good news. But the situation was odd, I supposed. I had just gotten used to Allison springing things on me.

"Fine," he finally said. "I'll take care of it."

"Call me when you get back."

"Okay," he said. And then I changed my mind again. I wanted to see my sloth. And I wanted to see him, too.

"Look, you know, I'll come, too," I said.

"You don't have to," he said.

"I'll see you in half an hour," I said, and hung up before he could argue.

I was wide awake now. I looked at my shoes again. They seemed okay this time. Then the phone rang.

I hesitated. Was it Chris trying to talk me into not coming? But it might be Allison again. I'd better answer it.

"Hannah, it's Beth. I left a message earlier—"

Oh great. "I have to go out in one minute," I interrupted.

"I won't take long. I wanted to make sure you heard about this before it was in the paper. Because I feel like I broke a promise. Look, I am really sorry. I know I swore that this wasn't going to turn into some kind of muckraking. But I can't help what I found, and it's too late—"

Oh, God, Beth and her excuses before she even tells you what she's making excuses for. I didn't have time for this.

"I don't care about that," I interrupted again. "What did you find out?"

"Well . . . That company isn't just working on growing the plant and harvesting the drug. They're working on having a monopoly on it. Not just by having a patent and that kind of thing, but by having an exclusive source."

"So? Anyway, how can they do that? It grows wild. They can't own the whole rainforest."

"No, but it turns out the plant is very endangered, and there's only a few places left that it grows. Most of the other locations are in the hands of ranchers and developers—"

I broke in. "So they buy them up and take them away from people who were going to cut down the rainforest. That's great, what's wrong with that?"

"That would be great. But the thing is, the more limited the source is, the higher the price they can get for the drug. So they don't want those lots to be preserved. And it's not just that they aren't buying them. They've been working to prevent those people from selling to other conservation groups that want to buy up those parcels."

That was crazy. Why destroy a source of something so valuable? "That doesn't make sense. If you had more of it, you'd have more to sell. And surely they have the money to offer as much as necessary for the land. Why would they want less of the geese that are laying the golden eggs?"

"That makes sense to people like me and you," she said. "But every time one of those plots has gone under the bulldozer, their stock has skyrocketed."

So they were making money on destroying an endangered species. At least one, the plant, and probably lots of others that lived there, too.

Just as I thought that, Beth said, "And there's this thing about a bird. A new species that was just discovered, and the company destroyed its only habitat. I don't understand the whole thing—they discovered the bird a few years ago, but they only decided it was a new species last month. Can't they just tell by looking at it? But anyway, it doesn't matter. The whole deal looks really bad for her."

I didn't have time to explain to her about species. That they're something we invent because nature doesn't come in neat packages. Scientists make up the packages so they can publish papers about them and we have names we can use, but disagreements happened at the margins all the time. You could argue for years about whether the bird was a species or a subspecies or just some kind of regional variation.

But it didn't matter, because Beth was right. Allison might or might not have destroyed a bird species, but that's what it would say in the newspaper. Reporters wouldn't understand or care about the details, and it this case, maybe they were right not to. The story was a symbol of everything she and the drug business had done. And it would certainly destroy the image she'd spent years building.

"You understand this is a big deal," said Beth, echoing my thoughts. "You've seen her press clippings. And the article I wrote. She wants you to think she's the queen of rainforest conservation. Everything about her life is based on that. But in secret, she's doing the opposite."

"Yeah." I'd wondered how much of what we were doing was for show. Seemed like now I had the answer.

"And you know that guy who was murdered? He was in on the deal, too. But he sold his stock before he died. I wonder—"

"I have to go," I said, hanging up.

I dialed the phone again in a frenzy. Everything had all clicked into place. Allison was the only one who could have done all those things: the slothnapping, the chutes, training the elephants, persuading Victor to take something that was drugged. And she had a motive, a bigger one than I'd ever imagined, a secret that would destroy her whole carefully constructed life. And Victor had known it. Victor was breaking up with her because he found out the truth about the company they both had stock in. And he was going to tell the world. So she had to kill him. All her other powers, to fire people, change their jobs, ship their favorite animals away . . . none of them were enough this time. He had to be silenced for good.

The phone rang and rang. Chris wouldn't have left the building yet to meet Allison in half an hour. It wasn't that long a walk. But if he was amusing himself in an exhibit, he knew he couldn't get to the phone before the machine picked up. He wouldn't run after it.

"Pick up, dammit," I said, desperately. But I got the machine.

"Chris—never mind about meeting Allison. I'll go by myself. I don't have time to explain. Don't go. I'll see you soon."

I was wide awake now, almost hyperventilating as I ran to get my coat. Because I had to get there first. Because maybe that was what was wrong between Chris and Allison. What if he knew her secret, too? That's why she'd tried to kill him with the booby-trapped chute, right? She thinks I'm coming now. But if he shows up instead, well, she's smart enough to grab the opportunity. Just the two of them alone, the zoo dark and closed. Who's going to contradict her if he's killed in some kind of accident? Animal keeping is a dangerous business.

I ran down the stairs and flew down the street.

The secret entrance in the fence worked just like she said. It was a long run down the road through the dark woods. But with my eyes used to the dark, it was easy to follow the road. This was my turf, and I was comfortable. I was here in the dark all the time. I got to work before the sun came up a good part of the year.

When I got to the tiger exhibit, I looked all around in front and didn't see anyone. Good. I had beat Chris here. Allison wouldn't try anything with two of us here. And I would be safe. She had no way of knowing I'd figured out her plan. I'd grab my sloth and get out. Then Chris and I could figure out what to do next.

"Hannah, over here," I heard. "Climb up."

I turned toward the voice. Allison was on the wall of the tiger enclosure, the inner wall. I was standing in the public area at the outer wall. In between the two walls was a grassy moat.

"Where is she?" What was up with my sloth, dammit? What was Allison doing on the inner wall of the exhibit?

"She's in the moat. Go around that way. I left the gate open. Walk on the wall and you can get here."

Easy for her to say. It was dark. These weren't the familiar roads I'd been running down anymore. I could just see that there was a connecting wall beyond the gate she'd unlocked. It looked like it was possible to stand on the connecting wall, but it definitely wasn't really designed for walking.

I climbed onto the wall gingerly. I wasn't sure how far the drop was on either side. I wasn't that familiar with the exhibit. I didn't think it was too high. But it wasn't heights I was afraid of. Falling down was the part that worried me.

But I wanted my sloth. Before Chris got there. And then I wanted out. I didn't have time to be fearful. I repeated that to myself as I crept carefully along the wall.

"Where is she?" I said. "Is she okay? Are you sure she's alive?"

"She's fine, relax."

As I got closer to the inner wall I saw a movement in the exhibit and gasped. "Allison, why are the tigers out?"

The big cats were always brought indoors for the night. They weren't supposed to be out, and surely it was a bad idea for her to be sitting on the inner wall of their exhibit while they were in it.

"They love to come out at night. It's so unfair to keep them in, don't you think? Sometimes I come and give them a little walk. That's how I found the sloth."

She sounded cheerful and cheeky about the whole thing. Breaking the rules in her own private playground. The tigers were her favorites. She liked the elephants, but the statue in front of her house was a tiger.

I crept out to where she was on the wall. The tigers weren't too close, but they were watching us. I tried not to get my back to them or stare at them either. I was an animal lover, but I wasn't an idiot. I didn't have any illusions about what they'd do to me if I fell into their enclosure.

Finally I reached Allison, and she pointed down into the moat. "See?" she said.

I could barely see what looked like a rounded lump of straw. I wished I could tell if it was breathing, I didn't know how she could feel so sure it was okay.

"I'll jump down and hand her up to you, then you can help me back up. Here, give me a hand for a minute," she said.

I was totally focused on the sloth in the moat below me, sitting perfectly still, trying not to breathe myself so I could see if there was any motion of breathing. So I didn't see Allison come at me.

She knocked me over, and I was on my back on the wall. My right side was hanging off into the tiger exhibit. She had her knee in my chest and her hands around my throat, and her face was just inches from mine.

"I'm so sorry, Hannah, but I think it would just be better to finish what I started."

Her eyes looked like the tigers'. No malice really. Just business.

I couldn't try to push her off me with my hands. I needed them to keep myself on the wall. I closed my eyes. I was so stupid, it was amazing I'd stayed alive this long, really. Noble of me, trying to protect Chris and all, but so stupid to think that he was the one she was after. Maybe it would be better to just let her eliminate me from the gene pool.

She started to try to push me into the tiger enclosure. My arms were bent at a strange angle, and I felt them starting to weaken. I had read how when an animal is about to be killed by a predator, its body is flooded with a chemical that makes it calm. I waited for the feeling.

But it didn't come. We were near a corner, and I got my foot against the wall at a right angle to the one I was lying on. I had just enough leverage to resist her. Part of me didn't want to die, even if it was just my right foot, and it wasn't going to let the other parts drag it along.

I opened my eyes and saw the tigers approaching this interesting event curiously.

We were pretty evenly matched. She was bigger than me. Everyone was, after all. But I had the wall to help me and she was awkwardly balanced on top of me. For a moment nothing happened as we pushed against each other.

I closed my eyes and felt tears behind them. My ankle was starting to weaken. I wasn't sure I could last much longer.

I needed to save the sloth, I told myself. I needed to stay alive long enough to tell Chris that he'd been right and I was sorry.

I gave a last push with my whole body, with all my strength, and she toppled backward. She just saved herself at the last second from falling off. I jumped down off the wall into the moat and grabbed the sloth. I didn't know the way out, but at least now she couldn't get me in with tigers without knocking me out and carrying me out of the moat.

The sloth wasn't dead. I backed up against the outer wall as far as I could get from Allison and still see her. She was lying awkwardly on the wall, breathing heavily. I just stood there frozen like prey waiting for her next move.

What she did next was sit up on the wall and rearrange her hair. Then she crossed her legs and sat there kind of casually, like she was on a chair in her office instead of a tiger exhibit wall at five in the morning.

"I suppose it's not worth the bother. Now that it's all going to come out anyway. I've just always hated the idea of not finishing what I've started." She looked at me sternly. "It would have been easier at Small Mammals. I was very cross with you when I called and found that Chris is there instead. Of course I'm not surprised that he would counter my orders, but I thought you understood the chain of command better than that."

"You tried to kill me before, didn't you," I said.

She just looked at me and gave a shrug. Just business, it seemed to say.

I felt a stab of anger. "You almost killed Chris instead."

She scowled. "That was sloppy. That was not at all what I intended. I wanted him to be alive and suffering," she said angrily, adding, "No one does that to me," mostly to herself.

She continued, her tone softening, "That wasn't what I meant for you. It wasn't personal. I needed you dead, but you don't suffer after you're dead. Like the animals, some have to die so others can live," she said, as if this was a simple explanation anyone would understand.

"It's too late now, though," she continued. "Our friend the reporter called me. I have to give her credit. You didn't even know the significance of what you said, but you gave her all she needed. Of course, you didn't see the documents that connected me to the drug company by accident. Victor put them there. I think he knew he wouldn't be safe. So he had a backup plan."

I didn't say anything. She was going to keep talking. She was so used to talking and having people listen.

"He wasn't stupid. I don't go for the stupid ones. But I underestimated him. He planted copies of those papers in many of the files that he knew other people would see. I'm not even positive now that I've gotten rid of all of them. My staff has been very confused about my sudden penchant for doing my own filing," she said, as if this were funny.

They would be. They thought she never did her own dirty work. We'd all thought that.

"But he wasn't smart enough to be careful of what I gave him to drink. Why didn't he think of that? A woman's weapon." She laughed. "And Dad was a pharmacist. Victor should have known I can get into the hospital and take anything I want. Too obvious, you'd have thought," she said, shaking her head in disappointment, like he should have made it a little harder. "Still, there was no way he could have guessed why I wanted to have a late picnic in the Elephant House after it was closed. It's just the sort of thing I do, after all."

So she hadn't had to move the body very far. Maybe not at all. Victor wouldn't have questioned her if she told him to come with her into the yard. It was the sort of thing she did.

"But why the elephants?" I was surprised to hear myself interrupt her. But I had to know. If she'd given him a drug to knock him out, why not just kill him with poison? Why that bizarre stunt?

She shrugged. "Just for spite. I thought afterward perhaps I'd been a little too arrogant, that it might draw suspicion to me. But everyone was so busy thinking about who might have wanted to get at me by killing him. It's interesting how useful it's been to have such divided opinions about me," she said thoughtfully.

"Was it hard to get one of them to do it?" I asked.

"I had to work up to it for while. But they're used to learning new things. We do a very good job with elephants here, you know."

I sat there digesting this for a moment, as if it were just an interesting training problem, and then something occurred to me.

"How did you catch the sloth by yourself?"

"I used the old sloth crates that fit in the holding."

Yeah, the crate I'd found on top of the exhibit. She knew about my fear of heights, so she'd felt safe that I'd never go up there and see it. "We used to use them when I was curator. I had to wait a couple of nights, but eventually she just went in and slept in it," she explained. "It's much easier that way. It's a shame you don't still use them. But I know the vets are much busier now. You can't just reschedule for the next day if the animal isn't cooperative. It's too bad."

I nodded, hardly thinking about how bizarre this was. A normal conversation about animal management between zoo employees. One of whom had just tried to kill the other by tiger attack.

She shook her head kind of sadly and continued, almost as if talking to herself. "It's too bad Victor was afraid of the scandal himself. He wanted to convince me that we should both pull out, sell our stocks and sever our connections, and maybe no one would ever find out. It's his own fault he wasted time and gave me the chance to kill him. He didn't have the nerve to go directly to the press. That would have meant owning up to his own involvement."

She started to take her shoes off. I always remembered that detail later. Why did she take her shoes off? She didn't want the tigers to ruin them? Did she think they'd get hurt chewing them? They might swallow a heel or something? I still think about it.

"But I suppose I can understand his feeling. I don't want the publicity of a trial. It would be bad for the zoo. And I simply couldn't live in a prison," she said, not seeming to see the irony of the last statement, even though our animals had accommodations and treatment that couldn't really be compared to jail.

"It will look like an accident at first. Everyone knows I like to get up close with the animals." She smiled and hopped down off the wall and disappeared from my sight.

I was frozen in shock for a moment, and then all I wanted was to be as far away as possible. I picked up my sloth, and as I felt my way along with wall, I saw that there were stairs out of the moat near the connecting wall I'd been climbing on. She'd fooled me that I'd needed to climb out on the wall with her in the first place. I never knew the stairs were there. I needed to get out of the Small Mammal house and see the rest of the zoo more, I thought wildly, but now what I needed to do was run there as fast as I could.

But it was hard to climb the stairs and carry the sloth. Especially listening to the noises coming from the tiger exhibit. I couldn't help jiggling the sloth and making her agitated. I knew how strong she was, and if she wanted to get away, she could. Or she could hurt me badly. I could carry her when she was sleeping in a ball, but now I was having problems. I realized that Allison must have drugged her, and now she was coming out of it. I was in over my head. I started to panic.

"Hannah," I heard. It was Chris calling my name. Right on time. I'd never heard a more beautiful sound.

"I'm down here," I called, overwhelmed with relief, unable to control the tremor in my voice.

"What's going on?" he said, running down the stairs into the moat. "Where's Allison?" He looked at me with bewilderment. I must have been disheveled from the struggle. I felt like I'd been hit by a truck. But mostly, I was standing there holding a sloth.

"Help me with her," I said.

The animals came first. He took her from me. He could hold her better in his strong arms. I wasn't going to argue.

"What happened? Where did she come from?"

"Please," I said weakly, "let's put her back first."

We walked quickly in the dark back to the building, silence between us. We went directly to the exhibit and climbed in. Chris put the sloth gently on the ground next to a tree. She was completely awake now. She looked back at the two of us with her friendly alien sloth eyes, and then climbed up into the tree. I felt my eyes water. No one was going to take my sloth away again.

After we had watched her climb up and settle down, Chris turned and looked at me again. "Hannah, are you okay? What's going on?"

"Allison," was all I could say. I knew it didn't make sense. I struggled to construct a sentence.

Before he could say anything else, Chris's radio crackled. Then we heard the police officer on duty was calling for backup and an ambulance.

"It's too late. She's dead," I said to no one in particular, rubbing my eyes. "I should apologize to the police. I guess they do patrol at night." I'd assumed they just ate doughnuts, since they let my sloth get stolen twice. But of course, Allison would know how to outwit them. It wasn't their fault.

Chris was looking at me like he was concerned I had lost my mind. I guess you couldn't blame him. "Hannah, who's dead?"

"You were right," I said groggily, overcome with weariness as the adrenaline ebbed away. "You're always right. Why don't I learn?"

I felt like I couldn't stay awake, even standing up. But I kept trying to explain.

"Allison. She went in with the tigers. To kill herself. She killed Victor. You were right. She tried to kill me, too, just now, again, but—I don't know. She decided it wasn't worth the trouble anymore."

I rubbed my eyes again. It didn't help me wake up. I just couldn't explain things any better right now.

"But she gave me the sloth back first, so everything's okay," I concluded. That was what was important, right?

He looked stunned, I guess. I was too out of it to really tell. Then he pulled me close to him and squeezed me so hard that for a second I couldn't breathe. I put my arms around him and wondered sleepily what he was so upset about. Everything was fine now. My sloth was back, and I was here in my wonderful sloth exhibit with Chris, and he was fine. Allison couldn't bother him anymore, ever again. I rested my head on his chest and thought how nice he smelled in a fresh clean shirt with no monkey poop on it. Everything was wonderful.

I could have stood there forever, half asleep in his arms. But then I remembered something. Suddenly I was wide awake.

"I have to make a phone call," I said. Beth had warned Allison what was going to be in the newspaper tomorrow. So Allison hadn't bothered to try that hard to kill me. So Beth had pretty much saved my life. And I could pay her back, just a little, if I got to the phone right away, before anyone else heard.

Chris let go of me reluctantly without saying anything. I think he'd given up on expecting me to make any sense. We climbed out of the exhibit and walked downstairs to the office in silence.

I pulled the crumpled piece of paper out of my pocket and dialed the number. Beth croaked "Hello?" I guess it was pretty late by then.

"You should get over here," I said, and explained the situation.

I knew she'd figure out a way to get in. And get the story before everyone else. She hung up without saying goodbye before I'd even finished. I hoped she was going to take the time to change out of her pajamas. Or, if she didn't, that she'd at least buttoned them up right.

I hung up, and the phone rang immediately. I stared at it stupidly, and Chris came over and picked it up. I wandered over to the couch and lay down. I heard him saying "yes" a few times and hanging up.

He came and sat next to me on the couch. I pressed my head against the side of his leg and closed my eyes. I was sleepy again. He put his hand on my hair, so gently that I could barely feel it. I had my sloth back. I was lying down with my eyes closed. Chris was here. All was right with the world.

"Are you okay? I need to go for a while now." He sounded unhappy. Why was he unhappy? I was perfectly content. "I wish I didn't have to leave you alone."

I guess I was still in shock, because I didn't understand what he was worried about at all. "I'm fine," I insisted. "Everything's fine now." It was kind of a stupid thing to say, and also kind of right.

I lay there dozing for a little while, I don't know how long. Then I began to wake up and go over what had happened in my mind. How long had Allison been trying to kill me? What had been part of the plan? Not the wombat. The wombat came first. But the wombat started the whole thing. Because then she roped me into doing all those other things, like that interview. And while preparing for the interview, I saw the papers that I mentioned to Beth.

After that, all the weird stuff started happening. The booby-trapped chute that fell down on Chris and me. The comings and goings of the sloth. She must have been planning all along to use the missing sloth to get me alone. All the time, she was still going ahead with the wombat exhibit and doing all those cool things for me, to keep me on her side. To blind me to her real intentions and distract me from what everyone else said about her.

The whole wombat thing had had a point before that, though. There was something else going on there. What she'd said about wanting Chris to be suffering. And how Chris was upset all along by her relationship with me, and not just because he didn't like her. She'd been using me to get at him somehow. I didn't know why, but I could see it clearly now.

But her plans had all gone wrong because of Beth. Because of her persistence, grabbing onto the story like a pit bull and shaking it until all the secrets fell out. Even if Allison were never caught for the murder, even if no one saw the connection, her whole life would collapse around her in a huge public scandal. She didn't want a scandal for the sake of the zoo, she had said. I wondered if that was true, and whether it would feel better or worse to believe it. I couldn't decide.

She'd killed Victor because he was going to reveal the secret. She was going to kill me because I'd seen the evidence and might eventually have realized what it meant. But at the last minute, she found out that I'd already inadvertently passed the evidence on to Beth, and it was too late to keep it from becoming public. So it wasn't worth the bother of killing me anymore. She gave it one more try, but when it didn't work, she gave up. And killed herself to escape the consequences. She went out on her own terms. Like you'd expect of her, I guess.

It seemed like such a human motive at first, but really, we were no different from other animals. People liked to think that animals only killed for food. But they'd fight for territory or mates. And maybe you'd think they didn't kill to save face, but status was important to other animals, too. If one monkey was head of a troop and someone else wanted to be, they'd fight, maybe to the death. What was the alpha monkey risking his life fighting for? And maybe killing for? Status. Being at the top of the heap. The same way Allison had killed someone who'd threatened her position in the world. The phone rang again. Chris said that the police were here and wanted to talk to me. I locked up the building behind me and walked back to the tiger exhibit. It was dark and I was alone, but now I had nothing to be afraid of.

There was much more waiting around than talking. Dawn was beginning by the time they let me go. Zoo management had finally all arrived, and Chris had to go to a meeting. I could almost laugh—no matter what happened, they reacted by having a meeting about it.

I wandered back toward the building. I was wide awake now and alone with my thoughts. That sleepy, happy feeling I'd had was a distant memory.

I sat down on a bench outside Reptiles and put my head in my hands. I saw now what a fool I had been. Chris had been right. And he'd tried to save me from the worst parts of myself, the parts that were fed by Allison's attention. He really cared about me, but I'd kept choosing to believe her instead. Making her game of hurting him work perfectly.

I hadn't seen any of it before. Because I wanted a wombat. Because I enjoyed her attention. It all made me feel important and special. Too important and special to pay attention to the people I should have trusted. I had been too stupid and wrong and full of myself to listen to the people who really cared about me. And I had been saved in the end by someone I'd been constantly cross and impatient with, whose help, even accidental help, I'd done less than nothing to deserve.

I was sure there had been no one in sight when I sat down.

But almost immediately I felt someone standing next to me. I looked up.

The look on Ray's face made tears come to my eyes. He sat down and put his arms around me.

"What are you doing here so early," I mumbled into his shirt, hugging him back hard.

Uncharacteristically, he didn't answer, except by tightening his arms around me.

"I should have listened to Chris," I said. "He was right all along. I was so stupid." I couldn't say that, worse, I'd even suspected him. Ray would understand, Ray would forgive my foolishness, but I couldn't say it.

"Shh," he said. "All that matters is that you're all right."

"But none of this would have happened if I—"

"No," he said. "It's not your fault. She could have picked anyone, and they would have reacted the same way."

"But—"

"Shh. It's happened before. You were just unlucky to be part of the end of the story. But now it's over."

He held me close with no silliness and no flirting, just comfort, and I closed my eyes and tried to feel worthy of it.

When it was time to start work, I wandered slowly the rest of the way back to Small Mammals on my own. But I felt like I couldn't face anyone. I couldn't stop thinking about how wrong and stupid I had been about everything, and how many times Chris had tried to make me see who Allison really was, and how I'd played right into her hands.

I went out back and sat on the grass behind the brick wall across from the lemur exhibit, where no one would be able to see me. I fell asleep lying on my side on the grass. I must have slept for a long time because when I awoke, the zoo was open and I could hear people walking on the paths behind the Small

Mammal House and exclaiming at the lemurs. It seemed like a normal day. Somehow Allison was getting her wish, as usual, at least for now. Her death wasn't disrupting the business of the zoo today.

I sat up, still groggy. I saw that someone was sitting a little ways away. Of course, it was Chris, the only one who knew my hiding place.

I looked away.

"Do you mind if I sit here?" he said.

"Of course not," I said, not adding, "but why would you want to?"

After a while he said, "I'm sorry about what happened. It must be hard for you."

I felt tears in my eyes. "I'm sorry I was so stupid. You tried to tell me. Why didn't I hear you?"

"I could have been wrong," he said. "She was doing so much for you."

"But they were gifts from the devil. You tried to warn me."

"It's not your fault. It's the way she is. It's hard to resist." He was still speaking of her in the present tense. It would take a while before we stopped feeling her presence.

We were silent for a while. "I wonder if I can still love the wombat," I said.

"You still love the wombat," he said. "It's not his fault how he came here. She can't touch that."

He put his hands in his hair and sat there with his elbows sticking up in that way I thought was so cute, and it made me want to cry again. I had to turn away.

"She was just using me to get at you, wasn't she?" I said. "That's why she was paying attention to me at first."

"I think so."

He would tell me now. Wouldn't he?

"For what?" I said.

He avoided my eyes. "No one rejects her. She gets to decide when it's over. If you break that rule, she can hold a grudge for a long time."

How stupid I'd been not to see it before. I'd had all the information to put this together all along, but I hadn't wanted to hear it. But what else could turn that bitter? That was why he thought Allison could have killed Victor over their breakup. He knew what he was talking about.

"I should have told you," he said sadly. "I should have trusted you. But she poisons everything she touches. Including me."

"No." I still loved both of them. "Not the wombat. And not you either."

He liked those stubborn, strong-minded women, I realized. But I hoped there wasn't anything else I had in common with Allison. I swore to myself that I'd jump in with the tigers before I ever did anything to hurt him.

I watched him staring down at the grass, avoiding my eyes, his expression so vulnerable I almost couldn't bear it. It made him look oddly younger, and at that moment, I was suddenly blinded by anger. I thought of how she had manipulated me, and I thought of her years ago, honing those skills by practicing on new baby mammals keepers—for instance, Chris when he was like sweet innocent Jeff, so young and full of enthusiasm. I was supposedly older and wiser. I halfway knew she couldn't be trusted. And yet somehow, every time she was nice to me, I fell at her feet. Imagine what she'd do to a kid like that.

And if he happened to be a cute guy, why not take the whole thing a step farther?

"If she wasn't already dead I'd kill her," I blurted out.

Oh, God. What a stupid thing to say. I should have had some deep, sensitive reaction to this secret he'd finally told me. But I was a total idiot instead.

Now I was the one staring at the grass, afraid to look at him.

My mouth needed a rewind button. My life needed a delete key. But I had neither, and all I could do was hold my breath and wait.

He leaned over and kissed me and then stood up before I had time to react. I looked up, and he was smiling at me in that way that made my brain turn to armadillo gruel.

"That's okay, but thanks for the offer," he said lightly.

I looked into his eyes. They were the color of the sky after it rained. My mind was suddenly quiet and empty of everything but a feeling of peace and safety.

After a moment, he put out his hands. "Hey, want to go see the octopus?"

I held up my hands, and he helped pull me to my feet. We stood there hand in hand for a long moment more than was strictly necessary. Then we ran down the path to be on time for the octopus feeding.

ABOUT THE AUTHOR

As a child growing up in the Bronx, **Linda Lombardi** liked to play with a basket full of plastic animals instead of human dolls. Later in life, she gave up a position as a tenured college professor to take a zookeeping job. Linda lives in Silver Spring, Maryland, with her pugs, and you can read some of her nonfiction writing about animals (and other things) at her website, www.lindalombardi.com.